The Crescent

A Viet Nam War Novel

1SG David Allin, USA Ret.

D1527116

Cover photo by the author, May 1969

Table of Contents

FOREWORD

In May 1969 elements of the 3rd Brigade, 25th Infantry Division battled with North Vietnamese Army units in a large stretch of forest west of Dau Tieng called the Crescent. The events portrayed in this book take place during those engagements, although some incidents have been added or altered, and all the people portrayed are fictional. The outcome of the battles was inconclusive, and they did not mark a turning point in the war. For those who participated in the firefights, including the author, the engagements were nonetheless very memorable; for everyone else, however, they quickly faded into the background of a long and pointless war. This book is dedicated to the men on both sides who died during those battles, as well as to those who survived.

The author wishes to particularly thank LTC J. Michael Hemsley, USA Ret., a very good friend who inspired this book and provided valuable background information about the experiences of junior officers during that period.

ONE

The overpowering roar of the gunfire was both terrifying and exhilarating. Virtually every gun in the mechanized infantry company was firing, sending a hail of bullets down the lanes between the rubber trees. It was Second Lieutenant Stephen Carr's first real firefight, and his senses were being overloaded. Not only were his ears being pounded, but he could also feel it in his gut—the metronomic pounding bass of the .50-caliber machine guns mounted on the armored personnel carriers, the baritone chatter of the M-60 light machine guns, the tenor rattle of the M-16 rifles, and the tympanic thump of the M-79 grenade launchers. It was a glorious cacophony of explosive force all directed at an unseen enemy, embracing Carr in the power of the American military and giving him an exalted illusion of supremacy and invulnerability.

The morning had started out calmly. After spending a night in Fire Support Base Wood, the company had moved out the gate and headed east around Dau Tieng base camp toward the Michelin rubber plantation. The previous day elements of the First Infantry Division had engaged a large North Vietnamese Army force in and around the Michelin, and Alpha Company had been directed to sweep some of the area to assess the damage caused by the overnight airstrikes and artillery barrages, as well as to secure the flank of the Big Red One troops who were seeking out the retreating enemy. They had found a few abandoned enemy bunkers, their leafy cover stripped away by flames and blast, but no bodies, weapons, or other evidence of the NVA.

At noon, when the company had paused to rest and dig into the C-rations, the Commanding Officer, Captain Raymond, had called Carr and the other platoon leaders over to his armored personnel carrier, or "track," as the troops referred to the blocky vehicles. He informed them that Bravo Company, which had been providing convoy security on the road from Cu Chi to Dau Tieng, had discovered an enemy ambush where the road made a 90-degree turn around the small Ben Cui rubber plantation west of the base camp. Bravo was heavily engaged with the large enemy unit, which was entrenched in bunkers the enemy had dug overnight, and Alpha was being directed to rush to their assistance. Raymond established the march order and sent the platoon leaders back to get their troops moving.

Carr ran back to his platoon only to find them already mounting up and cranking the engines. Carr's platoon sergeant, Staff Sergeant Samples, was yelling and gesturing to the troops to hurry and get the tracks in line. Carr was puzzled as to how Samples had known what to do so soon. He ran up to the wiry young man and got his attention.

"We're moving out to the Ben Cui," Carr yelled over the roar of the diesel engines. "Bravo Company ran into an ambush."

"I know," Samples answered curtly, turning away to angrily wave the one-one track's driver into place. First Platoon had four squads, and their APCs were numbered accordingly—one-one, one-two, one-three, and one-four. Shorter than Carr, Samples was chronologically the same age as the lieutenant, but his combat experience made him seem much older. His sandy hair and blue eyes were appropriate for his Southern California upbringing, but he had none of the laid-back attitude associated with surfers. He was all business, a hard-driving task master who was well-respected by the troops under him for his competence and fairness. In all his ROTC training, and in the Infantry Officer Basic Course, Carr had been constantly told to trust and learn from his NCO's, but so far Samples had been a very reluctant mentor. He only spoke to Carr when he had to, and then kept his comments to a bare minimum. Samples jogged over to the first squad track, climbed up the back, and clambered over the top to take a seat on the ammo can strapped down to the right of the machine gun turret. He never looked back at Carr.

"Sir!" Specialist 4th Class Miles called, waving frantically from beside the one-four, the fourth squad track. Miles, a small, brown-haired college boy with glasses, was the platoon RTO— Radio Telephone Operator. Carr ran over as Miles began climbing up the side of the APC, his back-pack radio making his ascent ungainly. Over his shoulder he told Carr, "We're moving out." To his left Carr could see the other vehicles of A Company lurching forward and raising clouds of dust. First platoon was tail-end Charlie in the convoy, and Carr knew they would be eating dirt the whole way. Hoping that Private First Class Chacon, the track's driver, wouldn't start moving yet, Carr put one foot on the top of the tread blocks and pulled himself up to take a seat on an ammo box strapped to the roof of the vehicle. He sat right behind Sergeant Delano Washington, the squad leader, who was perched on the open hatch cover behind Chacon. Spec 4 Hicks, sitting behind the 50-cal, handed Carr a CVC helmet attached to a coiled wire that stretched down inside the vehicle. The Combat Vehicle Crew helmet was shaped like a football helmet and made of some composite material. Inside were padded earphones, and dangling from the side was a small microphone, the wire mount for which had broken long ago. Carr laid his rifle beside the turret, pulled off his boonie hat, and squeezed the helmet down on his head. Through the built-in earphones, he could now hear the radio chatter of the company as it formed up and began moving toward the road back to Dau Tieng. Belatedly he realized that he was on the last APC of the platoon, and thus of the entire column. So much for leading from the front.

Roaring at full speed, the company had sped past the Dau Tieng base camp and crossed the bridge over the Saigon River. Following the dirt highway as it swung south toward the abandoned village of Ben Cui, the convoy made the sharp right at the village and came to a halt on the road. To their right, in the tall trees of the Ben Cui rubber plantation, they heard the gunfire, muted somewhat by the brush and smaller trees bordering the plantation that hid the engagement from their sight. Over the radio the CO explained that Bravo was in the process of disengaging and would soon appear on the road ahead of them. As soon as the other company was clear, Alpha would do a right flank movement and sweep northward through the rubber to dislodge the enemy. In theory, at least.

A week or so earlier Alpha had done a RIF—Reconnaissance In Force—through the Ben Cui, so Carr was sort of familiar with the area. The rubber trees had been planted with geometric precision, each tree about twenty feet from the next, in perfectly straight rows aligned with the compass. Over a hundred feet tall, the gray-barked trunks were as straight as telephone poles, with no branches until near the very top. The leaves of the separate trees all met high above the ground, providing a solid canopy that left the level earth of the plantation in permanent shade. Except for a few scattered bushes, the ground between the trees was covered only by grass and leaves, giving the plantation the feel of a well-manicured park. The enemy loved the plantations—the canopy protected them from air reconnaissance and attack, and the open ground below provided easy transportation of equipment and movement of troops. For political and economic reasons, the Americans had refrained from seriously damaging the plantations.

Ahead of Alpha Company, Carr saw the Bravo vehicles appear from the brush and climb up on the road, getting into a road march formation headed back toward Dau Tieng. As the last track slotted into place, the entire company began to move past Alpha at a measured pace on the south side of the road. Over the radio Carr heard Captain Raymond give the order to move off the road and then pause for dismount. All the tracks locked their right laterals and squirmed around to face to the north, then clanked forward off the road and into the brushy area that enclosed the rubber. After a few yards, the tracks all halted. "Dismount!" came the order over the radio, which those without headphones heard from the speaker inside the track, and individuals began jumping and climbing down, juggling their weapons and ammo. Only the driver, the 50-cal gunner, and one loader would remain on each APC, but with most crews having only five or six members, not many soldiers were left to form a line between the tracks. Most of the dismounted men put on helmets, but others had left theirs behind on the tracks. Carr had his helmet on, but with no chin strap, it bounced a little as he moved. Chin straps and rifle slings were virtually non-existent in Viet Nam, due to their propensity to rot in the heat and humidity. Miles, citing his need to keep the handset up to his ear, had foregone the helmet in favor of a boonie hat.

Carr's stomach felt queasy, and his hands were trembling slightly. This was his first meeting with the enemy, his baptism in fire, and he had no idea how he would react to it. He was tremendously worried that he would break down in terror, and show cowardice to the other soldiers. As Roosevelt had said, the only thing he had to fear was fear itself, but that was small consolation. Checking to make sure that Miles was following him, Carr jogged to the left so that he would be in the center of platoon line as it advanced. He found Sergeant Montoya of second squad and two of his men spread out between the one-two track and the one-three. As he approached them Miles called out from behind him.

"CO says to move out. Shoot anything that moves."

Carr nodded and pushed through the low bushes beside Montoya. Within a few yards they broke through the undergrowth onto the rubber plantation grounds. Off to the left there were shots, and the firing spread quickly up and down the line. Just as quickly the order to cease fire was passed along, and the eruption subsided. Keeping abreast of the APCs, Carr, Miles, Montoya, and two other men Carr barely knew yet advanced at a walking pace, their M-16s and M-79s held in front of them, ready to fire. The rows of rubber trees marched off into the distance, the open areas between them deceptively peaceful.

On last week's RIF through the rubber, during a short break, Carr had studied the trees to try and understand how they produced rubber. He saw that each tree had a deep trench cut into the bark that started about head-high and spiraled down around the trunk until it ended at knee level. Into the bottom end of the cut a metal trough had been hammered, extending out for about six inches. Below the trough was a rough pottery bowl suspended in a wire loop. Apparently the sap would ooze out of the tree, run down the spiral slash into the metal trough, and then drip into the bowl, where it could be collected and somehow later turned into rubber. Here in the Ben Cui the cuts had almost all healed. The Americans had declared the rubber plantations free-fire zones, where any Vietnamese were assumed to be enemy combatants, and American soldiers were free to fire at them at will. Thus, the plantations were mostly dormant, although some enterprising peasants had undoubtedly been sneaking in to harvest what they could.

More to make himself feel useful than anything, Carr waved at the one-two driver to speed up a little to stay on line with the rest of the platoon. The driver, with just his head showing above the rim of the hatch, nodded his CVC and adjusted his pace. The company was now well within the rubber plantation, and his platoon was on the right flank, by the eastern edge of the ranks of rubber trees. Where the last row of trees ended, bushes and small trees had sprung up in the sunshine, providing a border of greenery to their right that separated them from the road to Dau Tieng. From the corner of his eye Carr caught some movement from his left rear, and turned to see Staff Sergeant Samples run across behind him and disappear around the back of the one-three track, headed for the one-four. He saw that Montoya had also noticed Samples, and he gave Montoya a questioning look. Montoya just shrugged and kept moving. Despite his name, Montoya was a big, blond, blue-eyed Texan who liked to boast about his home state.

A moment later Samples reappeared and jogged back toward Carr. Meanwhile the one-four track slowed in relation to the rest of the line. As Samples came abreast of him, Carr asked, "What's going on?"

"Flank security," Samples answered as if it was obvious, and kept going toward the one-one track.

Annoyed at his platoon sergeant's brevity and usurping of his authority, Carr was also chagrinned that he hadn't thought of it himself. That line of foliage to their right would give the enemy the perfect vantage point to launch an attack on their flank, so it made sense to alter the orientation of the fourth squad's attention and slow it down so it could respond to any fire from the right. Mentally kicking himself for not thinking of it first, Carr turned to ask Miles if there was anything on the radio, but he never had the chance.

A single shot rang out, and then more and more until the entire line of tracks and men was firing wildly and indiscriminately to the north down the rows of rubber trees. Raising his own rifle to his shoulder, Carr pulled the trigger to no effect. Cursing, he rotated the fire selector switch from safe to semi-auto and tried again, relishing the recoil against his shoulder. He couldn't see any enemy soldiers, but since everyone else was firing, he did the same. That was actually the current policy of the Army, called fire superiority, the concept of which was to put so many rounds down range that the enemy was bound to be hit by one of them, or at least forced to keep their heads down.

Just like the TV show *Combat!* with Vic Morrow, Carr thought with pleasure. He dropped to a proper kneeling position and continued to shoot, aiming at a suspicious looking clump of bushes about one hundred yards away. Then the pottery bowl attached to the rubber tree just three feet to his left shattered. *Oh, shit!* he thought. They were shooting back at him. He hadn't even considered that as a possibility. Quickly he threw himself down into a prone position and rolled behind the tree with the shattered bowl, only then noticing that Miles, Montoya, and the others had dropped as soon as the firing had started. The rumor flashed through his mind that the average life expectancy of an infantry lieutenant in Viet Nam was about five minutes, which meant he was already way overdue.

"Eltee!" Miles yelled over the din, holding the radio handset to his ear. "CO says to keep moving forward." When the mass firing has begun, the entire company line had halted in place, which Carr hadn't really noticed, since it seemed like the obvious reaction. Nodding his understanding, Carr bit his lip and stood up behind the tree, took a deep breath, and stepped to his right. Feeling tremendously exposed, and remembering the statue at Ft. Benning, he raised his left arm and thrust it forward, yelling "Follow me!" It was ludicrous and hypocritical, for he was no hero, but it was expected of him. He was extremely gratified and relieved when the other men stood up and began advancing with him. The APCs also advanced, having heard the command on their radios.

Over the thunder of more than a hundred American guns firing at once, it was impossible to hear or know if the enemy was returning fire. Presumably they were in foxholes and bunkers below ground, impervious to the American bullets. The NVA and Viet Cong had developed the art of digging and camouflaging such fighting positions to a level that amazed the Americans, who had been known to fall into such unseen holes by accident. Suddenly the APCs all halted, and the dismounted men automatically dropped to prone positions. Carr did likewise, with Miles now following close behind. Miles scooted up to lay beside him, keeping the radio handset pressed to his ear.

"Sergeant Petty's hit," Miles informed him. It took a moment, but Carr soon remembered that Sergeant First Class Petty was platoon sergeant for second platoon. Behind them a crouched figure ran up the line. It was Spec 4 Allman, the first platoon medic, rushing to help Petty, in case it was more than the second platoon medic could handle. The company kept up its firing, although at a slightly diminished rate as they begin to worry about running out of ammo. After only a few minutes, Carr saw the two medics carrying Petty on a stretcher, heading back toward the road. Petty, a tall older man from Georgia, was bloody, but holding on to the stretcher with both hands.

No sooner had Carr returned to observing the lane in front of him than he heard a commotion coming from the third squad track to his right. He looked over and saw the barrel of the fifty-cal pointed skyward and no one sitting behind it. The driver's head was also not visible, nor was the loader in the cargo hatch behind the turret. "It's Knox!" Miles shouted beside him. Carr was pretty sure that Knox had been the one behind the fifty. Carr scrambled to his feet and rushed over to the back of the track. He grabbed the handle of the hatch set in the rear ramp and swung it down to open the door. Pushing through the narrow opening, he found the driver, Spec 4 Aiello, and PFC Johnson, the loader, hovering over Knox, who was lying on the stacked ammo cases that filled the front of the main compartment. The fronts of Knox's thighs were covered in blood. Behind Carr, Miles squeezed into the track as well.

"What happened?" Carr asked. He briefly noted that he felt safer inside the armored vehicle, but brushed that thought aside.

"Hot round. Misfire," Aiello said, unwrapping a field dressing.

"Round went off before it was fully seated in the breech," Johnson explained. His dark face was dripping with sweat. "He's got brass shrapnel in his legs."

Knox was moaning and cursing, pounding on the ammo cans in pain.

Carr turned to Miles and said, "Get a medic over here."

"Doc Allman's out at the road with Sergeant Petty," Miles replied. "There's been some other wounded in third platoon."

In other words, they all knew, there were no medics immediately available.

Aiello tied off the field dressing on Knox's right leg while Johnson did the left one. Then Aiello scooted backwards into the driver's compartment. "Let's take him out to the road. That's where the medics are, and they've probably got a dust-off coming in." He maneuvered onto the little seat and gunned the engine, which had been rumbling away at idle.

"Wait," Carr ordered. "Let me and Miles out." He wasn't sure Aiello was doing the right thing, but it seemed logical. Maybe that was standard operating procedure in this situation. He didn't have any other suggestions, anyway. Miles and he jumped out of the vehicle and slammed the heavy hatch closed. Johnson latched it from inside, and as Carr and Miles moved aside, Johnson's head appeared in the machine gun turret. Aiello, CVC helmet just above the rim of the driver's hatch, locked the right lateral and gunned the left tread in reverse, slewing the APC around until it faced the rear of the line.

The vehicle lurched as Aiello threw the automatic transmission into Drive and stomped on the accelerator. With a roar and a plume of diesel smoke from the exhaust pipe at the top front of the boxy machine, Aiello gunned it toward the road. He had gone only a few yards when the right front corner of the track slammed into the trunk of a rubber tree, making the tree vibrate like a tuning fork and causing a few branches and leaves to rain down from above. Aiello backed up a few feet and tried again, this time weaving around the tree and disappearing through the bordering foliage toward the road. Shaking his head, Carr took up a kneeling position behind the closest tree and prepared to resume firing, while Miles flopped down into a prone position nearby.

"Where the fuck is he going?" Carr had not seen or heard Sergeant Samples run up behind him. The man's face was red with anger as he glared accusingly at Carr. Samples' rifle, held only by the pistol grip, was pointing only a foot or so away from Carr, he noticed with concern. The sergeant was standing in the open, oblivious to the gunfire.

"Knox is wounded," Carr explained. "They're taking him out to the road for dust-off."

"Who told him he could do that?" Samples was visibly quivering with anger.

"The medics were busy. It seemed like the right thing to do."

Samples looked back at where the track had gone, obviously struggling to control his temper, before returning his focus to Carr. "We're in the middle of a fucking firefight, *lieutenant*, and we need every available gun on the line." Clenching his fist in exasperation, and shaking his head in disgust, Samples turned and jogged off after the departed track.

Feeling both guilty and pissed about the way the sergeant had treated him, Carr wrestled with his emotions and worried about what he should do next. "Miles," he called out. "Inform the CO about the one-three."

"Already did that, sir," Miles answered sympathetically.

Carr nodded. *What am I doing here?* he thought. *These guys know what to do better than I do. Am I just getting in their way?* He fought the sensation of despair and failure that was threatening to overpower him.

By the time Samples pushed through the now-shredded bushes and onto the road, the one-three track was parked diagonally across the road, and the rear ramp was down. Aiello and Johnson were carrying Knox by his knees and shoulders toward the company medics track, parked a few yards away on the side of the road. Doc Allman and another medic rushed over to help them load Knox into one of the stretchers inside the medics track. Samples waited until Aiello and Johnson walked back to their track.

"What the fuck?" Samples asked, his anger now better under control. The roar of gunfire from inside the plantation was lower in volume, but still present.

"Knox got some brass in his legs," Aiello explained. Johnson guiltily hung back, letting Aiello deal with their platoon sergeant.

"No, dickwad," Samples scolded, "why did you leave the line?"

"The lieutenant said we could," Aiello answered, a little whine coloring his voice.

"The lieutenant? He's a fucking officer, he just got in country, it's his first fucking firefight, and he's a dumbshit. Why the fuck would you listen to him?"

"He outranks us?" Aiello asked pleadingly.

"Fuck!" Samples spit to one side. "Get your asses back on line, right now!"

"What about the fifty?" Johnson meekly asked. "The round went off in the breech. It's probably messed up."

"Then fucking fix it! Are you retarded? Now go!" Samples wasn't as angry as he presented himself, but he needed to impress on these soldiers the urgency of the situation.

The two young men hustled into the back of their track and took their positions. While Johnson worked on the fifty, Aiello started the ramp rising up into place, the motor's whine piercing through the noise. Samples shook his head in disgust again and trudged back to the rest of the company.

He knew he had probably been too hard on them, but he was still seething about Lieutenant Carr. Samples suspected that Carr hadn't actually ordered Aiello to drive Knox out to the road, if only because he doubted the young officer had the balls to make such a decision, but Carr should have known better than to allow them to do so. Aiello and Johnson were young draftees with no real military common sense, while Carr was supposed to be a leader, with training for such circumstances. He had been in the platoon for only a couple weeks, and already he was being a real pain in the ass. Like all lieutenants, as far as Samples was concerned. And though he would never admit it, Samples resented Carr because the officer was taller, better looking, and better educated than he was.

The one-three track roared past him, so Samples followed it through the brush into the plantation, where he saw that the company had begun moving forward slowly. Only a few guns were firing as the men and APCs advanced, seeking out likely hiding places. When they caught up with the company, he made sure the one-three track got into the correct position, noting with satisfaction that Johnson had gotten the fifty-cal working again. Samples then fell into line between the one-one and one-two tracks, so he wouldn't be close to the lieutenant.

There didn't seem to be any return fire, and the open ground between the long lines of gray tree trunks was hardly disturbed by the previous hail of munitions. The trunks themselves were chewed up by the bullets, but seemed in no danger of falling as a result. Samples suspiciously eyed every bush or mound of earth, searching for any sign of the enemy ambushers. He had just about concluded that the gooks were all either dead or withdrawn when he detected an anomalous movement. Two lanes over to his left, in front of second platoon, and four rows to the front, a small patch of ground had trembled. It was right behind one of the trees, and there was no fire in that direction that would be disturbing the earth. It appeared to be just a pile of leaves and sticks, but Samples was instantly on alert.

No sooner had he brought his M-16 up to his shoulder than the pile of leaves lifted up like a trap door and a figure popped up from a hole beneath it. The man wore one of the green NVA pith helmets, and on his shoulder was the tube and conical warhead of a loaded RPG launcher.

"RPG!" Samples yelled, and began pulling the trigger. The enemy soldier swung the launcher to take aim as other Americans joined Samples in firing at him. The soldier jerked as bullets hit him, but he managed to pull the trigger anyway. With a booming back blast the rocket-propelled grenade shot out of the launcher toward third platoon. Samples followed the smoke trail with a feeling of dread, only to see it zoom past the company line and explode against a tree trunk behind them. The gook had dropped back down into his spider hole, probably dead, but no one was taking any chances. Virtually every gun opened fire again, many concentrating on the spider hole, and several M-72 gunners competed to drop their grenades into the hole. One finally succeeded, with a gratifying secondary explosion as spare RPG rounds went off.

The company had stopped moving when the RPG was launched. After the spider hole had been grenaded, a cease-fire order spread through the line. Samples went over to the one-two track and asked Vasquez, the fifty gunner, what was the hold up.

"CO says to wait one," Vasquez told him. Samples surmised that Captain Raymond was checking with battalion about what their next move should be. Meanwhile, Samples stepped back a few paces so he could check on all his troops. To his far right the one-four track was stopped along the edge of the plantation, about fifty feet back from the rest of the line. Spec 4 Hicks was standing on the treads so he could root around in one of the ammo boxes strapped to the top of the track, while Sergeant Washington, the squad leader, looked at something in his hand. Samples started walking toward them, ignoring the lieutenant as he passed behind him. Washington saw him approaching, and held up a hand grenade as Samples came up.

"There's something wrong with these grenades, Sarge," Washington said. Delano Washington was one of only two soul brothers in the platoon, the other being Dupar Johnson in third squad. He was medium height, with a muscular build and ebony skin, and sometimes had an attitude, but he was very competent.

"What do you mean, Del?" Samples asked, taking the grenade from him to examine.

"They ain't going off. We thought we heard some gooks talking a few minutes ago, over behind them bushes, so we tossed a couple grenades over that way, and they didn't go off. Weren't about to go looking for 'em."

"This one looks okay," Samples told him.

"I know, they came out of a new box. We pulled the pins and threw them, but nothing happened. I just noticed they got this other wire around them."

Samples sighed. "It's a safety bale," he explained. "It's new, at least since you went through AIT. Too many straight-leg guys were hanging grenades on their web gear and getting blown up when the pins got pulled by branches and vines, so the Army added this safety bale that you have to pull off first, before you pull the pin."

"Shit," Washington said. "Nobody told us about that."

"Yeah, well, I guess the general's got something better to do than keep us troops informed." Samples actually felt a little guilty, for he had known about the change and not told his soldiers. The mech guys rarely used grenades, except when checking out bunkers and tunnels, and up until now they had been relying on old stock they had been carrying for months. The subject just hadn't come up.

Arturo Chacon, the one-four's driver, stood up in his hatch and yelled down. "Hey, Sarge, the CO says to get ready to move out. Sounds like we're leavin'." Samples glanced down at his watch and was surprised to see it was almost five o'clock. That was the usual quitting time, because the tracks needed to get back into some sort of defensive position before dark. Driving the APCs after dark was too dangerous, because the night belonged to Charlie.

TWO

Carr, riding on the last track to roll through the gate at FSB Wood, was covered with a layer of fine reddish-tan dust. The APCs moved by fits and starts around the inside of the perimeter, pausing to wait as each track ahead of them pulled into the space designated for that vehicle and butted the front of the track up against the berm. Each squad had left one man behind that morning, along with all their extraneous equipment—cots, ice chests, laundry bags, spare water cans, gas cans, etc. If the company made contact, they didn't want the tracks crowded and burdened with unnecessary impediments. The men were left back both to guard their equipment from theft by other soldiers, and to allow at least one man a chance to rest. Of course, those stay-behinds usually ended up doing details for battalion, or shoring up their own section of the perimeter by filling sandbags and fixing the concertina wire, so it wasn't really a day off.

PFC Larry Jones was waiting for them when they finally pulled into their spot on the east side of the FSB and Aiello shut down the engine. Jones greeted them happily as they all climbed down and brushed off the dirt. Their equipment was all stacked neatly up near the berm, and the ice chest sat open, filled with ice and cans of soda. Carr eyed the sodas covetously, but knew he had to wait until the rest of the crew had their chance at them. It was an unwritten rule in the Army that leaders ate and drank last, after ensuring their troops had what they needed. Carr, his helmet left on top of the track, was still slapping at his dusty uniform when Samples strode up and addressed Sergeant Washington.

"Get everybody cleaning their weapons," he instructed. "First Platoon gets to top off first, so have Chacon watch the line at the fuel truck and go over as soon as he can. Make sure the water cans are full and give me a count on your ammo. I don't know yet what battalion has to give out, so we might have to redistribute what we have. Once the track's topped off and the weapons are clean, you can release the guys to go to the mess tent, a few at a time. Got that?"

Carr was standing there listening to Samples, but Samples never even glanced his way. As soon as Washington nodded, Samples hurried away, leaving Carr feeling useless. Washington began passing on the platoon sergeant's instructions to the rest of the squad, and they all got busy cleaning their weapons. Carr was the platoon leader, but he wasn't doing much leading, he realized. He stood there watching the others, and then looked down at his own dusty rifle.

"Want me to clean that for you, sir?" Jones asked, walking up and extending a cold can of RC Cola. Carr took the soda gratefully, but shook his head.

"No, I'll get it. Thanks."

"It's no problem, sir. I cleaned mine earlier, so I've got time to do it."

Carr really appreciated the offer from the young man, whose red hair and freckles made him look like Opie. "Why don't you go help Chacon with the refueling," he suggested gently. Carr had the feeling that if he let Jones clean his weapon, it would only further lower Samples' opinion of his lieutenant.

After cleaning his M-16, Lieutenant Carr cleaned himself as best he could. Removing the liner from his helmet and pulling out the flaps of the camouflage cloth helmet cover, he filled it with water and dropped in a bar of soap. He took off his jungle fatigue blouse and shook it as hard as he could to remove the dust, then hung it on the side of the APC. Using a brown towel dipped in water and rubbed with the soap, he wiped down his face and entire upper body, which felt very refreshing in the waning afternoon heat. Reluctantly he pulled his dirty shirt back on and buttoned it up.

Picking up his rifle, but leaving his pistol belt behind, Carr strolled along the platoon line, pretending to check on the progress his men were making with their evening tasks. He found Staff Sergeant Samples at the first squad's track, regaling them with a humorous story as they all cleaned their weapons. A couple of the men nodded at Carr, but Samples simply glanced at him and continued his story. With a sigh Carr turned away and strolled to the mess tent located near the center of the fire support base, just beyond the 105mm artillery battery. Inside the tent he went through the line, filling his tray with unidentifiable food, then found a seat next to a lieutenant he didn't know. They exchanged meaningless pleasantries as they ate, avoiding any discussion of the day's battle.

As Carr was dumping his tray and preparing to leave, Spec 4 Miles rushed into the tent and ran over to him. Miles was bare-chested, hatless, and without his ubiquitous radio. "Sir," he said breathlessly, "the CO wants you."

"Where is he?" Carr asked, walking quickly out of the mess tent.

"At his track." Miles scampered ahead, anxiously leading Carr back toward the company area. He peeled off as they approached the company commander's APC, parked a few yards behind the second platoon's tracks. The track's rear ramp was down, so Carr ducked his head and entered, taking a seat on the right side bench facing Raymond, who was studying a map.

"You wanted to see me, sir?" Carr prompted.

Captain Raymond's dark curly hair was all askew, and his piercing ice-blue eyes only glanced up at Carr for a second before returning to the acetate-covered topographical map on his lap. "Steve," he said sympathetically, "I know it's already been a pretty tough day for you, but it's not over yet."

"Sir?"

"Battalion wants us to send out a platoon ambush patrol tonight. They're hoping to catch the gooks moving south toward Saigon. The S-2 thinks they may be preparing another Tet-type offensive. I want you to take about half your platoon out tonight and set up along the most likely supply route."

"A night ambush?" Carr said dubiously. "I've never done that, sir."

"I know," Raymond said, his voice rough with fatigue. "It'll be good training," he added facetiously.

"Where am I going?"

Raymond turned the map so it was oriented toward Carr, and extended it for him to see as he traced the route with his finger. "You'll go across the road and head northwest for about two clicks, then head northeast into the woods here for three clicks. You'll head southeast from there for another three clicks, and set up along this clearing. The S-3 is having someone prepare a map for you with the route and waypoints added."

Carr chewed his lower lip as he stared at the map, his mind in turmoil. "Okay, sir. I'm sure Sergeant Samples can help me out."

"Samples won't be going out with you," Raymond said. "I'm worried the gooks might try a ground assault here at the FSB, so we're going to need leadership here as well. I'd suggest you take two of your squad leaders and about twelve men. Sergeant Rael, our Arty FO, will be going, too." That last comment pushed Carr's anxiety level up a notch. If the artillery forward observer was going out, that meant Raymond anticipated their making heavy contact that would require artillery support.

"Yes, sir. When do we head out?"

"It should be dark enough around twenty hundred. Make sure your men are travelling as light and quiet as possible. No helmets, minimal web gear. Maximum ammo, of course. Do you think you can handle this, Steve?"

"We did night patrolling in Ranger School, sir, so I know the basics. But this is a little different."

"Look, ninety-nine percent of AP's never make any contact. You'll probably go out, lie in the bushes for a few hours, and come back. Your main enemies will be bugs and lack of sleep. If you do make contact, you'll have mortars and arty support. Once they're zeroed in, you'll break contact and beat feet back here. No sweat."

Easy for you to say, Carr thought. Out loud he said, "Roger that, sir. I'll go start getting the men ready."

Raymond nodded, then pulled the map back and resumed studying. Carr realized he was being dismissed, and stepped down the ramp into the fading sunlight. He took a deep breath, fighting the fear that was welling up inside of him. The very idea of a night ambush patrol terrified him for some reason. With his mind swirling with all the things he needed to do to prepare, he trudged back to the platoon. He found Samples and pulled him aside.

"I'm taking out a platoon AP tonight," Carr told him.

"The whole platoon?" Samples asked without surprise.

"No, just fifteen or so men."

"Okay," Samples agreed. "When are we leaving?"

"The CO wants you to stay here. I'll take two of the squad leaders, Miles, Doc Allman, and ten more. You can pick them. Sergeant Rael will be going, too."

"Why can't I go?" Samples asked suspiciously.

"The CO thinks there might be an attack here, and wants you to be in charge of the platoon's defense." Samples didn't look convinced. "Figure out who should go out, and have them meet me at the one-four around nine-thirty. No helmets, pack light, but take plenty of ammo. Questions?"

"Negative." Samples pondered a minute. "Art—Sergeant Jamison—has the most experience with AP's, so he'll be one of the squad leaders. He can help you out. The hard part's gonna be keeping track of where you are. You got a good map and a flashlight?"

"Battalion's preparing a map for me. I hadn't thought about a flashlight. Does the platoon have one?"

"I've got one with a red filter. I'll have Art bring it with him."

"Thanks. Well, I've got to go start getting ready. Can you give me a list of names of those going out in an hour or so? I want to be able to do a headcount."

"Roger that." Samples spun on his heel and went to the one-one track, calling out for Sergeant Jamison. Belatedly Carr realized that Samples had never used the word "sir" in his conversation. Granted, Army policy prohibited saluting in the field, to avoid identifying officers as targets for snipers, but verbal forms of respect were still expected. Carr knew he would have to call Samples on it at some point, but this wasn't the time.

While he waited for Jamison, Samples was saying "Bullshit!" under his breath. He didn't believe that the CO had told Carr to leave him back with the tracks. He was the platoon sergeant, after all, and should be going out on the AP to make sure it didn't get screwed up by the green lieutenant. It was like they were saying he wasn't good enough to go out, or was too burned out to be trusted on such a treacherous mission. Due to the division-wide shortage of lieutenants, Samples had been the acting platoon leader for over three months until Carr arrived, and had clearly proven he was capable. The fucking officers were sticking together, though, and cutting him out of the action. "Fuck, fuck, fuck, fuck, fuck!" he muttered.

"Sarge?" Jamison said, looking at Samples with a puzzled expression. The young sergeant had walked up without Samples noticing. Samples cleared his mind and got down to business.

"The lieutenant's taking out a platoon AP tonight," he told Jamison, trying to keep the anger out of his voice. "I want you to go with him to keep his shit straight. I'll have George go, too." George Montoya was the squad leader for the third squad, with seven months in country. "Get five guys from first and second squad, and I'll have Montoya get five from the other two squads. Get volunteers if you can, volunteer some guys if you have to. Make a list for me as soon as you can. Tell them to travel light, no helmets, but plenty of ammo. They're supposed to meet with the lieutenant at the one-four around nine-thirty, but I want to check 'em out first."

"Gotcha," Jamison affirmed. "What about guard duty here? We'll be really short-handed."

"Yeah, I know. Look, get with Reedy and work out a schedule so that there's one guy awake between your two squads. You can have the guys on watch all sit on the one-two, or switch back and forth, I don't care. As long as someone's awake."

"Roger that. " Jamison turned away and called out to Spec 4 Greenberg, who was sitting on a cot writing a letter. "Hey, Simon, wanna go for a walk?"

Samples left Jamison to his recruiting, and walked down to the line to find Montoya. He passed Miles, who was handing out mail, but didn't bother to ask if there was anything for him. He knew there probably wouldn't be. His folks and siblings weren't much for writing letters, and he wasn't interested in any letters from his ex. He found Montoya and told him the same things he had told Jamison, and then told him to come down to the one-one track as soon as he had his list ready.

While his two squad leaders went about their tasks, Samples strolled over to the company headquarters area and wandered around until he found Jesse Rael, the arty FO, sitting on a stack of C-ration cases reading a letter. Rael was a short Hispanic guy from Los Angeles with a knack for numbers. Whenever the company needed artillery support, Rael could bring the fire down right on target, usually after only one marking round. He looked up from his letter when Samples came to a stop in front of him.

"Hey, Jesse," Samples said cordially. Samples liked and respected the young sergeant. "Did you hear?"

"About the AP? Yeah. Sucks."

Samples chuckled. "I know. Hey, man, my Eltee is in charge, and he's never done this shit before, so I'm kinda worried. You gonna be able to take care of him for me?"

"Like how?"

"You know, help him read the map, not get lost. You know what they say; the most dangerous thing in the Army is a lieutenant with a map."

Rael shrugged, smiling at the old joke. "Sure thing, Free." The platoon sergeant's nick-name in the company was "Free" Samples, although nobody called him that to his face except Rael. "Got you covered. Do I have to change his diaper, too?"

"If you don't mind," Samples laughed.

Rael shook his head wearily. "Fuckin' AP led by a green lieutenant. Ain't that the shits."

"Hey, how you gonna act?" The worn catch phrase didn't require an answer. "Thanks, man," Samples told him, lightly tapping Rael's shoulder with his fist. "Take it easy."

Returning to the one-one track, Samples climbed up on top and dug into his ammo can. He found a secretary-sized spiral notebook and a ball-point pen, and sat down to begin preparing for the AP roster. He put a heading on two pages, and numbers down the sides. He planned on making two copies, one for the lieutenant, and one for himself, in case the lieutenant didn't come back or lost someone in the process. Next he told Dale Gunn, the one-one driver, who had just finished checking the engine, to go find Reedy and Washington and ask them to come see him.

A few minutes later Jamison and Montoya climbed up on the track and handed him their lists. Reedy and Washington were right behind them. The five of them went over the names of those going on the AP, and Samples copied the names onto the pages in his notebook. Next they discussed the guard roster for those staying behind, with Samples insisting that he be included in the rotation. Washington and Reedy wrote up the guard roster, and everyone returned to their own squads. Samples climbed down and got a cold soda from the ice chest, which had just been replenished, steeling himself to go talk to Lieutenant Carr. He winced when he saw what kind of soda he had pulled out. It was a Wink, a grapefruit soda that was barely tolerable when cold, and tasted like battery acid when it was warm, as it usually was.

Carr was alone inside the one-four track reading the letter he had just received from his wife. He held the page up at an angle to catch the fading light coming in through the cargo hatch overhead. The inside of the track was painted a light apple green, with narrow metal benches running down each side. Behind the benches were storage areas filled with canvas and waterproof bags, miscellaneous equipment, and an M-60 light machine gun that Chacon occasionally mounted in front of his driver's hatch. Strapped to the right sidewall was the long black tube of a 90-mm recoilless rifle, since fourth squad was the designated weapons squad. They never used it, as it just wasn't an appropriate weapon for jungle fighting. In the storage area up near the engine compartment was the ammo for recoilless, packed in long cardboard tubes strapped vertically to the wall. On the left side of the interior, on a rack bolted to the wall just behind the driver, was the track radio, a heavy metal-encased device the size of a fat briefcase. The front third of the interior, between the benches, was filled with closely-stacked dull green ammo cans— mostly for the fifty-cal, along with some M-16 and M-60 cans. The crowded compartment had already begun to feel like home to Carr.

Outside someone had a radio tuned to AFVN, listening to yet another playing of everyone's favorite song, "The Letter" by the Box Tops. Carr's letter from Sarah was mostly concerned with the everyday activities of her and her family, combined with heartfelt declarations of love for him. Carr had been in Nam only a couple weeks, and already the simple events of home seemed almost fantastical. No wonder the soldiers always referred to the United States as "back in the World." It was an entirely different planet compared to what they were experiencing here.

Outside, PFC Chacon, the one-four's driver, was banging on the track shoes and cursing in a mixture of English and Spanish. Carr had overheard him earlier complaining to Sergeant Samples about not having the proper tools. Samples had told him the tools were on order, but Supply was not known for their promptness in filling such orders. The platoon sergeant had then mentioned, in a suspiciously off-hand manner, that the battalion commander's track never went anywhere, and probably had a full set of tools. "Yeah," Chacon had replied. "That's right."

"Lieutenant?" Samples was standing on the open ramp, leaning down to hold out a piece of paper.

"Come on in, Sergeant," Carr told him, folding up the letter he had been reading. Samples hesitated, then stepped in and sat on the bench opposite Carr.

"Here's the headcount you requested," Samples said, holding out the piece of paper again. This time Carr took it and glanced at it.

It was a neatly printed list of names and ranks, the men who would be accompanying Carr on the ambush patrol.

"Thank you. Is there anything I need to know about any of these men?"

Samples took a moment to consider the question. "Well, Jamison's the most experienced, so I'd have him walk point. Be sure you get the flashlight from him. Montoya can be tail-end Charlie, to make sure no one gets lost or left behind. You need to keep Rael close to you. He's good with a map, and you'll need him to call in arty if you make contact. You may have to come down on Jones—he's a talker. Make sure Miles has a spare battery with him. Otherwise I don't see any problems."

A young man in clean pressed fatigues appeared in the ramp opening. "Lieutenant Carr?" he asked.

"Yes."

"Here's your map, sir." The young man handed him a folded map encased in plastic, and then hurried away, back to the battalion headquarters bunker presumably.

Carr unfolded the map and stared at the grease-pencil lines and words drawn on it. Carr looked up at Samples. "What do you think?" he asked. Reluctantly Samples crossed over and sat beside Carr so he could see the map. He traced the lines with one finger.

"They've got you going northwest into the rice paddies, then northeast into the woods until you hit the Rome Plow, and then southeast to the ambush area. Crossing the paddies will be fairly easy; you can see the stars and Nui Ba Den." Nui Ba Den, Carr knew, was an extinct volcano, also called the "Black Virgin," a conical mountain rising above the otherwise flat terrain that served as a point of reference for miles around. An American encampment at the peak was continually illuminated with yellowish streetlamps. "Once you enter the woods, though, it's going to be rough. You can't see the stars, and you can't travel in a straight line, even if you wanted to. You got a compass?"

Carr pointed to his pistol belt lying on top of the fifty ammo. Attached to it was a small pouch that contained an Army lensatic compass. "Yes. I even know how to use it," he said, instantly regretting the snide remark. Samples didn't react.

"Jesse will have one, too," Samples continued, referring to Sergeant Rael. "The key to a successful night AP is not getting lost. Anything else is secondary. Now the map shows a clearing here where you're supposed to set up, but these maps are old and out-of-date. There might be a clearing, and there might not. The boonies grow pretty fast here. And even if there is a clearing, it might not be what you expect. It could have bushes growing head-high, which would pretty much cover any gooks walking through there." Samples stopped talking and just studied the map.

"Anything else?" Carr prompted.

Samples shook his head. "Just don't get any of our guys killed," he said evenly. With that he left.

The last glow from the setting sun had faded, but a half moon rising in the east cast a bluish glow that barely outlined the dark figures of the men as they milled around just inside the gate of the fire support base. There was muted talk and occasional stifled laughs. Carr peered through the darkness, trying to identify the various men. With all of them dressed and equipped the same, and their faces in shadow under their boonie hats, it was almost impossible. Only the two men carrying M-79 grenade launchers—called bloop guns by the soldiers—were easily distinguishable. Carr checked the barely glowing hands of his watch, and saw that it was now ten o'clock. "Sergeant Jamison," he said, just loud enough to be heard over the murmur of the men's conversations. Carr directed the remark in the general direction of the group, since he was unable to pick out which one was Jamison. He was relieved when one of the men stepped forward.

"Yes, sir," he said. The other men went silent.

"You'll take point. I'll be right behind you, then Miles and Sergeant Rael. Sergeant Montoya?" Carr paused until he saw one of the men raise his hand. "You'll bring up the rear. The rest of you men fall in behind Sergeant Rael. Stay in line, keep up, and keep quiet. Any questions?"

"How far out we going'?" someone asked.

"About eight clicks."

"Shit," someone else muttered. Carr ignored the remark.

"All right, let's move out." Carr motioned to the two men who were the gate guards that evening. They carefully grabbed the coils of razor wire and accordioned them to either side of the entrance road. Jamison strode forward through the gate, and Carr followed close behind. The others fell into line behind them. Once they were out of the gate, they followed the entrance road to the main road and crossed it into the dry rice paddies on the other side. The only sounds were the shuffling of their boots and the occasional clack of magazines in their carrying sacks. Most of the men had Claymore bags stuffed with spare magazines, and the bloop gunners had special vests with multiple pockets for the large grenade rounds. Carr had only the two ammo pouches he had been issued, pouches designed for the old M-14 magazines, now clipped to his pistol belt. He had stuffed three of the M-16 20-round magazines into each, and barely managed to clip the canvas lid shut. He needed to get a Claymore bag like the rest of the men, because one of those green cloth bags with a shoulder strap would hold more than a dozen magazines.

As they crossed the first rice paddy, Carr turned and walked backwards for a few steps, striving to see the line of men behind him. As far as he could tell, they were all there and keeping up. He spun back around and scanned the sky and horizon to make sure he had his bearings. Using the Big Dipper as his pointer, he found the North Star, just where he expected it to be. Below and to the left of the North Star he saw the twinkling yellow lights of Nui Ba Den. As long as they were traveling through the open rice paddies, he wouldn't need the compass to maintain his directions. He wondered if the local farmers let their water buffalos roam free at night. He would hate to run into one of those beasts in the dark—they notoriously disliked Americans, and would charge at the slightest provocation.

More worrisome was the danger that the VC or NVA had set up an ambush of their own, somewhere in these rice paddies. The wide open flat terrain, with only foot-high dikes separating the dry paddies, left few hiding places for such an ambush, but the gooks were skilled at traveling by night and quickly digging in. Carr's eyes had fully adjusted to the darkness, and the wan moonlight revealed the geometric pattern of the dikes, with no ominous mounds or unexpected shapes breaking the outlines. Quietly the patrol trudged northwestward, snaking over the east-west dikes and across a narrow ditch that was still wet at the bottom. Carr knew he should have been counting his steps, in order to determine how far they had gone, but he hadn't. It was easier to count paddy dikes. Knowing the average size of a rice paddy, he had worked out how many paddies would take them two kilometers from the FSB. It wasn't exact, but it was easier than counting paces.

When he thought he had gone far enough, Carr halted the column and took a look around him. According to the map, the tree line to the east jutted out in line with the place they were supposed to turn northwest, marked on the map as checkpoint alpha. To his eyes, however, the dark fuzzy strip appeared uniform. He turned and quietly spoke to Sergeant Rael.

"What do you think? Is this checkpoint alpha?"

Rael studied their surroundings for a moment. "Could be," he admitted.

Jamison joined them, whispering hoarsely. "I think we've gone at least three clicks, maybe more."

"Okay," Carr told them, "then let's start moving at a 45 degree heading. We should hit the tree line in a couple hundred meters." He opened his compass and steadied it at waist level to take a reading. Looking up from the compass, he spotted a distant break in the tree line that would make a suitable visual point for reference. He pointed it out to Jamison, and the patrol resumed movement in the new direction. Behind him Carr could barely hear Miles as he called in the checkpoint on his radio.

It wasn't long before they left the rice paddies and entered the band of heavy brush that bordered the thick woods. Although not technically a jungle, the woods were an imposing and difficult forest, with tall leafy trees, dense underbrush, and a network of thorny vines. Once they entered the woods, they lost all visual orientation under the dense canopy of leaves. Keeping an eye on his compass, Carr strived to keep them moving in a straight line, but it was difficult because of the detours around tree trunks and thick clumps of thorns. Eventually, as expected, they came to the Rome Plow area.

A large section of the woods in this area had been knocked down by Rome Plows, giant bulldozers that simply pushed the trees over and ground them into the earth. Left behind was a jumble of tangled limbs and tree trunks that made passage extremely arduous. The patrol had pushed through the foliage until they reached the first of the fallen trees, and there they halted. Jamison and Montoya had the men spread out and kneel down while Carr and Rael consulted their maps.

"I think we're about here," Carr said, pointing to a spot on his map that was slightly west of their planned route. Miles was holding the flashlight over their shoulders, its red filter barely illuminating the map and altering the colors. The Rome Plow strip ran east and west, and marked the point where they were to turn southeast.

Rael consulted his own map, and then grunted his agreement. "Yeah," he said. "If we follow the edge of the Rome Plow east about a hundred meters, we should be able to hang a right and enter the wood line where we were supposed to."

"Sergeant Jamison," Carr called softly. Jamison was a few feet away, watching and listening for any movement among the fallen trees of the Rome Plow. He edged back to where Carr and Rael were squatting. "We're going to head east along the Rome Plow a hundred meters, then we'll cut back into the woods at an angle."

"Roger that, sir," Jamison whispered, then passed the word to the rest of the men. Cautiously they formed up into a line again and began pushing through the underbrush that bordered the Rome Plow. The plowed area was an almost perfect rectangular strip cut into the woods, stretching far off to the east. They skirted it for a couple minutes before making a right turn back into the woods. The Rome Plow had been relatively well lit by the moonlight, but the woods were as dark as sin. They paused after entering the wood line while Carr took a compass reading, and then pushed on deeper into the gloom. Miles quietly called in that they had passed checkpoint Bravo. The ground cover was less dense here, which made the going easier, but the random massive tree trunks kept them from moving in a straight line. Carr kept consulting his compass, tapping Jamison on the shoulder frequently to redirect him.

The dimness under the canopy of leaves limited vision to only a few feet, and the bushes and vines tugged at their clothes and scratched their hands and faces. Carr was very aware that they were traveling slower than he had hoped. They sometimes ran across trails that beckoned them to take an easier route, but Carr knew that way led to more danger. While they might be just game trails, they were more likely something used by the gooks to transport men and supplies south toward Saigon. In the darkness of the woods, the gooks would hear them coming long before they could see them, and set up an ambush for the Americans that would turn the tables.

When Carr's watch said it was after eleven, they came to a very small clearing, really only a gap where one tree had fallen and no others had yet filled in behind it. Carr called a short halt, and the men quickly dispersed around the perimeter of the clearing. A small circle of the sky was visible overhead, but not enough to reveal the North Star or any other familiar constellations. Again, Carr and Rael squatted down and consulted their maps in the crimson glow of the flashlight. Carr traced the line on the map, trying to compare it to the woods they had just traversed. His finger stopped on the line a short distance from the ambush site.

"Think we've made it here?" he asked Rael.

"Fuck if I know, sir," Rael replied. "Maybe. But these fucking woods. . ." He shook his head.

"Yeah, how can we be sure," Carr mused. "There are no landmarks, and we can't see more than a couple meters."

"We could call for a marking round," Rael suggested. Carr's confusion must have been evident. "We can have the mortar guys send a star shell right here on this reference point." The map had included several reference points, each with a label such as "beer", "cars", "cities", etc. The theory was that the patrol could call in its location by saying they were three hundred meters south of "Budweiser", and any gooks listening in would be unable to pinpoint them. Each time they re-used one of the reference points, they would choose another name in the same category, such as Miller or Pabst, and this would further confuse the enemy. Carr quickly grasped what Rael was suggesting. A star shell above a certain reference point could provide a location from which Carr could shoot a back azimuth with the compass. Tracing a line on the map from the reference point along the back azimuth would give them at least an approximation of their location on the route of march. Two marking rounds, at different reference points, would give them an even better estimate, but would also alert the gooks that there was someone in the area. Carr considered the pluses and minuses.

"Not yet," he told Rael finally. "That opening is so small, we might not even see the star shell, and even if we did, the gooks would know we're out here somewhere. Let's assume we're where we're supposed to be, and keep moving toward the big clearing. If we don't find it, then we can call for marking rounds."

"Your call, sir," Rael said.

Constantly checking his compass, Carr led the men through more of the woods, although it all looked the same to him. After thirty minutes they had found no big clearing. The woods had thinned a little, but the sky was still only barely visible between the between the trees. Carr felt totally lost. On the bright side, he thought, he wasn't consumed with fear. He knew he was in a dangerous situation, but what he was experiencing was rational concern and unease, not irrational fright and alarm. So he wasn't a coward, he told himself ruefully, just incompetent.

Stretched out on the metal bench seat of the one-one track, Aaron Samples was asleep, sort of. The track radio, on the far wall, was turned down very low, emitting a low rush of static interrupted by briefly-whispered status reports by the men on guard. Samples was able to doze without really hearing the messages as his brain automatically categorized them as non-essential and ignorable. Dale

Gunn, the track's driver, was asleep on the other bench, while someone from second squad stood watch on top of his own track.

"Golf four six, this is three three Alpha Papa, over," the radio murmured. Samples was instantly awake. That was Miles calling in from the ambush patrol. G46 was battalion, which had insisted on controlling the patrol directly. Samples put his feet down on the floor and leaned across the track to turn up the radio volume a little. Gunn kept snoring.

"This is four six, go ahead, over."

"Four six, this is Alpha Papa, request a star shell at reference point Budweiser, over."

"Say again." The battalion radio operator's voice had a tinge of disbelief.

"I say again, we need a star shell at Budweiser, over."

"Wait one." Samples knew the guy who had radio watch would be waking up the duty officer. Depending on who that was, he might make a decision on his own, or wake up the battalion commander. Either way, he would have the radio operator ring up the mortar guys on the land line and have them start preparing. After a few minutes a new voice came on the radio.

"Alpha Papa, this is Golf four six Delta, do you have contact, over?"

"Negative, four six, we just need to confirm our position, over."

"Roger. Wait one." Silence for about thirty seconds, and then the voice at battalion said, "On the way, over." Samples heard the deep pop of a mortar tube from across the fire support base. Shaking his head, he muttered, "Stupid shit lieutenant."

"Wha?" Gunn groaned, squirming on the bench.

"The lieutenant's lost," Samples explained succinctly. He turned on the red light that dimly illuminated the inside of the vehicle.

"Yeah, so?"

"He's calling for star shells."

Gunn sat up and rubbed his eyes. "Why?" Gunn had only been in Nam for a couple months, and as a driver had never been out on a platoon ambush.

"So he can take an azimuth from it and figure out where he is."

Gunn started to ask another question, but stopped when the radio squawked again.

"Four six, this is Alpha Papa. Request another star shell, this time at Cadillac, over."

"God fuckin' damn," Samples cursed. "They might as well put up a fuckin' neon sign tellin' the gooks, 'Here we are'."

"Wait one, over," the voice at battalion said. After a moment he came back on and said, "On the way, over."

There was no radio traffic for a couple minutes. Then a new voice came on the radio. "Alpha Papa, this is four six Lima, put your Papa Lima on." Samples groaned. He knew that was the battalion S-3, and he sounded pissed. Major Moore, the S-3 Operations Officer, was not known for his patience with subordinates.

Samples waited, and after a few seconds he heard Lieutenant Carr's voice. "Four six Lima, this is Alpha Papa Romeo, over."

"Are you at checkpoint Charlie now?"

There was a long pause before Carr answered. "Not sure, sir, over." Samples winced at the violation of radio procedure. Carr should not have said 'sir,' but his fear of the battalion staff had apparently overridden common sense.

There was another long pause. Samples could just imagine the major cursing as he consulted with whoever else was in the command bunker. Finally the radio fan whined into action as the major's voice came over loud and clear. "Alpha Papa, set up where you are and provide hourly sitreps. Do you copy? Over."

"Roger. Good copy, over." Even over the radio Samples could detect Carr's chagrin.

"Four six, out." The major had clearly emphasized that the conversation was finished.

"That boy's gonna have some serious 'splainin' to do in the morning," Samples said with a chuckle. He checked his watch before turning the red light back out. He had twenty minutes until his guard shift started—not enough to get back to sleep. "I'm going on guard," he told Gunn, who had already lain back down. Pulling himself up through the cargo hatch, he scrambled over the ammo boxes and junk lying there and jumped down to the ground. He walked the short distance over to the one-two track and quietly called up to the man sitting in the machine gun turret, Fred Aiello.

"Hey, Freddie, I'm takin' over guard now. Go get some zees."

"Roger that, Sarge," Aiello answered, standing up to stretch.

"Where's Merrill sleep," Samples asked. "He's after me, right?"

"He's got a cot on the other side of the track. Be advised, he's hard to wake up."

"Not for me," Samples warned jokingly. Back at the one-one track he climbed up and took a seat behind the fifty-cal machine gun, making sure the pork-chop microphone has hooked on the edge of the turret, it's coiled cable stretching down to the track radio inside, just above Gunn's head. Adjusting the folded canvas bench cushion nestled in the concave side of the turret hatch cover, he positioned his boots on either side of the machine mount and began sweeping his gaze across the dark fields in front of him. It was boring but necessary duty.

The half-moon was almost directly overhead, bathing the empty rice paddies and fields in a ghostly light, broken by the dark tree line a few hundred meters away. Samples had been on duty for over an hour, struggling to stay awake and worrying about his men out with the lieutenant. If any of those men was killed or injured as a result of that officer's stupidity or ineptitude, there would be hell to pay. Samples didn't believe in fragging, the rumored practice of some enlisted men to roll a fragmentation grenade under a troublesome officer's cot, but he was beginning to at least understand the motivation behind it. Viet Nam was a screwed-up war, with no discernible goals and misleading reports of success from senior officers. It seemed to Samples that the officer corps was continuing the war purely for the benefit it would have on their careers, at the expense of the enlisted men who actually had to fight and die.

There was a pop as a mortar round launched from the tube, and with a start Samples realized the sound had come from in front of him, not behind. It had to have come from within the wood line off to the east. He grabbed the mike, pressed the rubber-covered button on the side, and yelled "Incoming!" as loud as he could. Then he pulled up his feet and dropped down inside the turret hatch, continuing to hold down the mike button. "Mortars in the tree line to the east!" he announced as he waited for the first round to complete its high arc and explode somewhere inside the perimeter. There were two more pops from the tree line just before the first round exploded just a few yards to the right front of the one-one track. Samples heard the shrapnel patter against the front and side armor, and then clods of dirt rain down on the roof. The next two rounds fell behind him somewhere, but he didn't have time to figure out exactly where. He stood up on the ammo cans and stuck his head up through the hatch enough to grasp the wooden handles of the fifty-cal. Over the radio someone called out "Open fire!" unnecessarily.

Pushing the butterfly trigger with both hands, Samples was dismayed when nothing happened. He realized the gun had not been charged, and quickly grasped the charging handle, dragging it backwards twice. With the gun now ready, he again pressed the trigger just as he heard more pops from the woods. Crouching low to see through the triangular mount beneath the gun, he began firing short bursts to rake the line of trees to the east. Every fifth round was a tracer round, helping him correct his aim as he fired. Over the pounding blasts of the machine gun, he heard more mortar rounds falling inside the perimeter, but paid them little heed.

The red streaks of the tracers seemed to float across the fields before disappearing into the woods, although occasionally one would ricochet up into the sky. Other guns joined his in spraying the wood line, while mortar rounds continued to fall, some outside the perimeter, but most within. To his left Samples felt, more than saw, that Gunn had popped up in the drivers hatch and was firing the M-60 light machine gun he had mounted on a pintle clamped to one of the headlight brackets. Only the Alpha company tracks faced the east, limiting the number of guns that could be brought to bear on the enemy, but all of them were firing in a swelling wave of explosive clamor.

Somewhere from within the perimeter American mortars began counter-battery fire, launching mortar rounds larger than those of the enemy, and these began exploding in the trees. A couple parachute flares popped overhead, the bright white flares swinging underneath the parachutes, bringing the rice paddies and fields into sharp relief. Samples saw that some of the trees in the wood line were actually falling, having been cut in two by the stream of bullets from the base. As American mortars continued to raise clouds of dust and leaves somewhere within the woods, Samples noticed that no more enemy mortar rounds were coming in. At the same time, his fifty-cal clicked to a halt as the last rounds from the ammo can were fired. Flinging the empty can over the side, Samples ducked down and grabbed a fresh ammo can to pull up through the hatch. He jammed it into the ammo tray, and then took it out and turned it around so the lid would open the right way. Flipping open the catch and allowing the lid to flop open, he grabbed at the linked bullets and fed the first one into the gun's mechanism. A couple cranks of the charging handle and the gun was loaded and ready to go again, but a cease-fire order came over the radio and was repeated along the line.

The last of the small arms and machine-gun fire echoed away, but the crunch of mortar explosions still reverberated occasionally. Someone had realized that the parachute flares did more to make the fire support base a target than help against the gooks, who were dug in within the woods, and those had all sputtered out as they neared the ground. Samples swept the area in front of him with his eyes, willing them to regain their night vision. He could detect no movement, but he was well aware that the gooks were masters of approaching a perimeter at night without being seen. He was starting to relax a little when new shots rang out. They weren't American guns. By the deeper crack and different rhythm, Samples knew immediately they were AK-47s.

Some came from the wood line, but a few came from the ditch that ran alongside the road off to his left. Then an RPD machine gun opened up from the woods, its green tracers flying toward the tracks to his right. Immediately Samples pressed the fifty-cal's trigger and began pouring fire toward the tree line, sweeping his red tracers across the area where the RPD had been firing. Other guns opened up along the perimeter, some toward the woods, and some raking the ditch. The heavy mortars resumed their fire, walking the rounds left and right along the wood line, while some enterprising M-79 gunners launched grenades toward the nearer stretches of the ditch. After a minute or so, Samples and the other men paused their firing to take stock. No more enemy guns were firing. Samples hoped they had killed them all, but he realized that it was more likely that they had simply melted back into the dark. Along the line he could hear men checking their weapons and loading new magazines, ready for the next onslaught. Fortunately, it never came.

THREE

The sun had just risen when Lieutenant Carr and his weary patrol trudged through the gate of the fire support base, ignoring the sarcastic "Welcome home" remarks from the gate guards. Sending the rest of the patrol on to their individual squads, Carr peeled off at the company headquarters element to go see Captain Raymond, with Sergeant Rael following. Carr found the CO sitting in the back of his track, the ramp lowered, eating from a paper plate. Raymond looked up at Carr and smiled.

"Steve, how was it?" Raymond asked pleasantly. Carr was relieved that he wasn't being dressed down as soon as he showed up, although he expected it would come soon enough.

"Not so good," Carr admitted, sitting down on the bench opposite his commander. He eyed the bacon and scrambled eggs enviously. "We didn't really get lost, but we weren't sure exactly where we were, either." He looked around and noticed that Rael had disappeared. He had hoped the young sergeant would be there to back him up.

"I heard the calls for marking rounds," Raymond said. "The S-3 wasn't exactly pleased."

"So I gathered. Those woods were pretty heavy, and we couldn't get our bearings. Rael and I thought a marking round would help us get better oriented, but we couldn't even see the first one at all. We barely saw the second one, and it didn't help all that much. Then the major said to just stay where we were, so we did."

"Well, those things happen," Raymond commiserated. He took another bite of his breakfast. "Did you ever hear or see any movement?"

"Not a thing, but we did hear all the gunfire from here. What happened?"

"We had mortars and a small ground attack on the east side, in front of your platoon. A couple of minor injuries, but nothing serious. The CRIP platoon is out checking to see if the gooks left any bodies behind. Not likely." The Combined Reconnaissance and Intelligence Platoon was a fairly new innovation in Headquarters Company. A mix of Americans and South Vietnamese, they did independent patrols and talked to the villagers. That independence had led to disquieting rumors about their activities.

Carr nodded, and then changed the subject. "Am I going to have to face the major, sir?" he asked plaintively.

Raymond grinned. "Not today, Steve. I'm sure he's over it by now. Look, I've got a meeting with the colonel in ten minutes, about what our mission will be for today. Why don't you go get some breakfast and clean up a little. We'll probably be moving out in an hour or so."

"Roger that, sir," Carr replied, buoyed by the reprieve. Ducking out of the commander's track he hurried back to the one-four track, where he was met by Miles, who was holding two paper plates piled high with breakfast. Miles had already ditched his radio, helmet, and rifle somewhere. His brown hair pointed in all directions, and his green eyes sparkled as he gave Carr an encouraging smile.

"You better eat something, sir," Miles said, handing Carr one of the plates. "It's a long time till dinner."

"Thanks," Carr told him, taking one of the plates. He set the plate down on the end of the bench inside the track, then climbed in and sat down beside it, dropping his helmet on the floor and laying his rifle on the bench beside him. Clearing some gear out of the way, Miles took a seat on the bench across from him and began eating. Carr picked up his own plate, pulled out the white plastic spoon he always carried in his shirt pocket, and dug into the scrambled eggs. They were reconstituted powdered eggs, of course, but he was so hungry he didn't care.

Fortunately, Mile was too busy eating to talk. Carr was hoping Miles didn't become a problem. Carr appreciated having at least one member of the platoon who didn't treat him like a pariah, but Miles' puppy-dog affection was a little cloying. It could become a problem for the boy if the rest of the platoon regarded him as a teacher's pet, and a problem for Carr if Miles started assuming authority he didn't really have. Carr had been warned about this problem in his training back in the States, so he knew he would have to be wary with Miles. Which was too bad, because he really liked the timid young man.

Folding a piece of soft white bread around the greasy limp slice of bacon, he took a bite and thought about his report to Captain Raymond. He hadn't told the commander everything, and never would. It had been the Arty FO, Rael, who had pressured him into the requests for marking rounds, but Carr wasn't going to use that as an excuse. He was an officer, the man in charge, and he could have refused. But he didn't. That was his fault, and his alone. He despised leaders who blamed their subordinates for their own mistakes, and he wouldn't be one of them.

The fact that they had not found the ambush site specified for them was nobody's fault, in his opinion. With no visible landmarks or way to accurately determine distance, the chances that they would end up where they were supposed to were astronomical. Carr had heard that most ambush patrols didn't even try to find their designated area; they just went out of sight of the base or laager and found a comfortable place to sleep. They would rotate the duty of being awake to call in sitreps at the required times, and in the morning return none the worse for wear. Carr had at least tried to follow orders and set up an effective ambush. Although they had been unable to find the clearing that battalion had chosen—one that might not even exist—they had stumbled across a trail that appeared to have been used recently. Setting up a few feet to the west of the trail, the men had taken up prone positions in a line wherever trees or bushes gave them a little cover and concealment. Carr had even considered setting up the field manual preferred L-shaped ambush, but without knowing which way the gooks would be coming from, if at all, he decided that wouldn't work.

Per policy, the men were to maintain a 50% guard ratio. That meant the men would pair up, and one of each pair could sleep while the other kept watch, switching off every hour. Carr had buddied up with Miles, of course, and he told Miles to go to sleep while he took the first watch. Miles readily agreed, and was soon on his back with his head nestled in his helmet as a pillow, sleeping like a baby. With total silence, the patrol melted into the forest background. Keeping the radio handset next to his ear, Carr had wiggled around on the ground trying to get comfortable, hoping he wasn't near an ant hill or poisonous snake. Once he had settled in, the darkness and spookiness of the woods, silent except for the muffled adjustment noises of the men who were still awake, swelled around him.

Suddenly Carr was terrified. It was the unreasoning fear of a child who was scared of the monster under his bed—logically he knew it didn't exist, but he wasn't about to get out of bed and find out. Hands trembling, knees quivering, Carr felt the terror sweep over him like a heavy blanket. His left hand gripped the radio handset in an iron fist, and his right hand clutched his rifle like it was a magic talisman. *I could die tonight!* Carr found himself thinking. While he had always recognized on a certain level that he could be killed or wounded in Viet Nam, until now it had not really sunk in. Now, suddenly, it was real and possibly imminent. They were just over a dozen men, armed only with rifles, deep in what was actually enemy territory. Since they had been unable to accurately establish their position, they could not call for mortar or artillery support if attacked. There could be hundreds of gooks in the surrounding woods, and not necessarily on the trail. What if they were attacked from behind?

Carr gritted his teeth and tried to shake the terror, but with only limited success. His ears were attuned to the slightest sound, and he kept imagining the snap of a twig or the crunch of a foot on fallen leaves. His rational mind told him that since he didn't know where he and his men were for sure, the enemy was unlikely to know either, and the woods went on for miles. The chances of any gooks stumbling over them were infinitesimal, but that didn't really quell the dread that clutched at his chest. On the one hand, he wanted to get up and run screaming through the woods, and on the other he wanted to curl up in a fetal ball and pretend the outside world didn't exist. Neither option was practical, so he just lay there and trembled.

To his left Miles breathed heavily, not quite a snore. To his right Sergeant Jamison sniffed, and Carr could tell he had reached up to scratch his nose. As quickly as it had appeared, Carr's fright disappeared. If Miles and Jamison weren't worried, why should he be? Carr took a deep breath and calmed himself. He checked the glowing hands of his watch, and saw that he had another half hour to go until he could wake Miles. That was manageable, even boring, as long as the terror didn't return.

"If you're done, sir, I'll take your plate," Miles said, bringing him out of his reverie. Carr handed him the soggy paper plate and rubbed his face. Time to shave, he decided.

A few minutes later he was standing beside the track, holding his upturned helmet half full of soapy water in his left hand while he shaved with his right, staring at a small polished steel mirror hanging by a string from one of the lifting shackles. He heard Sergeant Samples' voice, and half turned to see him consulting with Sergeant Montoya. Samples broke away from Montoya and walked past Carr calling for Washington. Almost as an afterthought, he looked over at Carr and said, "The CO wants to see you at his track."

"When?" Carr asked.

Without looking back as he walked around to the other side of the one-four track, Samples said, "Five minutes ago."

Seething, Carr quickly finished his shave, dumped the water from his helmet, put the helmet liner back in, grabbed his rifle, and hurried over to the company headquarters area. The other two platoon leaders, Mel Baron of Second Platoon and Jay Fawcett of Third Platoon, were already there inside the CO's track, along with the mortar sergeant, Holmes.

"Come on in, Steve," Captain Raymond said, waving at an empty space on one of the benches.

"Sorry I'm late, sir," Carr apologized. "I just got the word."

"No sweat," Raymond assured him. "I just came back from the command briefing at battalion. Gentlemen, we are going to the Crescent today."

From studying maps of the AO—Area of Operations—Carr knew that the Crescent was a quarter-moon-shaped stretch of heavy forest just to the west of Dau Tieng, curling around to the east toward Tay Ninh. In fact, Carr realized, his ambush patrol had been in the lower end of the Crescent. To the north of the Crescent was

War Zone C, and then the Cambodian border. To the south were the Boi Loi Woods, the Ho Bo Woods, the Trapezoid, the Iron Triangle, and eventually Saigon. These thick forests and jungles provided numerous routes from the southern end of the Ho Chi Minh Trail in Cambodia to the South Vietnamese capital. Hence the many operations and efforts to cut the supply lines.

"According to the S-2, the gooks that ambushed us in the Ben Cui yesterday have pulled back to base camps in the Crescent. Our job is to seek them out and destroy them." Raymond spread out a map on an up-ended C-ration case and pointed to it. "Our company will sweep northwest from the main road here. Charlie will go in through the Ben Cui over here, and Bravo from here in the west. In theory it's a pincer movement, with us driving the gooks into Bravo and Charlie. We'll see."

Everyone studied the map, and Raymond gave them time to come up with questions. After a minute, Sergeant Holmes asked, "Mortars going on the sweep?" It was a valid question, because the mortar tracks usually set up somewhere within range of the sweep and then waited for any calls for fire.

"Afraid so, Sam," Raymond answered. "Here's the plan for our company. We'll roll out of the FSB in reverse order, third, second, and first platoons, and then the mortars. Headquarters element will fall in between second and third. We'll head down the highway to around here, and then turn northwest into the woods. Jay, make sure you guard our right flank, and Steve, the same for the left. Sam, you'll move out last, and keep your mortar tracks about a hundred meters behind the headquarters element. If we make any contact, you'll have to set up quick."

Holmes nodded his understanding, but clearly wasn't happy about it.

Raymond continued. "Battalion figures we'll meet up with Bravo and Charlie by 1400 if we don't make contact. That's almost seven clicks through thick jungle, so I have my doubts. Anyway, it's important that we stay on line and don't get ahead of ourselves. We don't want any casualties from friendly fire now, do we?" Everyone nodded their understanding. Due to the restricted visibility, maintaining a company-sized line through heavy forest was extremely difficult.

Raymond checked his watch. "We're rolling out at 0830. Get 'em ready."

Samples and the four squad leaders were gathered behind the one-two track. The rest of the men in the platoon were either standing by their tracks, or already mounted up. All had their helmets and pistol belts on, their bulging ammo bags slung over their shoulders, and the weapons in their hands. Samples already knew the plan for the day. One of the battalion radio operators used to be in the platoon, and he had told Samples what he had overheard during the battalion command briefing earlier. Samples had relayed an abridged version to the squad leaders, but they all had to wait and hear it from the lieutenant. When Samples saw Lieutenant Carr come out of the CO's track, he quietly spoke to the squad leaders without turning around.

"Remember, guys, pay attention and act dumb. That shouldn't be too hard." The other men chuckled, knowing Samples was joking.

Carr looked surprised as he approached Samples and the others. That was just what Samples had intended. He wanted to show the lieutenant just how unnecessary he really was. He suppressed a smile as he saw drops of water still dripping from Carr's helmet.

"Everyone's ready?" Carr asked. Samples nodded. "Uh, good work, sergeant." Carr paused to gather his thoughts, and Samples tried to look bored.

"Okay," Carr continued, "we're going to sweep the Crescent today. S-2 thinks the gooks that ambushed us yesterday are hiding out in there. It's a battalion sweep, with us driving northwest from the road, Charlie coming in from the Ben Cui, and Bravo from the west. March order for our company will be third, HQ, second, us, and mortars. Questions?"

"Nope," Samples said, speaking for everyone. As he hoped, this made Carr a little flustered.

"Okay." Carr looked around, brushing a stray drop of water from the front of his helmet. "We're rolling at 0830. Sergeant Samples, make sure everyone's got a full ammo load and a full canteen."

"Already checked," Samples said smugly.

"Okay," Carr said again, lamely. They all heard the diesel engines cranking up down the line in third and second platoons. Carr looked at his watch.

Before the lieutenant could say anything else, Samples turned away and began yelling. "Mount up! Crank 'em up! Let's go kick some gook ass!" With some satisfaction he watched out of the corner of his eye as Carr turned and hurried down to the one-four track, anxious to not be left behind. Samples observed his men scrambling on top of the tracks and taking their places on the ammo boxes strapped there, and reveled in the rumble of the tracks' engines as they started up, belching black smoke from their exhaust. One by one the drivers electrically raised the rear ramps of the blocky vehicles, locking them in place. Although he had experienced it dozens of times, the sights and sounds of his platoon preparing for battle still stirred his blood. Having confirmed that everyone was ready, even the lieutenant pulling on a CVC helmet, Samples strode over to the one-one track and clambered aboard.

Diesel smoke enveloped him as he stood beside the machine gun turret and gave the hand signals for the platoon to back out of their fighting positions and line up on the road. Bracing himself with his knee against the turret side, he remained standing as the one-one track backed and turned, so he could observe the other tracks doing the same. Satisfied that the vehicles behind him were in proper order, he turned to face the front, gazing over the tracks of second platoon to see if the third platoon tracks were moving yet. After a few moments, with gouts of dirty smoke and jerks as the drive wheels took up the slack in the tread links, the APCs up front began to move. As third platoon eased forward, the headquarters element—the CO's track, medics track, and mechanics track—

pulled in behind them. Second platoon began to move, and when their last track had started to pull away, Samples waved his arm for first platoon to follow. Roaring engines and clanking treads drowned out any voices. The company was on the move.

The rainy season, in theory, should have already started, but except for a shower two weeks earlier, this part of Viet Nam was as dry as a bone. The company of APCs rumbling down the dirt highway like a steam train threw up billowing clouds of reddish dust. Leading the last platoon in line, Samples was soon covered in a fine layer of silt, and he kept blowing and wiping at his M-16 to keep it as clean as possible. With a wry smile only slightly tinged with guilt, he figured the lieutenant would be even dirtier. But, as the troops frequently said, "it don't mean nothin'."

When they reached the designated area, Captain Raymond had all the tracks do a hard left and roll off the road into the low brush that bordered it and stop. Roughly a hundred meters way the forest began, a dark and brooding line of trees that marked the edge of the Crescent. With the engines now at idle, Samples heard the CO come over the track radio inside.

"Recon by fire," he ordered, "for exactly one minute. At my command." Raymond paused to allow all the squads get ready. Since they were all still mounted, only the 50-cal and mounted M-60 machine guns would be firing. "Fire!" With a thunderous roar the guns of Alpha Company erupted in a stream of bullets, the tracers arcing redly, visible even in the bright morning sun. Samples shifted his position to avoid the stream of hot shell casings that flew from his track's machine gun as Greenberg triggered textbook five-round bursts that lashed the distant trees. Keeping one eye on his watch, at one minute he placed a hand on Greenberg's forearm as a signal to stop. The rest of the company came to a sputtering halt as well, responding to the cease fire call repeated on the radio.

His ears were still ringing from the noise, but Samples listened intently for any possible return fire. Aside from the idling diesels and the snaps and clunks of weapons being reloaded, everything was quiet. Over the radio came the expected order: "Dismount!" Samples repeated it in his best command voice, urging his men to quickly get into position. The driver, 50-cal gunner, and one loader stayed on each track, while the rest of the men climbed or jumped down and formed a line about ten feet in front of the tracks. Samples made sure everyone had their helmet on, and spread them out evenly. With only six or seven in the average track's total crew, the line of dismounts looked pretty sparse. Samples took a position near the center of the line, and he was annoyed when Lieutenant Carr and Miles joined him.

"Nice day for a walk in the woods," Carr said. Samples resisted a smart-ass reply. He knew the officer was just trying to be friendly, and was aware that he himself was actively fighting the urge to do so in return. His dislike of lieutenants was well founded, and he wouldn't let this one change his mind.

"Another hot one," Samples managed to answer mildly.

Miles, standing the requisite two feet behind and to the left of the lieutenant, had the handset pressed to his ear. Even he was wearing a helmet today. "CO says to move out," he announced.

"Okay, let's move out!" Samples yelled, waving the men on either side of him forward. He ignored the look of exasperation that flashed across Carr's face at being cut out of the chain of command. Behind them the APCs began crawling forward at a walking pace, crushing the vegetation that the dismounts had to wade through. Stepping carefully, the men on the ground watched for booby traps and mines while trying to avoid the thorns and sticky vines that pulled at their trousers.

"Don't get too far ahead of the tracks!" Carr yelled beside him. Samples rolled his eyes at the unnecessary command. His men knew what to do and how to do it, and didn't need any prompting from a fucking new guy lieutenant.

"Lenny!" Samples yelled at PFC Sorenson, who had gotten ahead of the rest. "Stay on line!" Samples guessed that Sorenson, like all of them, wanted to get into the woods where it was shady and the undergrowth was much thinner. It was vital, however, that everyone remain abreast of each other, in case a firefight broke out. Otherwise there was a chance for someone to get hit by friendly fire. Belatedly he realized he had just done what he had mentally chastised the lieutenant for doing. He kicked the log he was stepping over in self-contempt.

Suddenly there was yelling behind him, and he turned to see the crew of the one-three track jumping off and running in three different directions. All three were yelling as they scampered away from the stopped vehicle. "Watch out!" "Dud round!" "Arty round!" Carl Tenkiller, an Indian from Oklahoma and the driver of the vehicle, had slid down the front glacis and run over to where Samples and Carr stood.

"We ran over a dud artillery round!" he reported breathlessly. "Bobby saw it, but I wasn't able to stop in time. It's under the left tread. What are we gonna do?"

"Where's your weapon?" Samples admonished him. Dud or no dud, no soldier was to be without his weapon when in a combat zone. Behind him Samples heard Miles reporting the incident to the commander.

"In the track, Sarge," Tenkiller replied sheepishly.

"If it's a dud," Carr asked, "what's the problem?"

Samples groaned. "It could still explode," he explained impatiently. "If it does, it'll blow the left side of the track off, and we won't get a replacement for months, if ever." Samples grabbed Tenkiller's arm and pulled him toward the idling vehicle. "Let's go take a look." Over his shoulder he called out, "The rest of you set up a defensive perimeter and get down."

Samples stopped when he realized Carr was following him. Facing the lieutenant, he told him gently but firmly, "You better stay back, lieutenant. No point in both of us being killed." Carr nodded and backed away with a stricken look on his face.

Samples continued walking toward the track, with Tenkiller reluctantly following. When he got within a few feet he stopped and carefully pulled a small bush aside. There under the left tread, its pointed nose sticking up at an angle, was what appeared to be a 105mm artillery round. *Better than a 155 or 8-inch*, he thought. The 105mm howitzer was the smallest of the three main artillery pieces in use in Viet Nam. The 155mm cannons, and the 8-inch guns, used much larger rounds with more destructive power. A 105 round would probably just blow off a couple road wheels. He was also glad that the pointed end with the detonator was not in direct contact with the tread blocks. Tenkiller had stopped the track after only three or four of the tread blocks had passed over the round, so it was much closer to the front of the track than the rear.

"Okay, Carl," Samples told the nervous driver, "get back in there."

"Sarge?" Tenkiller asked anxiously

"Go ahead, get back in the driver's seat and close the hatch. I want you to back up very slowly while I ground-guide you." Tenkiller's face was ashen. "Don't worry, it's only a 105. You might get bounced around a little, but you'll be okay. I'm the one who could get his shit blown away."

Visibly shaking, Tenkiller went around to the far side of the track to climb on top, then carefully stepped around the machine gun turret and lowered himself into the driver's compartment. First he lowered the driver's seat so his head was below the hatch opening, and then reached up and unlatched the open cover. Gently he pulled the round hatch cover down until it locked in place. Samples took a position about fifteen feet to the right front of the track, giving himself a little cover if the round went off.

"Miles," Samples called out, "ask him if he can see me in his vision blocks." Around the driver's hatch was a ring of solid glass periscope blocks that ostensibly allowed the driver to see where he was going when the hatch was closed. They were notoriously difficult to see out of, especially when they were covered with dirt.

"He says he can see you," Miles reported after a minute.

"Okay, everybody get down," Samples yelled. "Miles, talk him through it. Tell him to put it in reverse and watch my signals."

"Roger," Miles replied. Samples heard the clunk of the transmission lever.

Even though he knew it wouldn't really make much difference, Samples knelt on one knee, laid his M-16 on a bush, and raised both hands to shoulder height. "Is he ready?" he asked.

Miles mumbled into the handset. "Ready," he replied.

"Okay, back up very slowly. DO NOT use the laterals." While Miles relayed the message, Samples began gradually waving both hands toward the track, indicating Tenkiller should move straight back. The engine revs began increasing, Tenkiller being very tentative as he waited for the torque converter to grab hold. Finally, with only a subtle jerk, the metal behemoth began easing backwards inches at a time. Samples kept his hands in motion, pushing the track back until he thought it was clear of the round, and then he made both hands into fists, the signal to stop. Immediately the track shuddered to a halt. Samples held up a single finger and yelled out, "Wait one." Picking his rifle back up, he walked over to where the round was. The back of the round was buried in the dirt, but the detonator end still sparkled in the sun. The front of the APC was now two feet away.

"Tell him he's clear," Samples told Miles, "and to back up another thirty meters." Samples waited as the message was relayed and Tenkiller backed the track up almost to the road. There he stopped and popped open the hatch, sticking his head out to see where he had been. The dismounted men of the platoon all stood up, and heads came up in the other tracks. Samples saw Tenkiller's squad leader, Richard Reedy, and gestured to him. "Rick, walk Carl around this. I'll stay here to mark it." Reedy ran over and took a position a couple meters in front of the one-two.

Samples yelled out to Fourth Squad's leader, Sergeant Washington, "Del, bring me a block of C-4, a blasting cap, and some fuse." He looked over at Carr, who was waiting with the radio handset in his hand, the coiled cord stretched to the radio on Miles' back. "Lieutenant, tell the CO he can have the company move out now. Once you are all in the tree line, I'll blow this fucker in place." Carr nodded and spoke into the handset. Moments later the line of men and APC's again moved forward, with Reedy and Tenkiller guiding the one-two track wide around Samples and getting back on line with the others.

Washington ran up and handed the requested items to Samples before returning to his squad. The C-4 was about the shape and size of a thin brick, covered with brown waxed paper. It had the consistency of white modeling clay. The blasting cap was a small aluminum tube open at one end, and the fuse looked like thin brown clothes line rope. Samples knelt down and laid his rifle on some leaves. He reached into his ammo bag and retrieved a magazine, thumbing a single round out before placing the magazine under his arm. Using the pointed end of the bullet he punched a hole through the wax paper and deep into the side of the C-4. After wiping the end of the bullet on his trousers, he pushed it back into the magazine and returned the magazine to his bag. Turning his attention back to the C-4, he pushed the closed end of the blasting cap into the hole and squeezed the plastic explosive around it enough to hold it in place. Next he threaded the end of the fuse into the open end of the blasting cap and crimped the thin aluminum around it with his thumb and forefinger. Not a professional job, he thought, but good enough for Army work. Retrieving his rifle with his left hand, he rose into a crouch and cautiously laid the C-4 next to the artillery round, avoiding any touch that might jar it.

Slowly releasing the breath he hadn't realized he had been holding, Samples straightened up and looked around him. The rest of the company had continued their sweep, and the men and tracks were now disappearing into the shade of the woods. He reached into his pants pocket and found his Zippo. He didn't smoke, but had learned the value of always carrying a lighter. He opened and flicked it once to ensure it would light; the lighter flared as expected, so he closed it again. Stepping away from the arty round, he made a tight circle and eyed all the surrounding area to ensure there was no one waiting close by. Confident he was in the clear, he stepped back to the dud, again lit the Zippo, and leaned down to apply the flame to the end of the fuse. After a moment it spluttered to life, and Samples watched it for a few seconds while he put his lighter away to ensure it wouldn't go out again. It didn't, so he turned and began striding briskly toward the forest.

"Fire in the hole!" he yelled. The call was repeated on down the line. When he reached the wood line, Samples found the rest of the company stopped, with everyone sitting or kneeling. He walked over to Carr and Miles, knelt down, and said, "Cover your ears." A gigantic whump blasted the air and dirt and dust rose in a ball near the road. A few leaves and twigs fluttered down, and a light breeze wafted the dust cloud away. He considered the small explosion kind of anticlimactic; he had hoped for something more spectacular.

"Back to work," Samples bellowed as he stood up.

FOUR

Lieutenant Carr was hot, sweaty, thirsty, dirty, scratched, and tired, and it was still morning. They had been sweeping through the dense woods for over two hours, and had seen no sign of the enemy. Even in the shade of the forest the heat was oppressive, and every bush seemed to have long thorns that clutched at his uniform and left welts on his exposed skin. Because of the thorns, everyone had their sleeves rolled down, despite the heat. A perpetual network of vines clutched at his rifle or tried to trip him. The air was rank with the odor of rotting vegetation overlaid with diesel smoke and human sweat. His own perspiration gathered in beads on his forehead and then ran down into his eyes, stinging them with its salt. He had already drained his canteen, and was ashamed that he hadn't been rationing it like he had been trained to do.

The only excitement so far, at least since the dud round destruction, had been when the fourth squad's track had bumped against a tree with a mogator nest in it. Mogator was the name the GI's had given to a particular species of local red ant that lived in the trees. They had large mandibles, and used them to torture anyone who came in contact with them. If someone brushed against the tree or bush in which they had built their nest, the large ants would rain down on the intruder and bite with a frenzy. They weren't poisonous, and didn't sting, but they could sure bite the hell out of a guy.

The first indication that the one-four had hit a mogator tree was the yelling as the three men on board all jumped off and began ripping off their clothes. "Shit!" "Fuck!" "Goddammit!" "Ow!" Their curses flew as they stripped nude and brushed the ants off, hopping around at the same time to keep any ants on the ground from climbing back up. The rest of the platoon paused to laugh and applaud the antics of their fellow soldiers. They had all suffered from mogators at one time or another, and were glad it wasn't them now being tormented. Carr didn't join in the catcalls and merriment, in part because he felt that as an officer he needed to maintain a military bearing. He also realized that many of the ants had fallen inside the very APC that Carr would be riding on later, and for hours the climbing insects would be making their way to the top of the track and up the legs of the men on board.

"All right," Carr yelled, "fun's over. Let's keep moving." Although he couldn't actually see Second Platoon, he could tell by the noise of their tracks that they had moved out ahead of First, so they would need to catch up.

Miles spoke up beside him. "CO says we need to get back on line."

"I know," Carr said, and then spoke more loudly as he saw Samples come from behind a bush buttoning up his fly. "Sergeant Samples, please get the platoon back on line with Second." Samples scowled at him, but did as instructed. With shouts and hand gestures he pushed the men and tracks forward.

For the next thirty minutes the men pressed forward, the dismounts weaving around trees and bushes, and the tracks a few yards behind crushing the bushes and smaller trees. The noise precluded any chance of sneaking up on any NVA soldiers who might be out there. Worse, Carr realized, it gave the gooks plenty of advanced warning of their approach, allowing them to set up an ambush, or disappear, whichever they preferred. Although he had been out in the field only a couple weeks, Carr was already beginning to wonder if that wasn't the real strategy behind the deployment of mechanized infantry in this environment. Were senior commanders simply using the APCs as decoys, not-quite-sitting ducks sent to draw enemy fire and thus reveal the location of the gooks so the hellfire of artillery and airstrikes could be rained down on them? It made as much sense as anything in this bizarre war.

The men all looked up as a helicopter buzzed overhead. Glimpsed through the trees was a "loach", the egg-shaped Light Observation Helicopter used by the battalion and brigade commanders to monitor the troops on the ground. The chopper didn't stop and hover, it just circled once and zoomed off again. Carr saw one of his men give the chopper the finger.

"CO, sir," Miles said, handing him the radio handset. Carr kept walking as he squeezed the push-to-talk button.

"This is three-three Papa Sierra, over," he said.

"This is Yankee three-three," Raymond's voice came over the radio. "The BC says to hold up for a while, we're moving too fast for Bravo and Charlie companies. Have your men take a break in place. Smoke 'em if you got 'em, over."

"Roger that, out." Carr knew that the track drivers had been listening and were already responding, so he yelled at the men on the ground. "Take a break! Sergeant Samples, post security." Samples designated a couple men to go on forward for about twenty-five meters and maintain a watch for anyone who might approach. The rest of the men sat on logs or squatted, pulling out their canteens or cigarettes. Carr strolled briskly down the line to the one-four track and opened the rear hatch.

"What do you need, sir?" Spec 4 Eberhart asked. Eberhart was the designated loader for the day, and was standing in the open cargo hatch. He swatted at a red ant he saw on his pants leg.

"Just need to refill my canteen," Carr told him, reaching in for one of the black plastic jerry cans lying on the floor.

"Here, let me help you," Eberhart said, ducking down inside the track and taking the can from Carr. "Put your canteen down by the door," Eberhart directed while he unscrewed the smaller cap on the spigot in the lid, and cracked open the air relief valve. Carr did as suggested, and Eberhart tilted the can over until water began streaming out of the spigot. Quickly moving the neck of the plastic canteen to catch the stream, Carr felt the relatively cool water splash over his hand as some missed the narrow opening. It felt really good. Shortly the canteen was full and overflowed, the water washing over his hand and splattering on his boots. Eberhart jerked the can upright and began screwing the cap back on.

"Thanks," Carr told him, immediately taking a long drink. The water, despite the chlorination, tasted wonderful.

"No sweat, sir. A guy gets hot and thirsty humpin' the boonies."

"You got that right," Carr agreed, enjoying the innocuous and unforced conversation. He took another swig from the canteen, and then swung the heavy hatch closed and cranked down the locking handle. Feeling refreshed, he walked back to where Samples was talking to Jamison and Reedy. Miles was a few feet away, sitting on the ground with his heavy radio backpack leaning against a tree trunk. The three sergeants stopped talking when Carr approached, Jamison taking a casual drag on his cigarette. Carr once again felt like an outsider, the high school geek who tries to sit at the cool kids table in the lunchroom. Carr wanted to say something to establish his authority, but nothing came to mind.

Miles broke the uncomfortable silence. "Bravo found a weapons cache," he announced, the handset still pressed to his ear. "Some RPG rounds, some 60-mike-mike mortar rounds, and three AKs."

"Wonder how many AKs they really found," Reedy remarked with a sly grin.

"What do you mean?" Carr asked him, puzzled by the remark.

"AKs are good trading material," Jamison explained. "Whenever someone finds a few, they report some of them and keep the rest. Anything they report, they have to turn in."

"Air Force guys," Reedy said. "They pay good money for an AK, because they can sneak it back to the States on their planes."

Jamison jumped back in. "You know that our mail home is all screened, so if we keep one, we'll never get it home. You can take one SKS rifle on the plane back with you, but not an AK."

"I heard about a guy who mailed an M-16 home," Reedy said. "Took it all apart and put the pieces inside shit he bought at the PX, like coffee makers, to fool the X-ray machines."

"I don't know," Samples said doubtfully. "Maybe."

"What's an SKS?" Carr asked. The three men gave him a brief look of pity.

"ChiCom rifle, kind of like the old M-1," Samples said. "Gooks don't use 'em much anymore, now that they've got plenty of

AKs. I wouldn't want one. Too much hassle carrying it onto the Freedom Bird."

"You got that right," Jamison agreed.

"But an AK," Reedy said, "that's money in the bank. That's how Doc Allman got that thirty-eight he carries. Traded an AK to a fly boy."

Carr had noticed the revolver that Allman carried in a holster on his hip, in addition to his M-16. He had assumed it was something issued just to medics, for self-defense. Carr had already been told about the recent Division policy on carrying .45 pistols. Only captains and above were authorized to carry the old M1911 automatics, because too many young lieutenants had shot themselves in the foot practicing their quick-draw.

"Is that all you can take home, an SKS?" Carr asked to keep the conversation going. He was just grateful to be included.

"Nah," Jamison said authoritatively, "you can take home almost anything that isn't a weapon. One of those pith helmets, uniforms, canteens, shit like that, but who fuckin' cares. I don't even want to be reminded of this place when I get back in the world."

"Bet that," Reedy concurred.

"But I wish I could take home an RPG launcher," Jamison remarked wistfully. "No rounds, just the launcher. It's a cool piece of equipment, with the sight and all. But, nooo. I might get some rounds somewhere in the States and try to blow up an armored car or something. Like that would happen."

"Hey, maybe you could hide it in your ass," Reedy teased.

"Fuck you," Jamison rejoined with feigned anger, "and the horse you rode in on."

"Boys, boys," Samples admonished almost playfully. "Save your anger for the gooks."

"Fuck the gooks," Jamison said. "Fuck Viet Nam. Fuck the Army. Fuck the whole goddamn world." It was clearly a common refrain, as Samples and Reedy ignored it. Jamison didn't appear angry, and he took another drag off his cigarette. Carr wasn't sure he understood these men at all. They were bitter, cynical, and constantly derided the Army and their superiors, but were ready to go fight the enemy without hesitation or trepidation. In fact, they almost seemed to enjoy combat. Were they intrinsically different than him, or would he soon come to be just like them? Carr wasn't sure he wanted to know.

They all looked up as they heard the approach of a helicopter, and glimpsed the loach zooming by overhead.

"We're moving out again," Miles announced, struggling to his feet and adjusting the backpack.

"Confirm to the CO that we are on the move," Carr directed Miles.

"Did that, sir," Miles replied, trotting over to take up his position near Carr. The three sergeants quickly strode to their designated places in the sweep, calling their men to action. Carr again wondered just what his purpose was here.

"Okay, move out!" Samples yelled at the men, waving them on line again. "We've got miles to go before we sleep." Samples remembered that line from high school English class; he didn't know who wrote it, but he always liked it. As the sweep reached the two men he had posted as security, those guys stood up and fell into the formation. Behind them the tracks roared into motion, sooty smoke rising from their exhaust pipes and machine gun barrels jiggling as the gunners adjusted their perch. As noon approached, the heat had become even more oppressive, but Samples had become so inured to it that he hardly noticed.

He glanced over at the lieutenant, who was trudging along with the rest of them, and gave the guy credit for at least keeping up. Maybe that Ranger training actually helped. Carr was still green and goofy, but he appeared to learn from his mistakes, which was always a good sign. Last tour Samples had worked under a butter-bar second lieutenant who had kept falling behind, and who had frozen the first time they made contact. After only two weeks in the field, he was mercifully transferred to some headquarters job and never seen again.

Samples brushed some branches out of his way and pushed on through the woods, eyeing any suspicious mound of earth or pile of leaves that might hide an enemy bunker. They had seen no signs of enemy trails or activity, but that wasn't really surprising. The gooks were masters at leaving no trace behind. Gradually Samples became aware that the area in front of them was getting brighter, and after another hundred meters or so they broke out of the woods into a Rome Plow area. It was a couple hundred meters across, and stretched off to the east and west for several clicks in either direction. Tree trunks and branches were tumbled into random piles, baking in the sun. The giant bulldozers had pushed down all the foliage with their blades and crushed it with their giant metal treads, leaving wreckage like the aftermath of a major tornado.

"Hold up in the tree line," Samples called to his men. They all knelt or crouched near still-standing trees and bushes, watching the clearing carefully. Samples felt the lieutenant approach from his right and stand beside him, also gazing at the jumbled lumber.

"What do you think, Sergeant?" Carr asked him.

"I think it's a great place for an ambush," Samples replied. "Gooks could be in the far tree line, or in tunnels and bunkers in the Rome Plow, and we wouldn't know it until too late."

"I agree," Carr said. It seemed like he was about to add something when Miles interrupted. Carr took the handset and carried on a short conversation with the company commander, judging by the way he was talking. Samples noticed that Carr's face clouded, and his replies were reluctantly affirmative. Carr passed the handset back to Miles and didn't say anything for a minute. Finally he spoke.

"The BC says he flew over the Rome Plow and didn't see anything. We've been ordered to keep moving, in order to meet up with Bravo and Charlie on time."

"Fuckin' asshole," Samples spat, not caring that he was speaking to an officer about another officer. "He can't see jack shit from that chopper. He wouldn't know if gooks were out there unless they shot his sorry ass down, we should be so lucky."

"I know," Carr acknowledged regretfully. "We're heading straight north from here. Move 'em out."

"Okay, guys," Samples yelled out, "we're crossing the Rome Plow. Move as quickly as you can, but keep a good eye out for any movement. Don't lollygag and be sure to watch your ass." To their right Samples could see second platoon men easing out of the woods, and his own men began following suit. As they crept out into the open area, Samples felt terribly exposed, bending over into almost a duck-walk as he skirted the fallen trees. He remembered talking to a Marine once in bar in Saigon. They had discussed infantry tactics, and the Marine had told him that when they came to a clearing in the jungle, the Marines pushed directly through it to save time. Samples' Army training was to stay in the trees and go around the clearing, because they were prime spots for ambushes. Samples had thought at the time that maybe such Marine training accounted for the higher casualty rate that Marines suffered compared to soldiers.

This clearing, however, was too big to go around. The long rectangular open area extended far to the left and right, and was intended to remove cover for the gooks infiltrating south. Of course, the gooks just built tunnels under the Rome Plow areas and kept going, so the long-term benefit was dubious. Once he was out into the middle of the clearing, Samples took a slow look around the edges, trying to see where the strip began and ended. The western end, he knew, was at the rice paddies just north of FSB Wood, where Carr had gotten lost the night before. The eastern end was lost in the dust and haze.

"Sarge, over here!" Larry Jones, of fourth squad, was waving his rifle with one hand and pointing at the ground with the other. Samples ran over to see what he had found. "Right there," Jones said, pointing at a black high-top tennis shoe lying on the ground. Samples recognized it as standard issue for NVA soldiers.

"Don't touch it," he advised Jones. Anything could be booby-trapped, even a shoe. This one looked brand new, its laces tied at the top. Typically for something worn by the Vietnamese, it appeared to be a size suitable for American children.

"What is it?" Carr asked from behind him. He and Miles had rushed over to join them, as had several other members of the platoon.

"Spread out," Samples said sternly, "don't cluster." To the lieutenant he said, "You better get down. That radio antenna makes us a prime target for a sniper." With a worried look around him, Carr knelt down behind a tree trunk, and Miles quickly followed suit, reporting the find on his radio. Samples stayed standing, surveying the ground around the shoe and between the broken branches for any other clues as to how it got there.

"It's an NVA combat boot," he explained to the crouching officer. "Probably fell out of a pack some gook was carrying. Doesn't look like it's been here long."

"It's a tennis shoe," Carr noted with bewilderment.

"Yeah, that's what they issue. It's light and cheap, I reckon. Well, let's keep moving." Samples gestured for the men to resume their sweep.

"Should we collect it?" Carr asked, rising.

"Won't fit anybody in our platoon," Samples said, starting forward again.

Crossing the Rome Plow area was both tense and arduous. Out in the open, with dark wood lines all around, Samples felt naked and vulnerable, but he had to keep his eyes down to watch for vines and branches that could trip him up. Frequently he had to climb over fallen trees or through piles of branches, making him even more exposed. Around him the men occasionally cursed as branches snapped up to smack them or they lost their footing trying to climb across the jumble. Behind him the tracks roared as they struggled over the tangled mess, crashing down on the far side of massive logs, and backing and twisting to get around others. It was almost a relief when he slid over the final log and edged into the wood line with its welcome shade.

"Keep moving," he urged the men, who tied to stop and rest once they were out of the sun. Samples wanted to make room in the forest for the tracks following behind, getting them out of the clearing where they were most vulnerable to rocket-propelled grenades. Once all of the platoon's tracks were in the relative safety of the forest, Samples paused the sweep to allow the rest of the company to catch up before resuming the advance through the trees. He noticed that Lieutenant Carr and Miles had stayed with him, following close behind and to his right. Samples assumed the young officer had realized who was really in charge and was allowing him to do his job unhindered.

"Hey! Got something!" The call came from his right, where Jamison's squad was walking next to Second Platoon.

"Hold up!" Samples called to the men of the platoon, dodging bushes and trees as he ran to where he had heard the shout. He could hear Carr and Miles pushing through the brush behind him. Breaking through a thick patch of thorny bushes, he came upon Jamison and Spec 4 Reyes. The two men pointed a huge mound partially covered with black plastic sheeting, surrounded by thick bushes.

"Rice cache," Jamison said. "Big one."

Samples pushed through the leafy branches and lifted up one corner of the plastic cover. Underneath was a stack of bulging burlap bags, one of which had leaked a thin stream of white rice grains. Printed on the bags was the message, "Product of U.S.A."

Leaning in beside him, Carr asked, "That's American rice?"

"Afraid so," Samples said. "We give it to the South Vietnamese, and they sell it to the gooks. Everyone comes out ahead, except for us."

While Carr reported the find to the company commander, Samples had Jamison and Reyes pull the plastic off and start counting the bags. After a brief discussion, they decided there were forty-three bags, and each bag was marked as weighing fifty pounds. Samples did some quick math in his head as Carr reported the count to the CO. It was over a ton of rice.

"We've got to load it up in the tracks," Carr told him, after passing the handset back to Miles.

"What?" Samples said, not believing what he had just heard. "Whose fucking idea was that?"

"Probably the colonel," Carr told him, not without sympathy. "Captain Raymond didn't sound pleased with the idea either."

"Fuck me!" Samples cursed. "It's going to take at least two tracks to haul all this, and we aren't even done with the sweep yet. We oughta just blow it in place." He stood looking at the pile of bags, estimating the effort required to load it. He wondered why in the hell the U.S. was even sending any rice to Viet Nam, which produced more rice than any other country in Asia.

"Miles, tell Chacon to have Washington post security. Have Gunn and Tenkiller bring their tracks up here. What a bunch of shit."

Samples had Gunn and Tenkiller maneuver their tracks to either side of the rice cache and lower their ramps. Leaving only the 50-cal gunners in place, he directed the rest of the men, including the two track drivers, to form a couple of daisy chains to pass the bags from man to man into the tracks, stacking them neatly on the floors. Two guys from Second Platoon came over to help. It took only a couple minutes to get the bags all loaded, making stacks that reached halfway to the roofs of the APCs.

"Now I got a place to sit," Greenberg commented favorably. He was the designated loader for the one-one track, and usually the loader had to stand in the cargo hatch behind the machine gun turret.

"At least it's better'n them damn cows," Gunn said, heading back to the driver's compartment.

"Steers," Jamison corrected him.

"Steers?" Carr asked, looking befuddled.

While the men retrieved their rifles and helmets and again took their positions, and the drivers raised the ramps, Samples told him the story. "A couple months ago we were on a sweep with a company of ARVNs." Soldiers of the Army of the Republic of Viet

Nam were called ARVNs, rhymes with Marvins. Wearing the old-style US Army fatigue uniforms tailored to fit tightly around their slim bodies, they usually carried the Korean-era M-2 carbines, and were not highly regarded by the American troops. "We didn't see any gooks, but we did find four steers in an old rice paddy. The ARVNs insisted they were VC steers, and wanted to confiscate them. My guess is they just wanted them for dinner. At any rate, we had to load the damn things up in our tracks and haul them back to the ARVN compound, shittin' and pissin' in the tracks all the way. Took two weeks to get the stink out."

"Rawhide!" Miles sang with a cowboy accent.

"Seriously?" Carr said, shaking his head.

"Yep. Welcome to the land of the little people." Samples turned away and shouted, "Let's go!" The sweep resumed.

FIVE

More heat. More forest. More thorns. More vines. Lieutenant Carr was already fed up with it. Here they were busting their asses, and for what? A shoe? Stolen cattle? A bunch of misappropriated rice? If the protestors on college campuses back in the States knew what was really going on here, they would go completely ballistic. Or laugh their asses off. Carr was so thoroughly disillusioned after only two weeks in country that he couldn't imagine what he would be like by the end of his tour. His daydreams of being a heroic leader of men in their righteous fight against evil Communism had been dashed. Reality had hit him like a brick. Now his only dream was to make it out of here alive and sane.

Carr's bleak thoughts were shattered by the crack of a bullet breaking the sound barrier near his head. More rifle shots split the air, and Carr dropped to a prone position, trying to determine where the shots were coming from. The other men had done the same.

"Sniper!" Sergeant Samples yelled a few feet to his front. Several men fired their rifles at the surrounding foliage.

As quickly as it began, the firing petered out.

"You see anything?" someone said.

"I don't see shit," someone else replied.

"Anybody hit?" Carr called out, and was relieved when the response was a chorus of no's.

Everyone lay on the ground, peering through the underbrush and gazing at the treetops, looking for any sign or movement.

Way off to the right, more gunfire erupted, this time in the area where Third Platoon was. Again, it died off and quiet reigned, disturbed only by the idling diesels of the tracks halted behind them. Carr could hear Miles muttering into his handset, reporting their situation to the commander.

"Sergeant Samples," Carr said quietly, "what's the usual response to this sort of situation?"

"You mean after you change your shorts? Stay low and try to kill the motherfucker." Carr waited for a more useful answer, and eventually it came. "I'd say bring the tracks up on line and let the fifty-cals recon by fire."

"Sounds reasonable," Carr said. He turned his head toward Miles and reached for the handset. There was almost constant chatter and reports on the net. He waited until he could get through. "Yankee three-three, this is three-three Papa Sierra, over."

"This is Yankee three-three, go," came the response from Captain Raymond.

"We're going to bring the tracks up and use the fifties to recon by fire, over."

"Do it. All three-three elements, bring the tracks on line and recon by fire. Out."

Behind them the APCs revved their engines and began inching forward, careful to avoid any of the dismounts who might be hidden from view. As the tracks approached, Carr and the other men sprang into a crouching position and then ran back behind the lumbering vehicles, seeking shelter from any additional sniper fire. Once all the men were accounted for, Carr got on the radio and ordered the fifties to open fire. Immediately the thunder of the guns drowned out everything else, and ahead of them Carr could see the trees vibrating and shredded leaves fluttering in the air. After thirty seconds, he called a cease fire that was echoed on down the line for the rest of the company. There was no return fire.

Carr still held the radio handset, and heard as the CO told everyone to start moving forward again, but keep the dismounts on line with tracks. Carr relayed the order to Samples and the other men on the ground and gave the handset back to Miles. He could hear the clanks and clinks of fifty-cal machine guns being reloaded as the tracks started edging forward. Between the tracks the dismounted men cautiously kept pace, warily eyeing suspicious bushes and clumps of leaves in the trees. Carr was between the one-two and the one-three track, with Miles just behind and Samples alongside, the heat and thorns forgotten. The brief firefight had heightened their senses and introduced a level of tension that overrode any personal discomfort.

After five minutes they had found no evidence of previous enemy activity—no bunkers, no shell casings, nothing. They still had no idea where the sniper—or snipers—had been firing from. This part of the woods was denser than where they had been earlier, and much greener, as if it had a better source of water. The APCs had to keep dodging around trees and crushing bushes, while the men on the ground endeavored to stay out of the way of the branches that sprang back after the tracks had passed. It was slow going.

Carr was startled by a yell from PFC Merrill, the fifty gunner on the one-three track to his left. Merrill was pointing to something straight ahead, but he didn't seem terribly excited about it. Carr relaxed a little, relieved that it wasn't another sniper or ambush. Pushing through some leafy branches, Carr saw what had drawn Merrill's attention. Lying on its side was what appeared to be a fifty-gallon oil drum, painted olive drab. In the middle of this almost impenetrable forest, its incongruity was striking. How did it get here, and more importantly, why? Carr's first idea was that it was some sort of NVA provisions, maybe filled with cooking oil or something, but that didn't really make sense. It was too large to be hand-carried from North Viet Nam, and the gooks didn't have motorized transport in this area. Besides, there was no road or trail anywhere near it. The puzzle intrigued him, and he strode forward to inspect it.

"Lieutenant!" Sergeant Samples warned, just as shots rang out from ahead of them. Acting purely on instinct, Carr dived to the ground behind the drum, seeking its shelter from the gunfire. Miles plopped down beside him on his left, and PFC Sorenson from the Second Squad slid into the dirt on his right. Up on the tracks the fifty-cal gunners opened up, spraying the woods with random bursts of large-caliber bullets. There was a whang above Carr's head as a bullet ricocheted off the top of the drum, clearly indicating the fifty-caliber suppressive fire was not having the intended effect.

Miles was listening intently to the radio handset pressed against his ear, and Sorenson was now firing his M-16 around the right end of the drum. Carr, trapped between them, knew better than to raise his head, so instead he studied the drum itself. On the side of the drum facing the ground, mostly obscured by dirt, were faint stenciled markings. Carr made out "USAF" and some numbers, and a faint yellow line. The yellow line tripped some alarm in his brain, the vague notion that it symbolized something to be avoided. If he could just remember what it was.

The drum shook as more bullets struck it, and suddenly a white cloud spewed out of the upper side of the container and wafted down to settle on Carr and the other two men. It was a fine white powder, like talcum, and as soon as Carr took a breath he knew what it was—CS. A more powerful version of tear gas, CS in powder form was persistent and tremendously irritating. Carr's nose and throat burned, his eyes watered, and his skin felt like someone was spraying him with hot sauce. He wanted to wipe his eyes, but his hands and uniform were all coated with a film of white dust that rose back in the air every time he moved. Carr had his gas mask in its case on his hip, but realized it was too late for that. More bullets thumped into the drum, and Carr knew he had to get away from it, and fast.

Reacting more quickly than Carr, Sorenson jumped up and ran for the one-two track, scrambling up the back and diving into the cargo hatch, prompting an angry reaction from the loader, PFC Vasquez.

Carr tapped Miles on the shoulder and ran to the back of the one-three track, sensing that Miles was right behind him. His eyes were watering so bad he could barely see, and he was holding his breath to avoid inhaling any more of the stinging powder. He fumbled around until he found the handle for the rear hatch and jerked it open. "Water!" he yelled at Johnson, the loader who was crouched down inside. When Johnson didn't immediately respond, a look of stunned bewilderment on his face, Carr climbed in and searched for a water can. Behind him Miles dived through the hatch and sprawled on the metal floor, coughing and spewing.

Carr finally located a jerry can lying on its side. He jerked it upright and desperately twisted the large lid until it came free, as he sat down on the track's bench seat. On the floor Miles flopped around until he was on his side, his helmet rolling away. Carr tilted the can until water poured out and splashed over Miles' head, rinsing the worst of the CS powder away. Miles gurgled thankfully.

"Here you go, sir," Johnson said, handing Carr a towel he had pulled from a laundry bag behind the bench. Carr tilted the can again to soak the towel, before wiping his face and hands with the sopping material. The relief was wonderful. The burning subsided, and although he was coughing continually, he could at least breathe. Johnson had found another towel for Miles, who sat up, soaked it himself, and began wiping his face and hands. He, too, was coughing and wheezing. Above them the fifty-cal pounded away, but Carr hardly noticed. A figure appeared at the open rear hatch and then ducked in. It was Doc Allman.

"You two all right?" Allman asked solicitously.

"We'll live," Carr replied between coughs.

"Take you shirts off," Allman said. "They're covered in that shit."

Carr unfastened his pistol belt and gingerly unbuttoned his shirt, trying to avoid touching any of the inflaming residue. Miles had to struggle out of both his backpack and the web gear first. While Carr and Miles stripped, Allman set his helmet on the bench and put on his gas mask. He took the shirts that were handed to him and stepped out of the hatch, presumably to shake off the CS. No sooner had Allman left than Sergeant Samples jumped in. He looked at Carr and Miles appraisingly and nodded.

"Nasty shit, huh?" Samples remarked. Carr washed out his towel and resumed wiping himself down, concentrating on his arms and neck. Miles followed suit.

"What is a drum of CS doing out in the middle of the woods?" Carr complained. His coughing was subsiding, but still annoying.

"Fuckin' Air Farce," Samples explained. "The canisters are supposed to explode in the air and coat the woods with the powdered CS so the gooks can't go through here. 'Course, we can't either, the dumb shits. It's temporary, and only works in the dry season anyway. Same concept as the Rome Plows, or that defoliant they're spraying up north of here." Samples sniffed and made a face. "No offense, lieutenant, but you stink." With that he darted back out of the track.

Allman handed their shirts in through the hatch and pulled off his gas mask. "Wash 'em off before you put 'em back on," he suggested. "Keep you cool, too." After putting his mask back in its carrier, Allman took off. Outside and above them the gunfire had slackened off. Miles and Carr poured water over their shirts and pulled on the wet garments. They wiped down their web gear and helmets with the wet towels and put them back on, and then sponged off their rifles. Miles took extra time to wipe down his radio, especially the handset and coiled cable, before shrugging into the backpack straps. At last they were ready. While Johnson handed a full ammo can of fifty-cal up to the gunner, Carr and Miles stepped back out and closed the hatch. Back to the war.

After leaving Carr in the one-three track, Sergeant Samples sprinted through the bushes to the back of the one-two, where Sorenson was still dumping helmet-fulls of water over his head.

"You gonna be all right?" Samples asked him.

"Yeah, I guess," Sorenson replied, sniffling as water dripped off the end of his nose. "Fuckin' CS. They shouldn't leave shit like that laying around." He put his helmet back on, screwed down the cap on the water can, and lifted it back into the track through the open hatch. Samples then closed and latched the hatch for him while Sorenson retrieved his rifle. Both men remained close behind the track, sheltering from any possible enemy fire. Samples could see several guys huddling behind the one-one, and others lying prone behind trees and bushes. To his left he saw Carr and Miles climb out of the one-three, but they also stayed close to the back of the track. Above Samples the fifty-cal gunner, Pratt, let up on the trigger and called down to Vasquez to hand him another can.

"What's going on, Pratt," Samples called. Due to the noise of the guns, he had been unable to monitor the track radio. All along the company line the guns now stuttered to a halt.

"CO called a cease-fire," Pratt answered while opening the ammo can Vasquez had just passed up to him.

Samples took a quick glance around the side of the APC, but all he could see was forest. Across the way he could see Carr on the radio, the coiled mike cable stretching to Miles' back like a black umbilical cord. From inside the one-two track the radio blared at maximum volume, loud enough for Samples to hear it clearly. It was the Captain Raymond talking.

"Looks like they've pulled back," the CO said. "Let's start moving again, keep pushing them."

Carr looked over at Samples and yelled, "The CO says. . ."

Samples interrupted him. "I heard." Cautiously he stepped from behind the track and edged up until he was even with the driver's hatch. Tenkiller had raised his CVC helmet just enough to see over the rim of the hatch. "Take it slow," Samples told him. Tenkiller nodded and gradually upped the revs until the track began ponderously inching forward. To his left Samples saw Carr and Miles alongside the one-three, semi-crouching as they kept pace with the tracks. Sorenson was halfway between Samples and Carr, but hanging back nervously as he widely skirted the CS drum. Ahead there was nothing to see but tree trunks with their bark ravaged by bullets, bushes with shredded leaves, and dust particles sparkling in the sunbeams that occasionally pierced the overhead canopy.

Samples was carrying his M-16 at a modified port arms—the barrel angled up at forty-five degrees across his chest, but pointed generally down-range ahead of him, his left hand on the plastic hand guards around the barrel, his right hand on the pistol grip. He stepped to his left to go around a small thorn bush, when suddenly the rifle was torn from his hands. Something had hit the butt stock so hard it spun the rifle around and flung it to the rear. Samples' first thought was that a heavy branch had been run over by the one-two track and then snapped back viciously into his weapon, but then his mind registered the sound of a gunshot, one he recognized as coming from an AK-47.

"Hit it!" he yelled, probably unnecessarily, as he dropped to the ground and scrambled to find his rifle. Above him the fifty-cals opened up again, their pulsing drumbeat drowning out the shouts and rifle fire. Samples found his M-16 several feet behind him, and at first thought it was undamaged. A closer inspection revealed a hole in the plastic stock and a bullet lodged in the metal tube that housed the recoil mechanism inside. He knew the M-16 was trashed, although it could be salvaged for parts. He flipped the selector lever to SAFE, and dropped the magazine out. There was still a round in the chamber, but he would have to wait until he had time to disassemble the weapon in order to remove it. Belatedly he noted that both his hands stung.

He could see Carr, Sorenson, and Miles all prone a few feet away. Sorenson and Carr were both firing their rifles semi-automatic, while Miles huddled with the radio handset pressed to his ear. Even above the roar of the fifty-cals, M-60s, and M-16s, Samples could hear the occasional supersonic crack of a bullet coming the other way. Wherever the gooks were, they weren't terribly bothered by the blistering American barrage. A scene from an old movie about World War II flashed through his mind. Marines on an island in the Pacific were pinned down by Japanese snipers hidden in the trees. Maybe that was happening here. Grabbing his useless rifle, Samples clambered to his feet and darted back to the rear hatch of the one-two track. Jerking open the hatch, he dived in on top of the piles of rice sacks and threw his rifle into one of the storage racks behind the bench seat. Squirming past Vasquez, he pulled on the microphone cord that ran up into the machine gun turret and caught the pork chop mike at the end of the cord.

"Shoot the goddamn trees!" he yelled into the mike. "They might be hiding in the trees!"

Up in the driver's compartment, he could see Tenkiller with his seat as low as it would go, trying to watch the action through the periscopes. "Carl!" Samples yelled at him. "Give me your bloop gun." The M-79 grenade launcher was not a popular weapon among the troops, due to its single-shot capacity and limited usefulness in jungle fighting. Since the track drivers rarely dismounted, and usually had an M-60 machine gun available, it made sense to give them the bloop guns, which were shorter than an M-16 and thus easier to store while driving. Tenkiller passed the awkward weapon back to Samples. It looked like a toy shotgun, with a single short fat barrel and a wooden stock.

"Where's your ammo vest?" Samples demanded. The bloop gunners were issued vests with a bunch of pockets, like a photographer's vest, but with stubby explosive rounds instead of film canisters. Tenkiller rummaged around in the storage bin behind him and pushed the vest across the stacked cans of 50-cal ammo to Samples. On one side were the HE—high explosive—rounds, and on the other were the canister rounds. The HE rounds fire a small grenade that exploded on contact, while the canister rounds were just like shotgun rounds, firing a spray of BB-sized shot. There were other rounds available as well—CS rounds, smoke rounds—but they were usually left stored in an ammo can somewhere.

With the vest in one hand and the gun in the other, Samples pushed passed Vasquez and climbed out on top of the track to stand beside the fifty turret. Ignoring the incoming fire, he draped the vest over the side of the turret and pulled out a canister round. With a flip of the lever he broke the gun open and slid the round in, and then snapped the gun closed. A tree to his front had a suspicious-looking clump of leaves about forty feet up, so he raised the gun to his shoulder and squeezed the trigger. With a popping boom the shot burst from the barrel and the stock banged into Samples shoulder. The weapon had more recoil than he remembered, certainly more than an M-16. The spread of buckshot shredded the tree, and pieces of leaves fluttered down, but no other effect could be seen.

When he opened the weapon, the empty shell casing popped out on its own. Samples grabbed another canister round and reloaded. There was a metallic whang by his knees, and Samples glanced down to see the silver gash in the metal where a bullet had ricocheted off the flat olive drab side of the turret. No time to think about it now. He raised the gun to his shoulder and fired at a different tree top, with similar results. He fired two more canister rounds, but the incoming fire, though sporadic, continued. Maybe, he thought, they aren't in the trees after all.

If not in the trees, they had to be in bunkers, where direct fire from machine guns and rifles was unlikely to reach them. Samples leaned down to get an HE round, and sensed the disturbance of the air as a bullet passed over him. Standing up on the track like this made him a target, he knew, but he didn't care. He wasn't going to let the little bastards beat him.

"Sarge, get down!" Pratt yelled at him.

"I'm busy," Samples replied. He loaded the HE round and raised the gun at an approximately forty-five degree angle. He didn't bother with the folding sight—it required knowing the distance to the target, and even then was at best a guess. He pulled the trigger, and the grenade launched with the distinctive "bloop" explosion for which the gun was nick-named. The round arced through the trees and exploded beyond some distant bushes, raising a small cloud of dust.

"Too far," Samples remarked to himself. He loaded another HE round and aimed more to the right, raising the barrel higher to decrease the range. He popped off the round, and he could actually see it rising up and then falling about forty meters away, exploding when it hit a branch about ten feet off the ground. That was okay, Samples believed, because the shrapnel would spread both out and down, and thus be more likely to hit any gooks hiding in bunkers or spider holes. Again he loaded HE and aimed high, this time almost directly in front of the track. The result was a double blast. The round burst out of the barrel and hit a branch only a dozen feet way, exploding on contact. Samples felt the sting as several pieces of shrapnel hit him in the stomach.

"Shit goddamn it to hell!" he cursed, looking down at his shirt. There were small holes in the material, and spreading dark stains around them.

"You're hit!" Pratt yelled.

"No shit, Sherlock," Samples replied. The wounds didn't feel serious, and it wasn't the first time he'd been wounded. He reached down for another HE round, thinking about how he should aim better. Below him he could hear Vasquez on the radio reporting his injury as if he were in imminent danger of death. He loaded the HE round and looked around for a good place to aim it, but before he could fire, the radio blared a cease-fire order that quickly spread through the platoon. Samples knelt down beside the turret, making himself at least a little less obvious a target.

Doc Allman, his aid bag swinging, ran over to the track and scrambled up the side. Sitting down on one of the ammo cans, he laid his rifle down and said, "Let me see."

Samples scowled at him. "I'm okay. Just a scratch."

"I'm the medic here," Allman reminded him. "Let me make the medical decisions." Around them the forest was relatively quiet—no gunfire, just the idling track engines and quiet conversations among the men. Reluctantly Samples unbuckled his pistol belt, laying it neatly on the roof of the track, and then unbuttoned his shirt. He winced as he pulled it open, because the material had stuck to his wounds.

"More than a scratch," Allman reprimanded him while he dug through his aid bag. He found a gauze pad and doused it with orange liquid, then began gently swabbing the wounds. Samples gritted his teeth to keep from crying out at the stinging application. There were three punctures in his belly and lower chest; all were bleeding, but not profusely. After dabbing them with the antiseptic, Allman placed clean gauze pads over each and secured them with adhesive tape. "You've got some shrapnel in there," Allman told him.

"Take it out," Samples demanded.

Allman snorted derisively. "Yeah, right. I'm a medic, not a surgeon, and we're in the middle of a fuckin' firefight, in case you hadn't noticed."

"No one's shooting right now," Samples pointed out. He needed to get back to running the platoon.

"Yeah, at the moment," Allman said, repacking his aid bag. On cue, gunfire broke out up the line where Samples knew Third Platoon was located.

"Shit!" Samples spat, and buttoned up his shirt. Allman picked up his rifle and jumped down to return to Fourth Squad. Sample put his web gear back on, buckling the belt gingerly below one of the throbbing wounds. Deciding there was no point in being stupid, he grabbed the M-79 and ammo vest and jumped down into the cargo hatch next to Vasquez. He quickly loaded an HE round and leaned against the left side of the cargo hatch opening so he could aim around the machine gun turret, and then waited for something to shoot at. Almost as quickly as it had begun, the firing up at Third Platoon had subsided.

The track radio, mounted on the left inside wall near his hip, squawked. "This is Yankee three-three," Samples heard Captain Raymond announce. "All three-three elements, mount up and pull back. I say again, all three-three elements mount up and pull back. Out." Up and down the line Samples saw the men on the ground jump up and rush to climb on board the APCs, most choosing to jump inside the open cargo hatches and take up positions with only their helmets and rifles exposed. Sorenson appeared behind him, climbing up the back of the one-two and sliding on his butt across the open cargo hatch cover. Due to the stacks of rice, he could only drop part way into the track, so he squatted on the bags and turned to face the rear. Sergeant Reedy followed, saw how crowded the cargo hatch was, and clambered forward to sit on the driver's hatch cover behind Tenkiller.

"Everybody on?" Tenkiller yelled.

"Yeah, go!" Reedy replied, replacing his steel pot with the CVC helmet lying next to the hatch.

"Someone guide me back," Tenkiller said, clunking the gear shift into reverse.

"Straight back," Sorenson called out. With a roar of the engine and smoke from the exhaust, the track jerked into motion, rushing backwards.

"Not so fast," Reedy told Tenkiller. Samples unloaded the M-79 but kept a wary eye on where they had been. He knew better than to interfere with the operation of the track, instead letting the squad work together as an experienced team. A big tree trunk slid by on the right, and as it passed the front of the track, Sorenson called out.

"Right lateral, hard!" In response Tenkiller pulled on the lever, locking the tread on the right side, while the left tread kept digging into the earth, slewing the vehicle around until it was pointed back the way they had come. Throwing the gearshift into Drive and releasing the lateral, Tenkiller gunned the engine and the track surged forward.

Samples watched the other tracks of the platoon perform similar maneuvers, mentally critiquing the drivers' skills. He noted that Aiello jammed the side of the one-three against a tree, and had to back-and-forth it before he was free to move. Otherwise things went as expected, and the platoon followed its own trails back south, leaving the enemy snipers behind.

When they reached the Rome Plow area, the CO had the company set up a hasty defensive perimeter while he found a relatively unobstructed area in the middle of the clearing. The mortar tracks had parked a little to the west and were bombarding the contact area with HE. Leaving the M-79 behind with its owner, Samples jumped down and directed the platoon's tracks into position. Doc Allman approached, with Lieutenant Carr and Miles trailing along behind him.

"Come on, Sarge, you're getting medevacked," Allman told him, taking his arm. Samples pulled away.

"Bullshit!" Samples said. "I'm not hurt. I got things to do."

"They need to get that shrapnel out," Allman explained patiently.

"You can do that later," Samples protested. "Give me some tweezers and I'll do it myself."

"Sergeant Samples," Carr said sternly, "you've got to go. That's an order."

Samples stared at the young lieutenant, trying to figure out a way to buffalo him into letting him stay. Finally he sighed with resignation, knowing it was no use. He heard the approach of a helicopter, and saw the purple smoke now rising from the middle of the clearing. The mortar fire stopped to avoid hitting the chopper. "Aw, hell!" he complained, and began walking toward the plume of smoke. He hated riding in helicopters; they made him airsick, and he had seen too many of them drop out of the sky and burst into flames.

SIX

As the line of armored personnel carriers rolled down the road toward the entrance to Fire Support Base Wood, it occurred to Steve Carr with a touch of pride that he was in effect leading the entire company. After the dust-off in the Rome Plow, the company had continued back southeast until it reformed on the highway, and then headed back southwest in the reverse order from the morning. Now, instead of tail-end Charlie, the one-four track was at the head of the column, and Carr wasn't eating anyone else's dust. Or, for the time being, having to play second fiddle to Staff Sergeant Samples.

When they reached the turn-off for the gate, they had to stop out on the road. A 2½-ton truck, commonly called a deuce-and-a-half, was stopped in the middle of the gate, blocking the entrance. Somehow the truck had gotten its rear wheels tangled in the concertina wire used to block the entrance when the gate was closed, and now several soldiers were gathered around trying to undo it. Most were just standing there observing, while one guy, presumably the driver, rummaged through a tool box. "Tell the CO what's going on," Carr instructed Miles, and jumped down from the track.

Striding back along the left side of his platoon's vehicles, he motioned to each of the squad leaders to join him. He stepped off the road, across the ditch, to avoid some of the noise, and waited as the four sergeants climbed down from their perches on the tracks and came over to gather around him. When they were all assembled, he gave them their orders.

"Once we get inside," he told them, "have your drivers head straight for the fuel truck. We're the first ones here, so you should be able to top off right away. As soon as you're back in position on the berm, make sure everyone cleans their weapons. Take inventory and give me a list of any ammo you need." Carr glanced at his watch. It was still mid-afternoon. "We might go out again, so don't let anyone wander away. I'll let you know what the plan is after I talk to the CO. Any questions?" Carr felt good about himself, taking charge like this.

"Is Free coming back?" Reedy asked. Carr was annoyed by the question, since he inferred that the squad leader didn't trust him to be a competent leader in the sergeant's absence.

"Sergeant Samples is in Dau Tieng being treated for his wounds," Carr told them, although all of them should already know that. "He'll be back when the doctors release him. The wounds appeared superficial, so I suspect he'll be back in the platoon within a few days. Any other questions?"

"No, sir," Montoya said before anyone else could speak. He gave Reedy a quick dirty look.

Carr turned to look back at the gate and saw that the deuce-and-a-half had been disentangled and was now rolling down the entrance road, heading back to Tay Ninh or Cu Chi, wherever it had come from. "Mount up," Carr told the sergeants. They all ran back to their respective APCs and climbed back on board. Carr took his seat behind Sergeant Washington and gave the hand gesture for "forward," knowing it was probably unnecessary. The diesels growled and the treads clanked as the column moved down the entrance road and through the gate.

When the platoon reached the fuel truck, Carr dismounted and observed the refueling process, in part to learn how it was done, and in part because he didn't have anything else to do at the moment. As PFC Chacon pulled the one-four track up alongside the big olive-drab tanker truck, Spec 4 Eberhart climbed over onto the cargo hatch lid and released the filler cap at the left rear top of the track. The fuel truck operator, standing on a fender, handed across the hose nozzle so Everhart could insert it in the filler tube. Even standing on the ground on the other side of the track, Carr could smell the diesel fuel, its oily fumes permeating the area around the fuel truck. When the refueling was completed, Eberhart handed the hose back to the operator, snapped the cap back into place, and signaled to Chacon that he could leave. Meanwhile Sergeant Washington had jumped down the front of the track and prepared to ground guide Chacon back to their place on the perimeter. Washington began walking, and Chacon followed him like a pet elephant, making way for the next track in line.

Carr stayed to watch each of his tracks get refueled, and then followed the final one back to their parking place on the east side of the fire support base. As the one-one maneuvered up to the berm and shut down, Carr strolled on down the line to the one-four, where they had already set up a weapons-cleaning station. A tall and wide ammo can, labeled 20MM, was open on a small folding field table, and soldiers were dipping various parts of their disassembled M-16s into the liquid inside. Carr knew the can had gasoline in it, which was not the recommended solution for cleaning weapons, but it was available and efficient. He bent over as he went up the opened rear ramp and plopped wearily down on the bench. After a minute he took off his helmet and web gear, laying them on the bench beside him, and began disassembling his rifle.

Fifteen minutes later he was outside at the cleaning table reassembling his rifle. Hicks and Eberhart were up on the track dismounting the 50-cal so they could clean it. Chacon was up front with the engine cover propped open, checking the oil and other fluids. Sergeant Washington was inside the track counting ammo cans. Miles had left with a couple empty jerry cans to get refilled with water. Carr slid the charging handle into the upper receiver group, and then lowered the assembly onto the lower receiver group and locked it in place with the pin. He pulled the charging handle back to cock it, pushed the handle back into place, and dry-fired the weapon to ensure he had done everything properly.

"Good job today, Steve." Carr turned to find Captain Raymond standing beside him, looking at all the busy soldiers and nodding approvingly. Raymond had a boonie hat over his curly dark locks, no shirt, and his pants cuffs were rolled up above his boots. Only the black metal captain's bars on his hat distinguished him from the other soldiers in the area. No one in the company, however, mistook his lack of military decorum for slackness or lack of leadership. He was well respected by all the men, and not just because this was his second tour and he had lots of experience. He was a competent and fair commander, and Carr felt lucky to have been assigned to his company. "Looks like you're managing okay without Sergeant Samples."

"Yes, sir," Carr replied. When Carr had first arrived from Cu Chi and been assigned to Alpha Company, Raymond had warned him that Samples might be difficult.

"Frankly," Raymond had told him, "Samples doesn't like officers—especially lieutenants. Not sure why. The last platoon leader he had begged to be reassigned, and finally managed it. Samples hasn't had a platoon leader for the last three months, and he has obviously liked it that way. He's a very competent platoon sergeant, with tons of experience, and I've had no reason to complain about his leadership of the platoon. It wouldn't have bothered me if we never got a lieutenant for this platoon, but now that we have, that's fine, too. You've got your work cut out for you, though. If you can get on his good side, he'll really be an asset. Get on his wrong side, however, and you're fucked. He's been in the Army long enough to figure out all the ways to get around an officer and to make him look bad, without getting caught at it. So be careful." Carr had already discovered how true Raymond's words were.

"How is Sergeant Samples, sir," Carr now asked Raymond, as they stood in the bright afternoon sun. "Have you heard anything?"

"Not yet," Raymond replied, shaking his head. "Nothing about him or the other two either."

"Other two?" Carr hadn't realized there were other casualties.

"Atkins, in First Platoon, broke his wrist jumping off the track. Radavich in Second caught a ricochet in his butt. Could have been worse, I guess."

"What about Bravo and Charlie?"

Raymond shrugged. "After Bravo found that weapons cache, they held in place. They never made any contact, and should be pulling in any time now. Charlie got ambushed and lost a track to an RPG. At least one Kilo and several Whiskeys." Kilo was short for Kilo India Alpha—killed in action—and Whiskey short for wounded in action. The euphemisms were a way for soldiers to distance their feelings from the reality of war, but Carr sensed that Raymond still felt the losses, even for men he didn't know. "Charlie's going back into Dau Tieng for the night."

"So we're done for today?" Carr asked, trying not to sound too hopeful.

"Oh, yeah. We'll probably send out an LP tonight, but otherwise try to let the guys get some rest. They're arranging an Arc Light mission for tonight up in the Crescent." Arc Light was the code name for a carpet bombing raid carried out by B-52 bombers flying in from Guam. Carr had heard of them, but had no direct experience. The Listening Post would only involve three or four men, sent out a few hundred meters to provide an early warning of any approaching enemy.

"Oh, by the way," Raymond said, "there'll be a deuce-and-a-half coming by to collect those bags of rice later. I'm sure you'll be glad to get rid of them."

"Definitely, sir. What are they going to do with them?"

Raymond shrugged. "Probably give them back to the ARVNs or local district chief."

Carr cynically assumed that meant they would then be sold on the black market, and eventually end up back with the VC or NCA.

Raymond turned to leave, saying, "Well, I better get back to my track and find out what other bullshit Higher has for me." Then he stopped and turned back to Carr. "Oh, yeah, one more thing. Somebody stole the tools out of the colonel's track last night. The S-3's on the warpath about it. Just so you know." Raymond resumed his departure, leaving Carr to wonder just how much the captain really knew.

Stepping inside the track, Carr began rummaging through his personal waterproof bag in which he kept his clean clothes. "Sergeant Washington," he said over his shoulder, "we're done for the day. Would you please pass the word to the other squad leaders? And let Jamison and Reedy know a truck will be coming by to get the rice sacks. I'm going to clean up a little. I can still smell that damn CS."

"So can I," Washington replied. "No offense, sir."

"None taken. And please get the other squads' ammo requirements and consolidate them for me, will you?"

"No sweat, sir." Washington made a couple more notes on the small pad of paper he held and then headed back outside. As he was leaving Spec 4 Miles returned, a heavy water can hanging from each hand. He dropped them just outside. Carr climbed out holding a soap dish and a towel.

"Sorry, Randy," he told Miles, "I'm going to use one of those and take a shower."

"I figured," Miles replied. "Leave the can up there when you're done. I need one, too."

Carr lifted up one of the cans over his head and set it sideways on top of the track, with the lid sticking over the edge. He found an old poncho just inside the track behind the bench and spread it out on the dirt below the water can. Now all he had to do was undress, unscrew the cap of the small spigot on the lid, and stand under the resulting stream of water. Hardly a proper shower, but it was better than what the poor ground-pounders had to deal with.

Twenty minutes later, with all the dirt and CS washed off and a clean uniform, Carr was beginning to feel human again. With his boonie hat perched on his head, he stepped out of the track into the bright sun and breathed in the fetid air. As always, it reeked of diesel, dirt, and odors he would rather not identify, but it was far better than the CS he had inhaled earlier in the day. He left his weapon inside the track, knowing someone would always be there to watch it. PFC Chacon was sitting on the ground beside the road wheels, laying out some suspiciously new-looking tools.

"Going to replace a track shoe?" Carr asked innocently. Chacon visibly twitched, startled by Carr's appearance.

"Uh, yes, sir," the young driver answered, guiltily looking down at the tools. They still had the original paint on them, and next to them lay an equally new tool bag. Carr had no doubt where they had come from.

"Good. Good." Carr paused. "You know what you ought to do, PFC Chacon, is scratch the track number onto those tools with a screwdriver or something. You know, put 'A14' on them. That way, if they get, uh, misplaced, you'll be able to identify them."

Chacon's face was initially creased in puzzlement, and then suddenly transformed into a relieved grin. "Good idea, sir. I'll get right on that."

Carr chuckled to himself as he walked away toward the other tracks of the platoon. He saw Washington talking to Montoya at the one-three, and they kept up the conversation when he approached.

"All I'm sayin'," Washington insisted, "is that it will be in July. Not everybody, maybe, but most of us."

"That's bullshit, Del," Montoya replied, shaking his head. "Never happen, GI." Montoya turned to Carr. "What do you think, Eltee?"

"About what?" Carr asked.

"The pullout," Washington answered. "I heard they're pulling us out in July, sending us back to Hawaii." President Nixon had promised to start pulling troops out of Viet Nam, and it had already been announced that the 9th Division down in the Delta would be the first to go. Everyone had been required to fill out "dream sheets" indicating where they would prefer to be assigned when they departed Viet Nam. There were now daily rumors about which division would be the next to leave.

"Where'd you hear that?" Carr inquired with interest.

"I know a guy in headquarters company," Washington explained, "who knows a guy in Cu Chi that's got a friend at Division Headquarters, and that guy heard it from the Division Sergeant Major."

Carr raised one eyebrow and looked dubious.

"Hey," Washington asserted, "these are all reliable sources. Except maybe the Sergeant Major."

Carr and Montoya both guffawed. Washington grinned.

"Dream on, Del," Montoya said, slapping Washington on the shoulder. "You numbah ten, GI," he added with what was supposed to be a Vietnamese accent.

"Eat shit," Washington told him good-naturedly. He pulled a piece of paper out of his pants pocket and handed it to Carr. "Here's the ammo we need."

Carr looked over the list, not sure what he was supposed to do with it. Samples had always handled that up to now. Montoya apparently guessed at the problem.

"Just have the CO approve it, and Del and I can go pick it up."

"Sure," Carr said. "I was just on my way over to see him now anyway."

As if on cue, Miles came running up and said, "Sir, the CO wants to see you at his track, ASAP." Miles was shirtless, his boots were tied only halfway up, and his hair was still wet from his recent shower.

"On my way," Carr told the radioman, and strode toward the company headquarters area.

"I'll go with you," Miles said, catching up. "Stiles has a couple extra prick batteries for me." Stiles was the commander's RTO.

"Any idea what this is about?" Carr asked him.

"Nope, but he didn't sound happy."

When they arrived Carr found Captain Raymond and Major Moore standing beside the commander's APC. Miles darted inside the track to get his batteries. Raymond had put on his uniform shirt and bloused his boots, looking a little more strack than earlier. Major Moore was the battalion operations officer, the S-3, a tall auburn-haired Irishman with a bulbous nose and a red complexion that turned a deeper crimson when he was angry, which seemed to be most of the time. Although bare-headed, he was in full uniform, with starched jungle fatigues and spit-shined boots, with a .45 pistol in a leather holster clipped to his pistol belt.

"Glad you could join us," the major said when Carr walked up. There was a hint of sarcasm in his tone, and no welcoming smile. Carr came to a rough approximation of attention. This didn't bode well.

"Steve," Raymond said, "Major Moore believes someone from your platoon may have borrowed. . ."

"Stolen," Moore interrupted, his eyes narrowing.

Raymond continued. ". . .some tools from the battalion commander's track. Would you know anything about that?"

"Tools?" Carr temporized. "What kind of tools?"

"Track tools," Moore hissed, "what the hell do you think, lieutenant?"

"Sir," Carr said reasonably but assertively, "when I took over the platoon I did an inventory, and I did not find any excess tools. And if anyone had acquired additional tools lately, I would certainly know about it. Are these missing tools marked in any way, so that you could identify them?

Moore glared at him. "They're a brand new set," he declared angrily.

"And they're not marked? Well, I'll check, sir. I've had our drivers all mark their tools with their track numbers, so any new tools would certainly stand out." Carr noticed that Captain Raymond had his hand over his mouth, as if rubbing his chin, but Carr could tell he was actually hiding a smile.

"You do that, lieutenant!"

As if the idea had just occurred to him, Carr remarked, "If the tools aren't found, sir, you could probably order a new set from Supply. That's what we do." Moore's face now turned almost purple as he stifled a curse. The entire battalion was well aware that ordering new tools and equipment through Supply was an exercise in frustration. If the battalion commander personally went to the G-4 supply officer at Division and requested the tools, they might arrive in six months. Otherwise he was SOL.

Moore turned to Raymond with a scowl. "Briefing at 1800," he muttered. With a parting glare at Carr he spun on one heel and stalked away.

"That was interesting," Raymond said when Moore was out of earshot.

"Indeed, sir," Carr answered, forcing a blank look on his face. "The S-3 seems to be in a bad mood today."

"As always," the captain replied. "Don't tell anyone, but I think he got passed over for lieutenant colonel."

"Hard to imagine why," Carr said mildly.

Raymond chuckled. "Now about those tools. You go ahead and check your troops, and I'll tell the Major at the briefing that you couldn't find them."

"Thank you, sir," Carr said with a grateful smile. "Oh," Carr said as he remembered the list in his pocket, "can you approve this ammo request?"

"No sweat," Raymond replied, taking the piece of paper and scrawling his signature on it with a pen he pulled from his shirt pocket. "Anything else?"

"No, sir."

"Dismissed," Raymond told him with a friendly pat on the back. Carr turned and headed back to the platoon area. Miles came up from behind and matched his stride.

"Got my batteries," Miles told him, holding up the stack of three brick-shaped batteries for the radio. Miles was grinning. He had obviously overheard the conversation with the S-3.

"I see that," Carr said. "Better put them someplace secure."

"Roger that, sir." Miles skipped on ahead, snickering. Carr knew that the entire platoon would hear the story before evening chow.

Carr found Sergeant Montoya and gave him the signed ammo request, and then wandered through the platoon area checking on the men and offering suggestions on how to improve their defenses. He found two of the track drivers busy scratching numbers on their tools with pocket knives. They looked up at him, smiled, and nodded. The story had spread quickly, Carr realized.

Sergeant Reedy walked along the platoon line and told the soldiers that chow was being served. The men knew they had to go in shifts, and quickly agreed who would eat first. Carr was pleased that the platoon operated like a well-oiled machine, with the men all knowing what they should be doing and when. Of course, Carr acknowledged, most of that was due to the capable leadership and training of Sergeant Samples. He just wished he could find a way to break through Samples' barriers and develop a better working relationship with the platoon sergeant. Although Carr certainly hoped that Samples' wounds weren't serious and he would recover quickly, he had to admit it was pleasant being in charge himself, without interference.

Assured the platoon was managing well, Carr strolled over to the mess tent near the center of the fire support base. He got in line and waited for the cooks to dump the food onto the stamped metal tray. It was a typical Army meal—chili-mac, canned green beans, Wonder bread, canned peaches, a chocolate brownie, and Kool-Aid. Holding his full tray with both hands, Carr looked out over the rows of tables, trying to decide where he would sit. A hand was raised and waved at him. It was Terry Whiteside, a guy with whom Carr had gone through Ranger school. They had come in country together, and Whiteside had been assigned to Bravo Company. Carr smiled and maneuvered through the tables to sit across from him.

"How they hangin', Steve," Whiteside greeted him.

"Not bad, how about you?"

Whiteside shook his head. "Same ol' same ol'," he said, taking a bite of his chili-mac. Whiteside was the same age as Carr, but looked much younger. With wispy blond hair and startling blue eyes, he looked more like a fashion model than an infantry lieutenant. Realizing just how hungry he was, Carr dug into his meal. For few minutes both men ate in silence. Then Whiteside muttered something Carr couldn't hear over the noise of the other diners.

"What?" Carr asked.

"Fuckin' brigade commander," Whiteside repeated in a low voice. "He's always on my ass."

"What are you talking about?"

"Last week we were outposting down near Trang Bang," Whiteside explained, still keeping his voice down. "A couple of my guys set up ponchos like awnings from the sides of the tracks so they could have some shade, and the colonel flew over in his chopper. He saw the ponchos and landed to chew me and them out. Hell, we were just trying to stay out of the sun while we waited for the convoy to go through. We were in the middle of rice paddies, and no gooks could have snuck up on us. Coulda been worse, though. A few minutes earlier me and some guys were playing baseball with some of the farm kids. If the colonel had seen that, he would have shit."

"I know what you mean," Carr commiserated. His run-in with the S-3 came to mind.

"Did you hear what happened in Charlie?" Whiteside continued.

"Don't think so," Carr said, raising one eyebrow.

"They were outposting and the colonel flew over and caught them buying sodas and sandwiches from the Coke kids and sandwich mama-sans. Gave three of the guys Article-15s, and had them use CS grenades to run the kids off. Asshole." An Article-15 was administrative punishment usually handed out by company commanders, not brigade commanders. Applying them to soldiers for buying sodas and sandwiches seemed unduly harsh. Carr would have to remember that, because his men—and he himself—often bought refreshments from the kids who followed the GIs around whenever there was no chance of actual combat. Whiteside's and the Charlie guys' problem was that they had forgotten the prime rule in the Army—don't get caught, or, failing that, have a good excuse already prepared.

"Heard you guys found some weapons today," Carr said, changing the subject.

"Yeah," Whiteside said, brightening a little. "Mostly ammo. First platoon found this big bunker full of it. From what I saw, most of it was old and dusty. Looked like it had been there for a while. So you guys made contact, huh?" Whiteside sounded a little jealous.

"Yeah, snipers," Carr replied. "Had us pinned down for a while. I made the mistake of taking cover behind a big drum of CS, got that shit all over me."

"Somebody told me about that. We heard all the shooting, not sure if it was you or Charlie. And you had some casualties?"

"Three minor ones," Carr told him. "One was my platoon sergeant. Got shrapnel in his belly from his own M-79 round. He got dusted off to Dau Tieng."

"He'll still get a purple heart for it," Whiteside remarked. "How are you managing without him?"

"Better, actually," Carr told him. "He was the acting platoon leader for three months before I got here, and I think he considers me an interloper. He ignores me a lot of the time, or just works around me. My CO says he just doesn't like officers in general. Anyway, with him gone for now, I'm getting to know the platoon better and can make my own decisions."

"I should be so lucky," Whiteside said with a sorrowful shake of his head. "My platoon sergeant doesn't do anything. He's an old guy that's been in the Army too long. ROAD—retired on active duty. I'm pretty sure he's drinking a lot, too."

"Have you talked to your CO about him?"

"Yeah, but he says I'm lucky to even have an E-7 platoon sergeant. The other platoons have shake-and-bakes, an E-5 and an E-6 both fresh out of NCO school. I'm not sure which is worse. At least you've got someone who knows what he's doing."

"You're right," Carr admitted. "When we make contact, he's a good guy to have around."

"Me, I still haven't seen any contact yet," Whiteside grumbled. "It's always some other platoon or company." Whiteside was clearly a little envious of Carr's already greater experience. The young lieutenant was still burdened with the dream of being a combat hero, just as Carr had been when he first arrived. For Carr, however, the reality of contact had burst this bubble and left him drained and hoping only for survival. All the enthusiasm for battle that Officer Basic and Ranger School had engendered was now gone and replaced with a desire to stay alive and get home to his wife. Viet Nam was no longer a Great Adventure; it was a purgatory to be endured, a year-long sentence to hard labor.

Whiteside glanced at his watch and then picked up his tray. "Gotta go," he said, "make sure my platoon sergeant stays sober. Take it easy."

"You, too," Carr said. He finished his meal, dumped the tray at the garbage cans, and handed it to a KP who was dunking them in boiling soapy water. As he walked back to the platoon area, he was joined by Sergeant Washington.

"Got the ammo, sir," Washington told him. "Everybody's set."

"Thank you, Sergeant," Carr said. They walked together in silence for a minute. "CO said we'd have an LP tonight," Carr mused. "I guess I better check on that."

"I'll get some volunteers," Washington said. Carr knew that these men would actually be "volunteered" by the squad leaders, because no one wanted to go out and lay in the dirt all night if they didn't have to. Back at the one-four track the other men were lounging around enjoying the respite from work, reading paperback books or listening to AFVN on the squad's portable radio. Carr brushed his teeth, so he wouldn't have to do it in the morning, and then sat down to write his wife a letter.

The sun was getting low in the western sky when Carr emerged from the track with the letter, sealed in an addressed envelope. Casually he wandered over to the company headquarters area to drop the letter in the out-going mail sack. As he started back he saw the captain returning from the battalion headquarters area.

"Steve," Raymond called to him. "My track. Leader's meeting." Raymond then told his RTO, Stiles, who was messing with the microphone cord on his back-pack radio, to get the others.

Carr joined Raymond inside the track, but they remained silent until the other men arrived. First to arrive was Lieutenant Baron from Second Platoon. Baron, like Carr, had no platoon sergeant at the moment, due to Sergeant Petty's wounding the day before. Holmes, the mortar sergeant, arrived next, and behind him came Lieutenant Fawcett from Third Platoon and his platoon sergeant, Staff Sergeant Sotelo. Everyone settled onto the bench seats and waited for Raymond to begin. Before Raymond could speak, Stiles stuck his head in through the open ramp.

"Sergeant Samples is coming in through the gate," Stiles announced, holding the handset of his PRC-25 to his ear.

"He's what?" Raymond asked with surprise.

"Yeah, he's walking in from the road."

"He's supposed to be in Dau Tieng," Carr said, with a touch of disappointment.

"How did he get here," Holmes asked. "He can't have walked all the way."

Stiles consulted with someone on the radio before replying. "Apparently he got a ride with someone. A jeep dropped him off out at the road."

"Get him here," Raymond ordered. "Now." Stiles again muttered into the handset.

"He's on his way, sir," the RTO informed them after a minute.

"Gung ho idiot," Raymond muttered. "Could have at least spent the night there, maybe slept on clean sheets."

When Samples stepped up on the ramp of the CO's track and bent down to enter, he saw the various expressions on the faces of the men sitting inside. The two sergeants had accusatory looks, as if he had betrayed the enlisted men's code by not taking advantage of his break from the action. Raymond was trying to maintain a disciplinary frown, but not succeeding. Carr's face was a neutral mask attempting to hide disappointment. The other two lieutenants registered only mild surprise.

"Reporting for duty, sir," Samples told Raymond.

"What are you doing here, Aaron?" Raymond asked him with feigned anger. "You're supposed to be in Dau Tieng recovering from your wounds."

Samples shrugged. "They patched me up, and I felt fine. Figured I might as well get back to work. Besides, Dau Tieng keeps getting rocketed." The nightly rocket attacks didn't particular alarm him, but they did interrupt his sleep. And they were just an excuse anyway. He preferred to be in the field with his men.

"How'd you get here?" Carr asked. This close to sundown, few vehicles were out on the road.

"Caught a ride with an old friend of mine. MACV." MACV was the Military Assistance Command Viet Nam, the advisors to the South Vietnamese military. Samples' first tour had been with MACV. In a separate command from the regular Army, the MACV guys played by slightly different rules. They had no qualms about driving their jeeps and trucks alone through unpacified areas, depending on speed and daring to get them through safely.

Captain Raymond sighed with resignation. "Sit down," he told Samples. "We're just getting started." Samples suppressed a smile and took a seat.

"Okay, here's the deal," Raymond told them, consulting a small notebook. "We're sending out a four-man LP tonight. One man from each platoon, including headquarters platoon. Mel," Raymond looked at Lieutenant Mel Barron, "your radio will go out with them. Tomorrow only one guy per platoon will stay back, and that will be the guys from the LP."

Samples nodded approvingly. The LP guys wouldn't get much sleep, but would have a chance to rest up tomorrow. One guy per platoon was sufficient to guard against theft from the gear left behind.

"So what are we doing tomorrow?" Lieutenant Fawcett asked.

"Tonight," Raymond informed them, "there will be a B-52 raid on the Crescent. Intelligence thinks there's a big concentration of

NVA up there. The whole battalion will sweep the bombed-out area tomorrow, I guess to count bodies and assess the damage."

Samples had seen one of the Arc Light bombing raids before, in the daytime. The B-52s were so high you could barely see them, but the rain of thousand-pound bombs became visible as they neared the earth. When they hit it was like the worst thunderstorm imaginable, with the ground shaking and huge clouds of dust and smoke rising from the impact area. It seemed impossible that anyone or anything would survive such an onslaught.

"What time is the B-52 strike?" Fawcett asked.

"I don't know exactly," Raymond answered. "Probably after midnight. Better warn your men so they aren't surprised or think it's an enemy attack. Have your LP guys meet here at 2130, and I'll give them their orders. Any questions?"

Samples, like the others, just shook his head. As the first in, he was the first to leave, and head back to the platoon area. Carr caught up with him and fell in step.

"Sergeant Washington already has a list of men for the LP," Carr told him. "I thought each platoon was sending out an LP, so we'll have to choose just one from the list." Samples nodded and kept walking. He was mildly surprised that Carr had thought that far ahead. He was also a little annoyed, because it contradicted his poor opinion of the young officer.

"Are you really okay, Sergeant?" Carr sounded almost genuinely concerned. "Did they give you any kind of profile?"

"No heavy lifting," Samples replied sarcastically. "No, I'm fine. I'll have Doc Allman change the bandages every day, and he can take out the stitches in a week or so. No sweat."

Carr grabbed his upper arm and stopped him, then swung around in front to face him. "Look, Sergeant Samples," Carr said sternly, "the men and I need you to be fully operational. We can't be baby-sitting you if you can't hold up your end. Do you understand?"

Samples rolled his eyes. "Affirmative."

Carr stared at him a moment, then said quietly, "How about saying 'sir' every once in a while, too."

Samples clenched his teeth. This was no time to get into the problem, and besides, he knew he was in the wrong. "Yes, SIR," he bit out. "Is that all, SIR?" They glared at each other. Carr released Samples arm, and Samples walked around him, heading back to the one-one track. He didn't look back, even when Carr spoke again.

"Platoon briefing at one-four in ten minutes, Sergeant." Samples didn't even nod.

Samples was still fuming when he was greeted by Art Jamison standing beside the APC.

"Welcome back, Sarge," Jamison said with a smile. "How was the vacation in the base camp? Hump any round-eyed nurses?"

"Eat shit and die," Samples replied grumpily. "Where's my rifle?"

"Turned it in to battalion. Said they'd bring you a new one out from Dau Tieng later."

"What the fuck am I supposed to do meanwhile?" Samples was still irritated by his conversation with Lieutenant Carr, and was taking it out on Jamison. He knew it was unfair, but he couldn't stop himself.

"Throw rocks?" Jamison suggested facetiously. "Seriously, though, don't sweat it. We'll find you something. Maybe you can borrow Allman's thirty-eight. Or you could go all John Wayne and carry an M-60."

Samples scoffed at the suggestion. "What about my helmet and web gear?"

"Inside the track, on top of the ammo cans. Don't worry, we're looking out for you."

Washington and Montoya walked up and slapped Samples on the back, joking with him about his brief absence. Samples began feeling better, enjoying the camaraderie and good-natured insults of his fellow NCOs. Sergeant Reedy apparently heard the laughter and came out of the one-two to join them.

"So how was the joy ride on the chopper?" Reedy asked.

"No big deal," Samples told them. "Short flight."

"I've never been up in a helicopter," Montoya admitted. "Kind of like to go sometime, as long as it was voluntary and no one was shooting at me."

"Bet that," Washington agreed.

"Remember Dave Conklin, in Third Platoon?" Martinson asked. "Volunteered to be a door gunner? Man, what was he thinking? Sure, you get to sleep in a bunker and go the PX every day, but door gunners got to have an even shorter life expectancy than infantry lieutenants."

"I wouldn't do it," Reedy said. "I get airsick. I'd be puking my guts out."

"Poor baby," Montoya chided him. Samples laughed along with the others, while gently rubbing the bandages on his abdomen. His wounds were beginning to itch already.

"Hey, Sarge," Washington said, "you hear about Carr and the major?"

"What major?" Samples asked, shaking his head.

"The S-3, Moore," Jamison said. "Man!" All four squad leaders were chuckling.

"So what happened?" Samples asked.

"Chacon took your hint," Washington began. "He 'acquired' the tools out of the BC's track last night and Carr knew it. He saw Chacon using them this afternoon, and told him to mark the tools with the track number."

"Yeah," Montoya joined in, "and then the major got a case of the ass and went looking for them. Somebody must have seen Chacon, 'cause the lieutenant had to go see the major at the CO's track. Carr said he didn't think anyone in our platoon would do that, and then he fuckin' told the major they shoulda marked the tools like our platoon does. The major was fuckin' *pissed*."

"Miles was nearby and heard the whole thing," Washington added. "The CO backed up Carr, and later said he would square it with the BC. Major Moore is such an asshole."

Samples grunted but didn't say anything. It sounded like the lieutenant had done something right for a change, which kind of bothered Samples. The other sergeants were talking about the young officer with a measure of respect, which to Samples seemed like a portion of the respect they had been giving to him. As if there was a certain amount of respect available, and some had been taken from him and given to Carr. Logically Samples knew this was ridiculous, but it troubled him anyway. Samples had always thought his sergeants shared his total disdain for officers, lieutenants in particular, but now they seemed to have welcomed Carr as a fellow soldier integral to the platoon. He wanted to say something negative about Carr, but knew it would be misconstrued at best, and damaging to good discipline and order at worst. Instead he looked at his watch.

"Platoon meeting at the one-four," he announced, as if it was his idea. "Get all the guys over there now."

A couple minutes later they had all gathered beside the one-four. The men stood in a loose semi-circle, at the center of which was Lieutenant Carr. Samples took a position next to Carr, giving the other men a menacing look to quiet them down. "Go ahead, lieutenant," Samples said, to hopefully establish who was really in charge here.

"Okay, guys," Carr began, stuffing his hands in his pants pockets, "here's the plan. It's a company LP tonight, and we only have to send one man from our platoon." He turned to look at Samples.

Samples was uncomfortable. He hadn't yet checked with Washington to choose the volunteer. So he punted. "Del and I are working on that. We'll let you know after the meeting."

Carr turned back to the men. "Whoever it is, you'll report to the headquarters track at 9:30. The LP man will be the only one to stay back tomorrow." Samples saw some faces brighten with the realization that the ordeal of LP would be rewarded with a day of rest.

"Tonight," Carr told them, "there's going to be a B-52 strike on the Crescent. Sometime after midnight."

"You'll know it," Samples told them men. "They're noisy."

"And tomorrow," Carr said, ignoring Samples' interruption, "the whole battalion is going to sweep the bombed-out area, counting bodies and doing a damage assessment."

"What time we moving out?" Sergeant Reedy asked.

"Don't know yet," Carr replied.

"So be ready first thing in the morning," Samples interjected. "Fill your canteens, stock up on ammo, and put on clean socks."

"That's right," Carr agreed. "It's going to be a long day, so be prepared. And I'm sure the battalion commander, and probably the brigade commander, will be overhead, so look military and keep your helmets on. Any questions?"

There were a few head shakes. Then someone in the back began to sing softly, "Please Mr. Custer, I don't want to go." Others laughed.

"Knock it off," Samples ordered with mild irritation. He turned and looked at Carr. "Anything else, lieutenant?" When Carr shook his head, Samples turned back to the assembled men and commanded, "Fall out." The gaggle shuffled away.

Samples cornered Washington and said, "Who you got?"

"For the LP? Sweet, Pratt, Merrill, and Eberhart."

Samples pondered the names for a moment. "Let's make it Sweet. He didn't go out on the AP last night. I'm gonna check with him, see if I can use his M-16 tomorrow. I'll tell him he's the one for tonight. You let the other guys know."

"Roger that," Washington said with a nod. He walked away, looking for the other men to pass the word. Samples started to head back to the one-one track to talk to Sweet, and then noticed

Lieutenant Carr standing by with an expectant look on his face. Reluctantly he went over to the officer.

"Sweet's going on the LP," Samples told him. "I'm going to borrow his rifle tomorrow, since mine's all fucked up."

"Good idea," Carr agreed. There was a look of concern on his face. "Are you sure you're up for tomorrow, Sergeant?"

"Me? Why shouldn't I be?" Samples was insulted by the question.

"Well, you just got wounded, for one thing."

Samples' hand almost involuntarily went to his shirt front. "No big deal," he asserted. "I've been shot before."

"The men depend on you," Carr reminded him. "Hell, I depend on you."

"I know," Samples replied, feeling a little glow of satisfaction at the compliment. "I'll be there, one hundred per cent. . .sir." The last was added without sarcasm or rancor.

"Good enough," Carr said. Carr turned and ducked inside the track. Samples stared after him a moment, wondering what had just happened. Then he took a deep breath and went looking for Sweet.

It was well after midnight when Samples was awakened by the vibrations of his cot and the distant rumble of thunder. He sat up and slipped his feet into the boots left next to the cot, only tying the laces enough to keep from tripping over them. He stood up and walked to the back of the track so he could see to the north. Overhead the stars twinkled brightly, and Sergeant Jamison came out of the track to stand beside him. The far horizon was flashing as hundreds of bombs exploded, the string of bright eruptions illuminating the clouds of dust being thrown up into the air. The concussions, attenuated by the distance, washed over them like waves from a distant hurricane, pounding them repetitively. Samples looked up to try and pick out the bombers, but they were either too high or it was too dark. Nor could he see the bombs falling lazily through the air. All he could see was the staccato bursts of light that were undoubtedly blasting the forest to shreds. Even at this distance he could feel the tremendous power and destruction, a testament to the force the U.S. could bring to bear on an enemy.

After a few minutes the raid ended, and the smoke and dust were hidden by the night. The last reverberations faded and silence once again reigned. Samples tried to imagine what it must be like to be at ground zero during such an assault. Surely any NVA in that area were totally wiped out, their bodies blown to smithereens. Surely. Even their best bunkers couldn't survive the onslaught of thousand-pound bombs. Tomorrow should be a cake-walk. Unless, of course, the gooks were somewhere else when the bombs fell.

"Wow," Jamison said, still staring at the horizon.

"Yeah," Samples agreed. He returned to his cot, laid down with his boots still on, and stared up at the stars. Just what was he doing here, he wondered. What was his purpose in life? For that matter, what was the point of this war? These were deep thoughts, and Samples usually avoided such introspection. He didn't want to explore such topics now, either. He closed his eyes and tried to think of absolutely nothing, to wipe his mind clean. It wasn't easy, but somehow he managed and fell asleep.

SEVEN

Alpha and Bravo Companies were lined up on the perimeter road and ready to go out the gate by 0800, and there they sat. With diesel engines idling and men geared up and ready, they did the usual Army hurry-up-and-wait. By switching back and forth between the company net and the battalion net on the radio, Lieutenant Carr gathered from the chatter that the hold-up was with Charlie Company in Dau Tieng. They were taking on a company of Wolfhounds, straight-leg grunts that would ride out with them, but the real holdup was the reporters. Apparently some AP or UPI reporters and camera men were going to accompany the battalion on the sweep. Carr didn't like the sound of that. Having reporters along indicated that someone higher expected there to be some real action today. At least the civilians wouldn't be on any Alpha tracks.

Eventually Charlie was ready and left Dau Tieng, so the other two companies rolled out the gate at FSB Wood and headed northeast to meet them. Carr's platoon was the first in line, and his own track, the one-four, was in the lead. After rolling northeast for a couple miles, the road turned straight east, where they met the Charlie company tracks arriving from the area of Ben Cui. Carr could see the reporters on the first two Charlie tracks, with their pads and cameras instead of weapons. First Platoon stopped and waited for the rest of the battalion to catch up, while the tail end of Charlie caught up as well. Once everyone had arrived, the command came down to turn north and proceed into the woods.

For the first hour the men remained mounted, with the tracks basically performing a battalion RIF. The troops called it "busting jungle," as the blocky armored vehicles pushed through the brush and vines between the trees. Carr was sitting on the ammo box just behind Sergeant Washington, whose legs straddled the driver's hatch, his butt on a folded bench cushion placed on the open driver's hatch lid. The driver, Chacon, had one of the CVC helmets, and Carr had the other. Through the built-in headphones he could hear the radio chatter, and if necessary he could issue orders through the small microphone that dangled brokenly from the side. Beside him, inside the open machine gun turret, stood Eberhart, and behind Eberhart, in the open cargo hatch, stood Hicks. Both men rolled and leaned with the movement of the vehicle like sailors on an old wooden ship, almost effortlessly maintaining their balance with only a light grip of their hands.

Carr, not yet as skilled as the other crew members, held tightly to a canvas strap between his legs, swaying precariously as he simultaneously used one arm to fend off the branches that threatened to slap his face. On the other side of the 50-cal, on yet another ammo can, rode Doc Allman, casually holding on to the side of the turret with one hand, and behind him sat Jones, who looked bored. Looking back over his shoulder, Carr saw Miles sitting behind him with the handset of the PRC-25 pressed to his ear, observing the passing scenery with mild interest. The young men around him were alert, but none appeared anxious or even concerned. To them, apparently, it was just another day on the job, one at which danger and death were just part of the job description. Carr was not yet so sanguine.

The line of APCs moved slowly through the woods, in part out of a heightened sense of caution, but mostly because it was so hard to keep the entire battalion on line. The radio was busy as various drivers were told to speed up or slow down, since the drivers were unable to see much to either side beyond the tracks next to them. It was important to not let anyone get ahead or behind the others, in case anyone made contact with the enemy. Contact would result in the entire battalion opening fire indiscriminately, and that would endanger with friendly fire anyone who was not on line. Carr, from his elevated position on the ammo can, could just make out all four of his platoon's tracks, stretching off to his left, and three of the Charlie company tracks to his right. The Charlie tracks were crowded on top, what with the Wolfhounds and reporters on board in addition to their regular crews. The Wolfhounds soldiers, carrying more equipment than the mech soldiers normally did, looked uncomfortable. They probably felt exposed, Carr surmised, sitting on top of these noisy beasts like slow-moving targets.

Finally the word came down to dismount, and all the APCs halted to let their crews climb down. Only the drivers, 50-cal gunners, and loaders remained on board. As everyone moved out in front of the tracks to form a ragged line, Carr noticed that the reporters had chosen to continue riding on the Charlie company tracks. The aluminum alloy armor of the tracks probably gave them a false sense of security; they probably weren't aware that RPGs and machine gun rounds could easily pierce that armor. Carr shrugged and walked over to the area ahead of the one-three and one-two tracks, where Sergeant Samples was already standing, shouting and gesturing the men into the proper positions. Miles had followed him, his M-16 held loosely in his left hand by the magazine well, his right hand holding the ever-present radio handset to his ear. Carr held his M-16 tightly, his right hand on the pistol grip and the left grasping the hand guards around the barrel. He had six spare magazines in the ammo pouches on his web belt, and four more he had scrounged were jammed into the cargo pockets of his pants. Not as many as the other men carried, but he hoped they would be enough.

"Move out," Miles said, relaying a command he had heard on the radio. Before Carr could respond, Samples repeated the command loudly enough for the entire platoon to hear, and they all began trudging forward. Pushing their way through the vines and underbrush, the men of the battalion advanced through the forest, watching for any suspicious movement and ready to respond. Off to his right, visible occasionally through the foliage, Carr could see the Wolfhounds advancing stealthily. They looked a lot more professional than the rather rag-tag mechanized infantry, although that may have just been because they were better equipped. Behind him Carr heard the tracks start easing forward at a walking pace, maintaining about a fifty-foot distance from the men on foot. It was just like the day before: walking through the dusty forest fighting the oppressive heat, the clinging vines, and the annoying insects, waiting for the first gunshots that would signal an ambush.

After about three hours they came to the first of the bomb craters left by the B-52s. Carr was surprised by the size. There, in the middle of the forest, was a hole in the ground at least thirty feet across, and ten feet deep. It was as if someone had decided this was an excellent location for a swimming pool, and had already begun the excavation. Carr couldn't imagine what the explosion must have been like to make such a crater, but was amazed that the surrounding trees seemed only slightly damaged. He had expected to see all the trees leveled, like in the Rome Plow areas, but the bomb had only opened a hole in the forest canopy slightly larger than the hole in the ground. After a brief inspection, the men and tracks detoured around the crater and continued their sweep.

Fifteen minutes later they found a cluster of craters, and Miles informed them that the battalion would halt for a lunch break. Samples sent a couple men forward to stand guard, while the rest of the men took turns going inside the tracks to paw through the open cases of C-rations for their favorite cans. After waiting for the rest of the platoon, Carr searched through the remaining loose cans and packets, retrieving an unloved can of pork slices and a can of round crackers, to make a tasteless sandwich. He wasn't that hungry anyway.

Carr stepped back out of the track and looked around for a place to sit while he had his meal. He spied a fallen log that was partially shaded, and headed over that way, when he was intercepted by one of the reporters. He was a young guy with long dirty blonde hair and John Lennon glasses. He was wearing Army fatigue pants with the cuffs rolled up over combat boots, but he had on a brightly-colored Hawaiian shirt under one of those khaki vests with too many pockets. He had a canvas messenger bag slung over one shoulder. To top it off, he had a tan cowboy hat on. Carr was not impressed.

"Lieutenant?" the reporter called as he approached. "Can I talk to you?"

Carr continued over to the log and took a seat, propping his rifle beside him. "What about?" he asked, digging out his P-38 can opener and going to work on the dark green cans of food.

"I'm Dave Crockett of UPI," the young man introduced himself, standing directly in front of Carr.

"Davy Crockett? Really?" Carr grinned up at him.

"Just Dave," the guy said, flushing a little. "Look, I'd just like to get your take on this battle, and the war in general, if I could."

"Why me?" Carr asked, pouring the excess juice out of the can of pork slices.

"Mind if I sit?" Crockett asked, plopping down without waiting for an answer and pulling a notebook and pen out of the bag. "I want to tell the American people what it's really like for the GIs who are fighting this war, not what the generals want me to tell them."

"And what do the generals want you to say?" Carr already knew, but wanted to keep the guy talking and not asking questions, so he could have his lunch.

"Oh, they keep telling us about how we've got the VC on the run, and the South Vietnamese are ready to take over, and all that bullshit. They give us these big body counts that can't be accurate, and say our soldiers are dedicated to winning this war."

"I don't know about the VC," Carr told him, munching on crackers and pork. "Around here about all we have are NVA. And they don't seem to be on the run."

"See?" Crockett said enthusiastically. "That's what I mean. I want to know what's really happening."

"I'm having lunch, that's what's really happening right now." Carr pulled out his canteen to wash down the dry crackers.

"Well, yeah, but there's been some real fighting around here, right? And you've been in the thick of it, right? So you can tell me what it's really like."

"I've only been in country for a couple weeks," Carr protested. "Maybe you should talk to one of my sergeants."

"Why not you? You've been in some firefights already, haven't you?" Crockett was like an eager puppy begging for attention.

"A couple," Carr admitted.

"And you're an educated man. ROTC?"

Carr nodded. It was an easy guess, since most infantry second lieutenants in Nam were college graduates who had been in ROTC, the Reserve Officer Training Corps. The ring-knockers from West Point got better assignments, and the Officer Candidate School grads were few and far between. American universities were turning out ROTC officers by the thousands, many of whom, like Carr, had been in ROTC primarily to avoid the draft in the hope the war would be over before they graduated.

"So I'd like to hear your opinion on things." Crockett sat poised, pen in hand.

"C-rations suck," Carr offered.

"No, no, about the war."

"The war sucks, too. Ask anybody." Carr was slightly amused by the reporter's earnestness and obvious lack of experience.

Crockett waved his pen dismissively. "Like, what's the difference between the VC and the NVA?"

"Where they come from?" Carr suggested. The Viet Cong were local South Vietnamese guerillas fighting to overthrow the American-supported government, while the North Vietnamese Army soldiers were sent down by Hanoi to assist the VC.

"No, like their skills and capabilities. Which are harder to fight."

Carr shrugged. "I've only been here two weeks, and all I've seen are NVA. From what I've been told, the VC are lightly armed and just do hit-and-run attacks. The NVA soldiers are mostly draftees, just like ours. They wear uniforms and are led by officers trained in military tactics."

"So why haven't we been able to defeat them?" Crockett asked. "We've got more men and better weapons."

"You'd have to ask the generals about that," Carr replied. He knew better than to say something to a reporter that could come back and bite him in the ass.

"In your opinion," Crockett insisted. "I won't quote you."

Carr knew that was probably a lie, but he answered anyway. "What we're doing is like trying to kill a mosquito with a hammer.

They're too quick and mobile for us, and we're doing a lot of collateral damage in the process."

Crockett scribbled on his pad. "So what's the solution?" he asked without looking up.

"Beats the shit out of me," Carr replied truthfully. "I just work here."

"Should we invade Cambodia, or maybe North Viet Nam?" Crockett pressed.

"I think we should declare victory and go home. But I don't get to make those decisions."

"Right. Right. Okay, what about today? Is there going to be a battle?"

"Yes. No. Maybe," Carr said sarcastically. "Let me check my crystal ball."

"Seriously," Crockett insisted. "What are the chances? The general told us it was certain."

"And he should know," Carr said facetiously. "Look, we've made contact in this area the last two days, so we know there's NVA in the area. But whether we see any today is strictly up to them. They always know where we are, and we rarely know where they are, so they can either ambush us or hide from us, whichever they decide is best. After that B-52 strike last night, if I was them, I would have un-assed the area and be miles away, sleeping in a cool bunker or tunnel."

"Yeah, that bomb run was spectacular, wasn't it? We saw it from Dau Tieng. And now that I've seen the craters, I don't see how anyone could have survived."

"They probably couldn't," Carr agreed, "if they were in the area."

"You don't think they were here?" Crockett seemed unsurprised by the statement.

"The Crescent's a pretty big area," Carr explained. "The bombs only hit part of it. Could be they had already exfiltrated back to Cambodia or somewhere. We haven't seen any bodies yet."

"Yeah, and there's rumors they know where the strikes are gonna be ahead of time."

"Oh, yeah?" Carr hadn't heard that one.

"Yeah. I heard we have to notify the South Vietnamese at least twenty-four hours before a B-52 strike, so they can get any civilians or ARVNs out of the way. And if the South Vietnamese know about it, the commies will hear about it, too."

"Are you suggesting that the South Vietnamese government has spies who are working with the Communists?" Carr said with obviously feigned outrage.

"Oh, Heavens, no!" Crockett said with a laugh. Carr chuckled along with him.

Carr finished his last small sandwich while Crockett tried to think up more questions. Finally Crockett asked, "So what happens if you do make contact today?"

Carr looked at him and saw the worry on his face. "You mean, what should *you* do?"

Crockett nodded sharply. "Yeah."

"Get behind a track and hide."

"Wouldn't it be better to get inside the APC?"

"Probably not. The gooks have RPGs and like to shoot them at tracks. The shaped charges burn right through those aluminum walls and can set off the ammo inside. Behind the track is better."

"No shit?" Crockett made a face and looked down at his shirt. "And I guess I make a pretty good target, huh?"

"I guess," Carr admitted, "but when the shit hits the fan, everyone becomes a target."

"Okay, thanks. Oh, I just thought of something. What do you think of Nixon's plan to withdraw the troops?"

"It was a campaign promise," Carr noted.

"And he's really doing it, right? The Ninth Division?"

Carr remembered the conversation with Sergeant Washington, and decided to see if he could maybe make it come true. "And I hear we're next," Carr said blandly.

Crockett looked up sharply. "Yeah? Where'd you hear that? You mean this division?"

"Well, a very, *very* senior NCO in Cu Chi says it's going to happen. On July fifteenth."

Crockett's face was flushed with excitement at this potential scoop. "The division sergeant major?" he guessed.

Carr raised his eyebrows and shrugged. "I'm not supposed to say anything until it's officially announced."

"Cool!" Crockett breathed. He quickly wrote something in his notebook, underlining it three times.

Carr turned his head so Crockett wouldn't see his grin. It was a struggle to keep from laughing. When he had calmed himself, he stood up, saying, "I need to take a leak."

"Can I get your full name and where you're from, in case any of this makes it into the papers?" Crockett asked. "I won't mention you on the pull-out date, though."

"Sure," Carr said, and gave him the information. While Crockett wrote it down, he checked his watch. The lunch break should be over soon.

Samples saw Lieutenant Carr talking to the reporter and slowly shook his head. The reporter was a geek, a civilian, no less, and shouldn't be out here in the boonies. Lord only knew what Carr was telling him. Samples took another spoonful of beanie-weenie and guided it to his mouth.

"Why's that guy talking to the Eltee?" Reedy asked with a slightly peeved tone. Samples was sitting with Rich Reedy, Del Washington, Doc Allman, and Miles on the opposite side of a bomb crater from Carr and the reporter. The three sergeants were sitting on a log, while Allman and Miles squatted gook-style on the loose dirt thrown up by the bombs. Miles had taken off the radio, but was still connected to it by the coiled mike cord, with the handset clipped to his collar.

"Yeah," agreed Allman. "He ought to talk to us enlisted, get the real story. Besides, the lieutenant's only been here a couple weeks. What the fuck does he know, anyway."

"More than you," Samples suggested jokingly. "He's been to college, so now he knows everything." Allman rolled his eyes.

"I went to college," Miles pointed out.

"And see what good it did you," Samples said. "It got you here in the boonies carrying a fuckin' prick-25."

Miles frowned. "Yeah, I shoulda stayed in ROTC. I was sure the draft would end before I graduated."

"You coulda gone to OCS," Washington said. "You got a degree and all."

"Yeah," Miles said, "but then I would have had a four-year commitment, and still be just a butter-bar in Nam getting my butt shot off. No, thanks. Two hundred and ninety days. Short!"

"You ain't short," Allman told him. "I'm short. I'm so short I have to have a ladder to climb down off a dime."

"Don't get cocky, Doc," Samples said. "You still got a month to go. Don't go gettin' short-timer's attitude on me."

"I'm shorter than the rest of you assholes," Allman said petulantly.

"And we're all shorter than the lieutenant," Samples pointed out. "It's all relative."

"True that," Washington seconded.

There was a pause in the conversation as the men finished up their lunch. Then Miles spoke up again.

"Did you hear about the lieutenant and the major, Sarge?" he asked Samples.

"About the tools? Yeah, I heard."

"I couldn't believe it," Miles said, obviously anxious to tell the story again. "I was just inside the track talking to Stiles, and we heard the whole thing. Man, Major Moore was really POed." Miles was very religious, and avoided using profanity. Samples admired his dedication, especially when everyone else used foul language constantly.

"They were just fuckin' tools," Reedy commented.

"Yeah, but they were the colonel's tools," Miles explained. "I'll bet the colonel had ragged on the major about them, and the stuff just rolled downhill. Anyway, Lieutenant Carr told him off, but very politely. He knew that Chacon had swiped the tools, but didn't tell the major that. Even implied it was the major's fault for not marking the tools in the first place."

"Not bad, for an officer," Allman noted.

They all turned and looked across the crater at Carr, who was still talking to the reporter. Samples wanted to say something negative about Carr, but held his tongue. In fact, he couldn't think of anything at the moment.

"Could be worse," Washington said. "Remember that guy in Second Platoon a few months ago?"

"That doofy mother-fucker Applegate?" Reedy said. "Everyone called him Lieutenant Apocalypse."

"How come?" Miles asked, intrigued.

"Must have been before you got here," Samples told him. "He didn't last long. Came in all gung-ho, talking shit like he was John Wayne. Got a back-pack from somewhere, hung grenades on the straps, kept calling the company 'Action Alpha.' First time he was in contact, over in the Boi Loi Woods, got his fucking straps caught up in some vines. In the process of trying to untangle himself, he accidentally pulled the pin on one of the grenades. Managed to toss it a few feet away before it went off, but he still got some shrapnel from it. Got dusted off to Dau Tieng, and we never saw him again."

"He died?" Miles asked.

"Nah, I think the CO just told Higher not to bring him back out. Probably works at the PX or something now."

"Think we'll make contact today, Sarge?" Reedy asked conversationally.

"No tellin'," Samples answered. "Either we do or we don't. That's up to the gooks."

"Shit, I hope not," Washington said, wiping the sweat from his forehead with his sleeve. "We've made contact the last two days. Time for a break."

"Know what you mean, Del," Samples told him. "Getting shot at just fucks up your whole day."

"I need my beauty rest," Washington protested with a smile.

"I don't think you could ever get enough rest to be beautiful, Del," Reedy chided him.

"Fuck you," Washington responded mildly, without any anger.

"You know," Samples mused out loud, "I don't want to make contact, but when we do, it's kind of exciting."

"Yeah, you're right," Reedy agreed. "I'll be thinking about how I want to go back to the fire support base or wherever, eat at the mess hall, and take it easy, but when the firefight starts, that's kind of fun, too."

"Relieves the monotony," Samples said in a pedantic tone. Even though he was joking, he realized it was true. Most of the time they were working, walking, or just sitting on their asses, and it got boring. A firefight brought thrills, danger, and a sense of actually accomplishing something. And, if he were truly honest with himself, it was like being the hero in a movie or comic book, as it did when he played Army as a kid.

"Okay," Miles chimed in, "but I've had enough fun for now. I'm ready to go back to the FSB."

"Well, let's take a vote," Samples told them. "Everyone in favor of going back now, raise your hand." They all raised their hands. "Okay, Miles, you go tell the lieutenant we decided to call it quits for today."

Miles shook his head ruefully. "If only it were that easy," he said.

"How's your stomach, Sarge?" Allman asked professionally.

"Maybe a little indigestion," Samples answered.

"You know what I mean." Allman was exasperated.

"Fine. I'm fine. You can change the bandages this evening."

"So, what is that, your fifth Purple Heart?"

Samples counted on his fingers, remembering the other times he had been wounded. "I guess it is," he said. "Time flies when you're having fun."

Miles gave him a puzzled look. "I thought after three Purple Hearts you got to go home?"

"Most people do," Allman explained, "but not our Staff Sergeant Samples."

"Why not?"

"Because I don't want to," Samples told him curtly. "Hell, this one was self-inflicted. I'm lucky I wasn't court-martialed."

"Man," Reedy said, "if I had three Purple Hearts, I'd be on that Freedom Bird so fuckin' fast you wouldn't believe it."

"Bet your ass," Washington agreed.

Samples didn't want to explain his reasoning to these men. He wasn't even sure he understood it himself. He liked to believe it was a sense of duty and commitment to the men under him, but he knew it was more than that. He didn't really have much to go home to, and, as the draftees put it, he had found a home in the Army. He was doing something useful, something relevant, and something he kind of enjoyed doing. Why leave now, when there was still a war to fight?

There was a squawk from the handset clipped to Miles collar, and he grabbed for it. Samples saw that Carr was standing up and the reporter was headed back toward Charlie Company. Miles, still listening to the voices on the radio, gave a forward motion with his rifle.

"Break's over," Samples said loudly. "Everyone back on their heads." It was the punchline from an old joke that everyone had heard him tell numerous times. No one laughed. They just gathered up their gear, put on their helmets, and got ready to move out.

Within minutes the entire battalion was on the move again, the dismounts shouldering their way through the underbrush, the APCs lumbering along behind them. More forest, more craters, more dust, more annoying insects. Samples had seen it all before, and knew he would see it again, but somehow he didn't mind. It was all in a day's work.

EIGHT

Lieutenant Carr ducked under a low branch and jerked the barrel of his rifle free from yet another clinging vine. Over eleven months to go, and already he was uncertain he could endure it. The futility of it was almost unbearable. In the short time he had been in country, he had quickly realized the war served no useful purpose, and they could never achieve victory. American forces were going through the motions, doing all the things that had brought victory in WWII, and at least a stalemate in Korea, but here they were just wasting time—and lives. Despite the rhetoric from Washington and the Pentagon, there was no end in sight. The Communists were committed to victory, one that for them was clearly defined—reunite Viet Nam under Communist rule. The U.S. policy, if it could be called that, was to contain the Communists and prop up the notoriously corrupt South Vietnamese government in Saigon. The American goals could be achieved only if the Communists gave up voluntarily, a scenario that looked increasingly unlikely.

Carr looked back to be sure Miles was still behind him. Looking tired but resigned, the young man watched the ground directly ahead of him while he listened to the radio traffic through the handset held to his ear. Montoya and his men were a few yards to Carr's right, and to his left Samples, Reedy, and a couple others were spread out, dodging expertly through the trees and foliage. Everyone seemed to be doing their job, ignoring the heat, the dust, and the possible danger with a stoic acceptance of their lot in life. No one but Carr seemed to be bothered by the situation, or concerned about the eventual outcome of the war. Carr wondered if he were truly more thoughtful than the others, or whether perhaps they had simply surrendered to the inevitable. And did it matter?

"Bunker!" Montoya shouted, and everyone, Carr included, dropped into a crouch and scanned the area ahead of them. Behind him Carr heard Miles relay the report on the radio, and the tracks all halted in place. There was no gunfire, but Carr heard the rustling of leaves and turned to see Samples crossing behind him to join

Montoya. Carr stood and followed him, knowing he would have to make a decision of some sort.

Montoya stood beside a tree trunk, the upper limbs of which had been blasted clean of leaves. To his right front was one of the bomb craters, a ragged hole in the ground with a ring of dirt thrown up around it. When Carr and Samples arrived next to him, he pointed at an area directly across the left side of the crater. Carr could see that all the underbrush and lower limbs of trees had been stripped away, revealing a low rectangular mound of earth. On the side of the mound facing them, he saw a small opening that had been partially collapsed by the explosion.

"Any movement?" Samples asked.

"Huh-uh," Montoya replied, shaking his head.

"Let's check it out," Samples said, motioning with his head for Montoya to go right. Samples darted forward to the left side of the bunker, while Montoya moved a little more cautiously to the right side. After a moment's hesitation, Carr followed Samples. All three paused at the back corners of the bunker and then eased forward, keeping their rifles pointed toward the larger opening they found there. It was a remarkably well-made entrance, nicely squared off, with steps cut into the earthen ramp leading down inside. Carr marveled at the quality of the construction, which had survived the nearby bomb blast so well.

"Are you going in?" Carr asked Samples doubtfully.

"Not yet," Samples replied brusquely. He looked back at the men waiting patiently on the other side of the crater and yelled, "Somebody bring me a grenade!"

Carr saw Miles run over to the one-three track where the loader opened one of the ammo boxes strapped to the top and handed the grenade to him. Miles ran to where Carr and the other two were waiting and held out the egg-shaped device. Samples took it from him and worked the safety bale off.

"Better back off, might be secondary explosions," Samples warned. Carr followed Miles and Montoya as they hurried back to the company line. When everyone was clear, Samples pulled the pin, let the spoon pop off, and tossed the grenade into the bunker. Shouting "Fire in the hole!" he jogged to join the others.

A few seconds later there was a muffled "whump" and dust spewed out of the small aperture at the front of the bunker and the larger entrance at the back. There were no other detonations.

"When the smoke clears," Samples remarked, "I'll see what's in there."

"Let me do it," Carr blurted out, surprising even himself. He couldn't interpret the look Samples gave him. "I, uh, I've never seen the inside of a gook bunker before," Carr stammered, trying to explain his abrupt decision.

"Rock out," Samples said calmly, motioning toward the bunker like a theatre usher.

Immediately regretting his offer, Carr forced himself to walk back around the bunker and stop at the entrance. Smoke and dust was still rising from the hole. He knew that the grenade would have eliminated any threat waiting there in the dark, but an almost claustrophobic fear began to grip his insides. He sensed that others had gathered behind him, but his attention was totally focused on the deep shadows of the entrance. "I'll need a . . ." Carr started to say.

"Here," Samples told him, handing him a flashlight.

Doc Allman stepped forward and held out his revolver. "Trade you," he said. Nodding numbly, Carr passed Allman his rifle and took the pistol.

Excruciatingly aware that everyone was watching him, Carr knelt down and peered into the entrance. The dust had settled a little, the motes sparkling in the sunlight as they rose from the darkness. He rose to a crouch, trying to figure out the best way to go down, and settled on sitting on the top step and easing down on his butt. Awkwardly he pushed off each step, his boots leading the way, as he bumped down step by step, flashlight in his left hand and pistol held ready in his right. At about the same time his feet told him there were no more steps, he ducked his head under the top of the entrance so that his eyes were no longer blinded by the sun.

As his eyes slowly adjusted to the dimness, Car could see that the interior was still obscured by swirling smoke. He fumbled until he found the switch on the flashlight, and then swung the resulting yellow beam from left to right. The bunker was larger than he had expected, although the roof, made of closely-spaced tree limbs, was only about five feet above the hard-packed dirt of the floor. The walls were flat and properly squared off, and there were small blankets lying crumpled beneath the entrance and the firing aperture. He could see sticks above the two openings where the cloths had been hung before being blown down by the bomb blasts. On either side of the bunker were two crude cots made with tree limbs and dried grass. Carr could just imagine the life of the former occupants—covering the openings with blankets so they could turn on lanterns at night, sleeping on the home-made cots, eating cold rice, and waiting for the approach of the enemy. Now, however, other than the cots and blankets, there was nothing left behind. If anyone had been in there when the bombs fell, their bodies had been removed before Carr and the others had arrived, and all their possessions with them. But it didn't look like that to Carr. To him it seemed obvious that the gooks had evacuated the bunker before the attack. Perhaps they had known in advance, as the reporter had suggested.

Carr suddenly noticed that his fear had evaporated. He took one last look around, and then climbed back out of the bunker. He handed the pistol back to Allman, and the flashlight to Samples, then brushed off some of the dirt before taking back his rifle. The other men stood around expectantly, waiting to hear what he had found. Carr turned to Miles.

"Tell the CO the bunker's empty. Looks like they left before last night."

Looks of disappointment were apparent on the faces of the other men as Miles relayed his findings on the radio. Carr wasn't sure if they had hoped for souvenirs, or had hoped Carr would somehow disgrace himself. Regardless, Carr was satisfied with the outcome. He had faced his fears and overcome them. Again.

When Miles relayed the order he had heard on the radio, Samples bellowed it for all the platoon dismounts to hear: "Move out!" Once again the men began working their way north through the brush and around the bomb craters, followed by the rumbling armored personnel carriers. It was midafternoon, and the sun was burning down fiercely. Like the rest of them, Samples tried to stay in the shade, but that was difficult because the bombs had removed so much of the overhead cover. Besides, Samples acknowledged to himself, it wasn't really much cooler in the shade anyway.

As they continued to advance, Samples reflected on the lieutenant's performance at the bunker. Although Carr had obviously been reluctant to go down inside, he had done so anyway, and when he came out he was calm and assured. Inspecting a bunker that had already been cleared with a grenade was no big deal, but Samples had seen men—officers and enlisted—who had quailed at the very thought. Even after the grenade, there still could have been a booby trap of some sort, or the bunker might have hidden the entrance to a tunnel in which gooks had taken cover, only to come out shooting after the blast. Samples himself tried to avoid bunkers and tunnels, not just because of the danger, but because he suffered from a slight case of claustrophobia. He just hated being underground.

He glanced over at Carr, with Miles faithfully following him, and saw the same look of weary resignation on the lieutenant's face that graced most of the men in the platoon. Carr had lost that initial look of wonder and excitement that was worn by most lieutenants when they first arrived in country. It appeared he had quickly adapted to the mood of the infantry, the knowledge that his tour was a year-long sentence that he would just have to endure. Samples even felt a little sympathy for the man.

Rich Reedy angled over and began walking beside Samples on his left. "How long you think we're going to do this?" he asked conversationally.

"Till the BC gets tired, I guess," Samples replied. It was a reference to a common remark from drill sergeants in basic training, who would instruct their recruits to do push-ups until the drill sergeants got tired. The battalion commander, like the drill sergeants, wasn't actually doing anything that would make him tired.

"Fucker," Reedy quietly cursed the colonel. "This is a fuckin' waste of time. The gooks all di-di-maued." The troops often incorporated pidgin Vietnamese into their vocabulary. They had been told that *di di mau* meant "get out of here."

"Maybe," Samples agreed. "That bunker was vacated before the B-52 strike, looks like."

"Yeah, they knew it was coming and booked it for Cambodia, I'll bet."

"I would have," Samples said. "But you can't tell about the gooks. They're pretty hard core. Might have un-assed the area before the strike, then moved back in afterwards."

"You think?" Reedy said, wiping the sweat from his large nose. Samples shrugged. They walked on in silence for a few minutes.

"We won't laager out here, will we?" Reedy asked, a note of concern in his voice.

"Doubt it," Samples told him. "The whole battalion's out here. There's no place big and open enough for all of us. Besides, we left all our gear back at Wood."

"Forgot about that," Reedy sighed. "Hope they got ice and sodas for us back there."

"Might get some orange or RC," Samples suggested. It was a common complaint among the men that the base camp warriors got all the good sodas—Coke, Pepsi, 7-Up—while the grunts in the field got the dregs, like RC, orange, and grapefruit soda.

"Yeah," Reedy groaned. "Fuckers." Reedy complained a lot, but Samples considered him one of the better squad leaders in the company.

"What's Vasquez think he's doing?" Samples asked sharply. Reedy looked over at his crew member, who was about thirty feet away.

"Vasquez," Reedy yelled at him. "Where's your goddamn helmet?"

The young soldier looked back guiltily.

"On the track, Sarge," he called. "Kept getting tangled in the vines."

"Go get it."

"Aw, Sarge," Vasquez whined, but turned and walked back toward the one-two.

"You're lucky I don't make you wear the flak vest, too," Reedy loudly admonished him. While the mech guys generally used the Army-issued flak vests as seat cushions, Samples had noticed that the Wolfhounds working with Charlie all had theirs on. Extra weight, extra heat, they were just too much a hassle for his guys.

In a quieter voice Reedy told Samples, "Can't take him anywhere."

"Kids," Samples said sympathetically. He was only twenty-three himself, but already he felt much older than most of the other guys. He knew that Miles, who had graduated from college, must be about the same age, but he sure didn't act like it. And the lieutenant was about his age also. Samples, however, felt that he was the old man of the unit, the most mature and certainly the most experienced. It was sometimes a heavy burden.

Samples looked to his right and saw that Carr was listening to something Miles was telling him. Thinking there might be new orders coming down, he left Reedy and veered over to walk beside the lieutenant. "What's going on?" he asked.

Carr shook his head. "Not much," he said. "Charlie found a bunker, but it was collapsed."

"Hmm," Samples grunted.

"Those reporters are probably getting bored," Carr offered.

"Hell, I'm bored," Samples replied.

"How far do they usually go on these sweeps?" Carr asked.

"Varies," Samples answered. It was a fair question, but every sweep was different. "With the whole battalion out here, the BC really wants to get a body count or something. Make it look good for the reporters. But we can't stay out here too late, and still have time to get back to the FSB. I figure we'll keep going until about five, then pack it in."

Carr looked at his watch and sighed. "You're probably right." They went around opposites sides of a huge tree, and as they rejoined Carr said, "Bread and butter." Samples just looked at him. Carr saw Samples' expression and gave his head an apologetic shake. "Never mind." Samples saw Miles smirking behind them.

They walked in silence for a while, brushing aside branches and vines, and dodging around the occasional bomb crater. To either side Samples could hear occasional desultory remarks from the other dismounts, and behind them was the low growl of the tracks inching forward. Beads of sweat rolled down his face, burning when they got in his eyes, so he kept swiping his sleeve across his forehead.

"Did you ever watch *Combat!*, that old TV show?" Carr asked out of the blue.

"Vic Morrow? Yeah." Samples wondered where this was going.

"What was the lieutenant's name?" Carr asked, as if trying to prompt his own memory.

Samples shook his head. "Can't remember. Morrow was Sergeant Saunders, or Sanders, but I don't remember anyone else."

"I think it was Saunders," Carr said.

"Why?" Samples asked out of curiosity.

"No reason. I was just thinking that this is nothing like the TV show."

"Not hardly," Samples agreed. "They had exciting and interesting adventures every day, meeting beautiful French women and capturing Germans. We just hump the boonies and get shot at every once in a while."

"You think World War II was really like that?"

"Probably not. It was a TV show. They had to make it look fun to get ratings."

They walked in silence for a minute. "Hanley," Carr suddenly said.

"What?" Samples was confused.

"His name was Hanley. The lieutenant on *Combat!*."

"Oh. I guess so."

"Did you watch *Rat Patrol*?" Carr asked.

"I saw a couple episodes, I think. I was in the Army when that was on." Samples wondered where this exercise in nostalgia was leading, if anywhere.

"Wasn't as good as *Combat!*. Besides, the real rat patrols were British, not Americans."

"If you say so."

"It's just, you know," Carr struggled to find the words. "Viet Nam isn't like the TV shows. TV and movies don't show all the time you spend just doing nothing, sitting around or walking through the boonies. Shitting in the woods. Eating C-rats. Shaving in a helmet."

"True that," Samples agreed. He worried that Carr was going to get all maudlin on him.

Miles spoke up from behind them. "CO says to take a break." Behind them Samples heard the tracks come to a halt, their engines idling.

"Take a break in place!" Samples yelled out. "Smoke 'em if you got 'em."

NINE

Lieutenant Carr took a long drink from his canteen, and then shook it to gauge how much water was left in it. Not enough, he decided, so he walked over to the one-four track, opened the rear hatch, and pulled a water can over to the doorway. It took some juggling to open the spigot and line up the tilted can with the small opening in his canteen, but he managed to fill it with only minimal splashing on his hands and the ground. He screwed the cap back on the water can spigot, pushed it back inside, and closed the heavy hatch. He was just sliding the canteen back into the cover attached to his web belt when Miles walked up.

"CO wants to see you at his track," the young man told him.

Carr nodded. "Any idea why?" he asked as he picked up his rifle.

Miles shrugged. "He wants all the platoon leaders. I'm hoping he's going to tell you the war's over."

"Yeah, right, like that will happen." Carr trudged wearily down the line of tracks until he found the company commander's. Raymond was standing behind it, his helmet on top of the track, wiping his bare head with a handkerchief. Mel Baron and Jay Fawcett, the other two platoon leaders, were already there. Carr gave Baron a questioning look, and the other lieutenant just shrugged. Raymond finished mopping up his sweat and stuffed the brown handkerchief back in his pants pocket. He glanced at his watch, and then looked up at the gathered platoon leaders.

"The colonel isn't happy," he began. "He says we need to step it up. We haven't reached our main objective, whatever that is, and we were supposed to be there by now." He reached up behind him and felt around the top of the track next to his helmet until he found a map encased in clear plastic. He brought it down and held it in front of him, folded so that only a small portion showed. There were grease-pencil marks all over it. "We're here," he said, pointing, "almost all of the way through the bombed area. He wants to get to here," Raymond said, pointing to an area a short distance away on the map, "before we call it a day."

"What is that, about two, three clicks?" Fawcett asked, leaning over to study the map.

"About that," Raymond answered. "I figure we'll get there in another couple hours. By then it will be close to five, and we'll have to turn around in order to get back to the base before dark."

"About time," Baron remarked caustically.

"So how are we supposed to move more quickly?" Carr asked, honestly unsure what he was supposed to do.

"Double time, march!" Baron said sarcastically, using the parade ground command for a jogging pace.

"No, really," Carr said.

"I don't know," Raymond said, shaking his head. "Just keep them moving, don't let them fart around. Keep on line with Charlie, and if we aren't fast enough, we can blame them."

"Ah, yes," Fawcett said in a bad imitation of W. C. Fields. "A man who can smile when things are going to hell around him is the man who knows who he can blame it on."

They young officers all chuckled. Raymond looked at his watch again and said, "About time to move out." The lieutenants nodded and hurried back to their platoons while Raymond reached up for his helmet. Carr paused and turned his head, wanting to ask the captain another question, but then thought better of it. He needed to be a leader in his own right, and not appear dependent on the commander.

By the time Carr got back to the platoon, the men were already gearing up and getting on line. Miles acknowledged something he heard on the radio and waved his hand forward—there was no need to go through Carr or Samples to give the order. Once again the men plodded forward, their weariness beginning to show. Carr caught up with Samples and matched his stride.

"CO says the BC wants us to speed up."

"Easy for him to say," Samples replied.

"Yeah, well. We'll probably call it a day around five."

"That's what I figured. Even with everyone mounted up, it'll take at least an hour or two to get back to Wood. Don't want to miss that wonderful chow."

"Boy, I hope we have chili-mac today," Carr said facetiously. Samples just gave him a sour look.

They walked on, pushing aside branches and wiping sweat from their faces, through what seemed to be an endless forest. Only the occasional bomb craters broke the monotony. Carr actually found himself looking forward to dinner in the mess hall tent, even if it was chili-mac and warm milk. There would also be mail from home, and a chance to wash the dust off himself before going to sleep on a hard canvas cot. It was surprising how much he enjoyed such simple pleasures now. He was startled when Samples yelled.

"Hicks, stop your lollygaggin'!" Off to his right Carr saw Hicks respond to the command by hustling forward. "Guys are getting tired," Samples said to Carr.

"It's been a long day," Carr agreed. "Hell, I'm tired, too."

"Not like Ranger School, is it?" Samples asked a little smugly.

"Not exactly," Carr said. In fact Ranger School had been more strenuous and demanding than this, but Carr decided not to brag about it.

"Snake!" Montoya yelled, pointing up in a tree with his rifle. It took Carr a moment to distinguish the python wound around a branch ten feet off the ground. Montoya took aim with his M-16, but Samples shouted for him to back off.

"Don't shoot it, dickhead!" Samples ordered.

"Why not?" Montoya asked, still aiming at it.

"You'll destroy the natural balance of nature," Carr told him with feigned seriousness. "Besides, you'll start everybody else shooting, too. Don't want to wake the neighbors."

"It'd be fresh meat for the mess hall," Miles remarked. "Make a good belt, too."

"Shut the fuck up, Miles," Samples said. More loudly he shouted, "Keep moving."

"Give the snake room, Sergeant Montoya," Carr said. "It's his forest."

Montoya lowered his rifle with a disappointed scowl on his face and moved out, giving the snake's tree a wide berth.

"Most excitement we've had all day," Samples remarked. Carr didn't comment. He felt like his trip into the abandoned bunker had been the high point for him, but knew that was a commonplace occurrence for Samples.

A few minutes later they came to a line of bomb craters spaced close together. While the dismounts could weave their way through, the tracks had to be guided far to either side of the string of holes to find ground wide enough for them to continue forward. Samples and Carr were running back and forth, signaling the drivers which way to turn and guiding them around the tree trunks until they could reform on the north side of the obstacles. All the maneuvering consumed almost half an hour, with Charlie Company on the right and the rest of Alpha and Bravo on the left all halted to wait for them. Carr could just imagine the tirade from the battalion commander about the delay.

As soon as everyone was back on line, the battalion again surged forward. Carr joined Samples in the middle of the platoon line as they resumed the advance. Behind them Miles relayed a command from the CO: "Step it out."

"Son of a bitch!" Samples cursed, wiping his sweaty face with his sleeve. All the running and shouting they had done to lead the tracks around the craters had gotten both of them hot, tired, and dusty.

"Not our fault," Carr said.

"They'll blame us anyway," Samples said grimly. "Shit always rolls downhill."

"What are they gonna do," Carr said, repeating a line he had already heard often, "send us to Viet Nam?"

Samples snorted.

Carr looked at his watch again. "Almost quitting time," he announced.

"Thank God for small favors," Samples rejoined. "Man, I could use a beer right now."

There was nothing Carr could say. Beer was available officially only in the base camps like Dau Tieng, at the EM and NCO clubs. You could also get it from Coke kids, for a ridiculous price, but they weren't likely to see any Coke kids today. And troops were technically forbidden from buying drinks from the Coke kids anyway. In fact, Carr knew, enlisted men below the rank of E-7 were also forbidden to drink any hard liquor. Apparently only senior enlisted and officers were considered trustworthy enough to get really drunk. Strange war.

They had left the craters behind, and were once again in deep woods, only able to see clearly about fifty feet ahead of them. Tan tree trunks, dusty green leaves, stalks of grass sticking up through the dark earth—the same things they had been looking at all day. Finding an open space before him, Carr strolled ahead of the line, with Miles right behind him. The open area led to his right, bringing him more in front of the one-four track. He had just realized that he was far ahead of Samples and the others, and started to slow down. Then Carr heard a boom-whoosh and saw the smoke trail from a rocket zoom out of the brush to his far right and explode against a tree near one of the Charlie Company tracks. Almost simultaneously rifle and machine gun fire broke out, along with more smoke trails of RPGs. Carr dived to the ground and brought his rifle to bear in front of him. An ambush, a really big one. All he could think about was the fact that it had happened just as they were ready to turn around and go home. It fucked up his whole day.

Samples took up a kneeling position behind a large tree trunk and began firing semi-automatic at the woods in front of him. He couldn't see any of the enemy, but that was normal. He just wanted to make the gooks duck. He looked around, and saw all his men had hit the dirt and were now firing as well. Carr and Miles, however, were thirty feet forward of the line of dismounts. Miles had taken cover under a bush that offered no real protection, but he was pressing himself into the earth as he kept the radio handset to his ear.

"Miles!" Samples shouted. "Bring the tracks up on line." Miles gave an almost imperceptible nod and began talking into the mike. With the APCs several meters behind the line of dismounts, the 50-cal gunners couldn't fire for fear of hitting their own men. They needed all the firepower they could get. "Lieutenant!" Samples yelled angrily, "Get your ass back on line." Carr looked back, saw the situation, and twisted around to his left to face Samples. Using the Army-approved method, he laid his M-16 across his forearms and began low-crawling back on a diagonal toward the center of the platoon line.

"You, too, Miles!" Samples bellowed, but Miles was struggling. His radio had gotten tangled in the vines, and the more he pulled at it, the worse it got. The young soldier rose to his knees and began jerking at the mike cord, but suddenly stopped. A red splotch appeared on his shoulder and he collapsed in the dirt, his helmet rolling away.

"Shit!" Samples muttered angrily. The one-three track rumbled to a halt beside him and the fifty-cal opened up with its thumping cadence, blasting the woods in front of them. "Johnson!" Samples yelled at the gunner, "watch out! The Eltee and Miles are out front!"

"I see 'em," Johnson yelled back as he continued to pound bullets down range.

"Warn one-four," Samples told him. They had to yell to be heard over the din of battle. Samples was pretty sure he had heard the drumbeat of a heavy machine gun coming from in front of them. The gooks must have at least one .51-cal, which was bad news. A heavy machine gun meant they were facing at least a company-sized force of NVA. Looking over past the front of the one-three track, he saw that Carr had managed to crawl almost halfway back to the company line. Either he hadn't noticed that Miles was hit, or he didn't care. Either way, Samples had to act.

"Heads up!" he yelled at Johnson, taking off in a low running crouch toward Miles, dodging around Carr without a word. He plopped down beside the fallen soldier and nudged him. "Miles," he shouted, "how bad?"

There were now bits of shredded leaves in the boy's tousled hair, and Miles could only moan and shake his head slightly. Samples saw Carr drop down on the other side of Miles, pushing away at the vines and branches that surrounded them.

"What happened?" Carr asked, confusion clouding his expression.

"Caught in the vines," Samples explained. "Got hit trying to pull free." Overhead bullets were flying in both directions, punctuated by the thumps of RPGs and M-79 grenades.

"We've got to get him out of here," Carr said unnecessarily.

"No shit," Samples grumbled. "Let's turn him over, get him out of the harness." Carr nodded, and together they gently rolled Miles onto one side so Samples could pull the boy's arm out of the radio backpack shoulder strap. It was the arm below the shoulder wound, and Miles screamed incoherently at the pain, before lapsing into silence as he passed out. Samples pulled the limp body forward again so Carr could work the other arm free of the backpack. While Carr shoved the radio out of the way, Samples maneuvered Miles onto his back.

"How do we get him back?" Carr asked. All three were lying on the ground under a large bush, thirty yards from the relative safety of the tracks, with hundreds of rounds cracking through the air above them. Samples tried to think. They didn't dare stand up.

Wham! An explosion just feet way blasted them with dirt and leaves. Samples knew from experience it was an RPG, one that had been aimed at them. They couldn't wait any longer. He looked over at Carr to tell him what they should do, and noticed that Carr's face was bloody. "You hit?" he asked, staring at the blood. Carr gently felt his face with one hand, and then marveled at the blood on his fingers.

"I guess so," Carr said. "Not bad, though."

"Okay. We'll have to drag him. You take one arm, I'll get the other." Samples grabbed Miles under the armpit of the unwounded shoulder and pulled him around until his head was pointed toward the one-four track. He laid his rifle on Miles' chest to free his other hand, and waited while Carr scrambled around to the other side. Seeing what Samples had done with his M-16, Carr laid his rifle next to it and got a good grip on the RTO's upper arm.

"Ready?" Samples asked. Carr nodded, blood dripping from his chin. At first Samples tried low crawling while pulling on Miles, and Carr imitated him, but progress was too slow. Samples rose to his knees and elbows, jerking his head at Carr to do the same. In this manner they were able to move a little more quickly, although it was still very slow. They had to work their way around trees and bushes, and Samples was hyper-aware of the lead flying above him. Twice their rifles slid off Miles' chest into the dirt, and they had to pause to reposition them. After what seemed like an hour, but was in reality only a few minutes, they were beside the one-four track, where Washington and Hicks rushed forward to help them carry Miles behind the protective bulk of the APC.

Panting from the effort to haul Miles back, Samples asked Washington, "Where's Allman?"

Washington just shook his head. "Chacon called for a medic. They're all kinda busy right now."

"Fuck! Okay, let's get him inside." Together the four men carefully eased Miles through the narrow hatch in the rear ramp and laid him on one of the benches. Eberhart was standing up in the cargo hatch firing his M-16 around the side of the machine gun turret, while Jones fired off methodical bursts of 50-cal. Chacon, keeping his head down up in the driver's compartment, glanced back and spoke into the dangling mike on his CVC helmet.

Samples knelt down beside Miles and unbuckled the boy's pistol belt so he could unbutton the shirt. The front left side of the shirt was dark with blood when Samples peeled it back. Underneath was a blackened hole just above his left nipple. Carr helped Samples lift Miles' torso so they could pull the shirt completely off, revealing another hole in the boy's back. Both wounds were bleeding. Washington was already unwrapping a field dressing he had pulled from a pouch on his web belt when the hatchway went dark for a second as Doc Allman stepped in.

"Let me do that," Allman said, taking over. Samples and Carr continued to hold Miles up in a sitting position as the medic swabbed and covered the wounds. Miles moaned and opened his eyes.

"What?" Miles asked softly.

"You're hit, but you're going to be okay," Allman assured him, wrapping gauze around his chest. Miles nodded sleepily.

Eberhart suddenly dropped down inside and sat down heavily on the opposite bench. "I'm hit," he announced calmly. The interior of the track was already crowded. Washington and Hicks were sitting on opposite sides of the track at the back.

"God-mother-fuckin-damn!" Samples spat, livid at the further deterioration of the situation.

"Where?" Carr asked Eberhart. The skinny young man turned away and pointed over his left shoulder. There were several ragged holes in his fatigue shirt just below his shoulder blade, through which a little blood was seeping.

"Take your shirt off," Allman told him while he continued to work on Miles. Samples helped Eberhart remove the shirt and inspected the wound. It wasn't bleeding badly, and the holes in his tanned flesh were small. It appeared to be shrapnel wound, not a bullet wound, but the small pieces of metal could still have gone deep and punctured a vital organ.

"You having any trouble breathing?" Allman asked Eberhart as he tied off the last of the bandages on Miles.

Eberhart took a deep breath experimentally, and then shook his head.

"Good," Allman said, switching positions so he could start dressing Eberhart's wound.

"When you get done with him," Samples said, "you ought to take a look at the lieutenant."

"How come," Allman said without looking up from Eberhart.

"He got hit in the face," Samples said.

"It's not bad," Carr said defensively.

"Let me see," Allman said, not pausing in his ministrations. Carr leaned over and tilted his head so Allman could see the cut in his cheek.

"Wash it off," Allman said, wrapping gauze around Eberhart's skinny chest. Samples reached for his own canteen, as did Carr, but Chacon was faster, handing back a brown towel and an open canteen. Carr took them, soaked one corner of the towel, and gently dabbed at his cheek. In a few moments his face was clean, and the narrow slash on his cheek was only oozing a little blood.

"Get a Band-Aid out of my bag," Allman instructed Samples after quickly examining Carr's cheek. To Carr he said, "Take two aspirin and call me in the morning."

Samples found a large Band-Aid and applied it to Carr's cheek. Meanwhile Allman repacked his aide bag and looked at Miles, who now appeared very frightened. "He's going into shock," Allman remarked in a matter-of-fact tone. "Need to get him back to the Medics track, and Eberhart, too." He leaned close to Miles and assumed a gentle tone. "You're going to be all right, Miles. We'll get you dusted off so you can go to the hospital where there are clean sheets and pretty nurses. Okay?" Miles nodded numbly.

"Sir," Chacon called from the driver's compartment, his hand holding the dangling CVC mike. "CO wants a head count."

"I don't know about the rest of the platoon," Carr said plaintively.

"What have you heard?" Samples asked Chacon.

Allman spoke up. "Reyes is a Kilo, Pratt and Sorenson are Whiskey's." One dead, two wounded. Not at all good, Samples thought.

"That's all I've heard about," Chacon confirmed.

"Okay," Carr said, "pass that on. Let him know Miles and Eberhart are wounded, and that Sergeant Samples and I are here in this track."

"Roger that," Chacon answered, and began muttering into his microphone.

"Del, Greg," Allman said to Washington and Hicks, "I'll need your help. You two take Miles, and I'll get Eberhart. When we get outside, go straight back about fifty meters, then we'll cut right to get to the Medics track. Keep your heads down." The two men nodded their understanding and moved to a crouching position near Miles. The RTO nodded and tried to rise from his seat, but sat back down heavily. With Washington's help he tried again and hobbled toward the open hatch. Hicks climbed out first and held out a hand to help Miles through the small doorway.

Behind him Samples heard Jones grab another can of 50-cal ammo and hoist it up top. After helping Miles to the ground, Washington grabbed his rifle and jumped out behind him. Eberhart shuffled to the hatch and climbed out, followed by Allman. That left Samples and Carr inside the main compartment, with Jones standing in the TC hatch opening the ammo can and feeding the ammo into the fifty, and Chacon in the driver's compartment monitoring the radio. Samples went to the door and watched as the five men began stumbling through the woods, bent over to hopefully avoid being hit. Then Miles turned his head and called back, "Hey, Sarge, what about my radio?"

"Don't worry about it," Samples called back. A minute later they were all out of sight, hidden by the thick woods. When Samples turned back inside, he found Carr pushing past him to go outside.

"I've got to go get it," Carr said, stumbling as he stepped out the narrow opening. "His rifle's back there, too."

TEN

Lieutenant Carr straightened his helmet, got a better grip on his rifle, and peered around the back corner of the APC. He felt Samples jostle him as the sergeant also climbed out.

"Leave it, Eltee!" Samples argued.

"Hey!" Chacon called from inside anxiously. Carr and Samples both stuck their heads back in through the hatch, their helmets bumping into each other. "CO says we're pulling back."

"I'll be right back," Carr yelled at him. "You go ahead, I'll catch up." With that he took another quick glance around the left side of the track, and then sprinted in a crouch toward the location where they had just rescued Miles. He dodged from tree to tree, staying low as bullets broke the sound barrier over his head. For a moment he feared he had lost his way, but then he saw the bush, and the square edges of the radio. He dived for it and sprawled on the ground under the bush, immediately tugging at the straps of the backpack.

Carr felt someone land beside him, and his first thought was that an enemy soldier had just arrived to slit his throat. He glanced over to see Sergeant Samples, his face red with anger and exertion.

"What the FUCK are you doing?" he demanded.

"We can't leave the radio for the gooks," Carr explained. "They could listen to our comms, and even send us false messages." He had learned this in his training on communications intelligence and security, and it had stuck with him. It sounded reasonable, and as platoon leader he had signed for all the equipment in the platoon and would have to be responsible for any losses.

"Shit," Samples griped, "you don't think they've got their own goddamn radios? And look." Samples reached over to the radio and turned it on its side so Carr could see the back. A large bullet hole pierced the metal covering.

Carr tentatively touched the hole, sticking his finger part way in. He felt a little embarrassed. To save face, he low-crawled further under the bush and pulled back Mile's M-16, its front sight temporarily caught in the branches. "At least I got the M-16."

"Big fuckin' deal," Samples said. "We could have written it off as a combat loss. The gooks won't use it; they'll just sell it on the black market. We gotta get outa here."

Carr noticed for the first time that the roar of the gunfire had diminished considerably as the battalion broke contact. He also noticed that most of the remaining rounds that passed through the trees were coming from the withdrawing Americans. He and Samples were increasingly at risk from friendly fire. Samples scooted around to face the departing tracks, and Carr did the same, preparing himself to jump up and sprint for the one-four track, the only one still clearly visible. Carr could see Jones' head just above the 50-cal as the gun sprayed the woods to right of them. Then Chacon began backing and turning the track, so he could follow the rest of the company. Carr wasn't sure if the driver was just preparing for a quicker getaway when he and Samples returned, or had simply gotten too nervous waiting. In the end, it didn't matter.

There was a boom from their left rear, and a sparkling smoke trail as an RPG sped through the air and exploded against the side of the one-four. It hit just aft of the engine compartment midway up on the right side. Right where the rounds for the 90-millimeter recoilless rifle were stored. The track juddered to a halt and a huge explosion erupted up through the cargo and TC hatches. Carr saw Jones fly skyward a few feet, realizing with a sick sensation that it was only the upper half of Jones' body. More explosions ripped through the interior of the APC, blasting out part of the side where the RPG had struck and blowing the rear ramp off to bang against a tree. Flames shot out of the driver's hatch, and Carr knew Chacon was gone too.

"Oh, God damn!" Samples cried. "Oh, God Damn! Fuck! Shit!"

Carr was too stunned to say anything. With mounting horror he watched as the track shuddered and rocked from the repeated explosions, now joined by the staccato raps of the 50-cal ammo exploding in the cans like thousands of strings of firecrackers. White and gold flames shot into the air as high as the surrounding trees, burning the leaves and branches nearby. In less than a minute the last of the ninety rounds had gone off, but the machine gun ammo continued to rattle like pebbles in a tin can. The wooden ammo box strapped to the left rear top suddenly flared as the C-4 inside caught fire, sending a pyre of blinding brightness twenty feet into the air. C-4 would only explode when properly ignited with a blasting cap, Carr knew, but it burned easily and extremely hot. Now it looked like the tail of a Saturn 5 rocket pointed the wrong way. The wooden ammo case on the left side of the track was now burning, and Carr remembered that it contained the squad's hand grenades. Soon that box would be exploding in a different way.

The burning armored personnel carrier had cut off their line of retreat. Carr looked to the left and right, trying to find a path that would skirt the danger of the exploding ammunition and fire yet still give them cover from both enemy and friendly fire. Nothing looked promising. Due to the roar of the blazing track, it took Carr a few moments to notice that the other gunfire had virtually ceased. His heart sank as he grasped that the silence meant the battalion had pulled back out of range, leaving him and Samples alone behind enemy lines.

Somewhere behind them a police whistle blew three short trills. It made no sense to Carr at first, but then he realized it was a signal to the enemy soldiers of the ambush. Fifty feet to their left a couple soldiers appeared, walking forward toward the bonfire that had formerly been the one-four track and stopping a safe distance away. They were short slender men with baggy tan uniforms and dark green pith helmets, carrying AK-47 assault rifles. They smiled and chattered as they watched the vehicle being incinerated. They were joined by another soldier who carried an unloaded RPG launcher—a long small-diameter tube with handles and a sight. The first two slapped the third man on his shoulders in congratulations. Carr slowly brought his M-16 around and took aim, but Samples hand reached over and pushed the barrel back down.

"They're all around us," Samples whispered hoarsely. He gestured with is eyes over to their right, and Carr followed his gaze to see other NVA filtering through the trees.

Carr heard the distinctive whop-whop-whop of a helicopter, and looked up. The canopy blocked much of the sky, but he caught a brief glimpse of a loach flying very high just to their south. Then another chopper approached at high speed from the east, flying just above the treetops. As it flashed overhead Carr saw the distinctive dragonfly shape of a Cobra gunship. The enemy soldiers all ducked for cover as the narrow-bodied aircraft swung around and made another run above them. Carr caught a glimpse of the pilot and gunner gazing out of their cockpit at the burning hulk of the one-four track. They were obviously looking for survivors, and Carr desperately wanted to jump up and wave his arms, but common sense prevailed. He could see one of the NVA soldiers trying to aim his AK-47 at the chopper, but was unable to get a shot off as the Cobra flitted past over the trees.

The roar of the Cobra's blades moved a little farther away as it searched other parts of the recent battleground. The gook with the RPG launcher ran back into the woods and a moment later reappeared with an RPG warhead. He slid the narrow rocket tube into the front of the launcher until only the conical warhead protruded, and then perched the loaded launcher on his shoulder while he searched the scattered patches of open sky.

"Waste of time," Samples said quietly but authoritatively. Carr looked over at him. "RPG's too slow to hit a moving Cobra," Samples explained. Although they couldn't see anything through the trees, they heard the approach of more helicopters not far to their south.

"Dust-off," Samples said. Carr nodded in agreement. Medevac Hueys would be flying in low to pick up the wounded—and dead—Americans. Either they had found a clearing big enough to land the choppers, or the APCs had knocked down enough trees to open a space. The Cobra made another pass over the one-four, which was now burning brightly as the alloy hull ignited. The RPG gunner tried to track it, but was unable to get off a shot. The sound of the choppers to the south surged and then faded off to the east.

They were evacuating the wounded to the Dau Tieng MASH. The Cobra's distinctive sound moved to the south, and Carr could tell it was now circling high above the battalion. Then it, too, moved off to the east and the last remaining mechanical noise drifted away.

There was a pop in the woods about a hundred meters to their right, and the three North Vietnamese soldiers to their left turned their heads sharply at the sound.

"Marking round," Samples muttered ominously.

The police whistle blew again, this time two short blasts followed by one long one. The enemy soldiers turned and ran back to where they had come from. Carr watched as the one with the RPG launcher stopped and disappeared like magic about forty feet to the rear and east of Carr's position. A moment later he reappeared, his launcher unloaded, now carrying a pack and an AK-47, and another soldier appeared behind him, this one carrying a large canvas sack with the tailfins of several RPG rounds sticking out. Together they hustled to the rear as the first mortar rounds exploded in the woods where the marking round had hit.

"We're fucked," Samples said with resignation. "They'll walk the rounds down this way in a minute."

Carr turned to look at Samples, who was facing the other way and had apparently not seen the RPG team. "There's a bunker over there behind us," he said urgently. Samples spun his head around to look at Carr questioningly. "The gooks are leaving," Carr explained. "I saw them evacuate." More mortar rounds crashed into the woods, closer this time. And off to their east they heard the louder blasts of regular artillery rounds. Probably the 105s from FSB Wood, Carr thought.

Samples nodded. "Can't stay here," he admitted. "Where is it?"

"Follow me," Carr said, this time without irony. He sprang up into a crouch and zig-zagged through the woods to where he had seen the RPG team appear. Or at least he thought it was the right place. He stopped and looked around, Samples beside him sweeping the area with the barrel of his M-16.

"It's gotta be here," he said, searching the ground for clues. All he saw was dirt and leaves. The mortar and artillery rounds were ripping through the air and exploding ever closer to them.

"There!" Samples said, pointing to their left front. At first Carr could detect nothing but woods, but then he saw the small dark hole peeking out of the pile of broken branches. That must be the firing hole, Carr speculated, so the entrance must be a few feet behind it. He ran around the barely perceptible mound that represented the underground fighting position and spied the larger sloping hole of the entryway. Artillery rounds exploded only a few dozen meters away, now visible and not just heard. There was no time to properly verify the bunker was safe. Carr jumped into the hole and slid down the stepped entrance ramp on his ass, holding his M-16 in front of him like a lance. After the bright sun outside, he could barely see anything inside but the firing hole opposite, so he rolled across the floor and sat down with his back under the opening, sweeping his rifle left to right. There was no reaction from inside, and Samples followed him in a rush, his feet tangling with Carr's as he reached the bottom.

"Clear," Carr told him. Outside the barrage intensified, rounds falling all around the bunker, shaking the ground like an earthquake. Dirt trickled down from the roof, and smoke drifted in through the entryway. Carr scooted over to his right, to avoid being directly across from the openings, and Samples moved to the other side. Outside was a cauldron of fire, a constant rain of explosions that battered his ears and resonated in his stomach. As his eyes adjusted to the dimness of the interior, he saw that it was virtually empty except for him and Samples, and they exchanged worried looks across the space between them. It was about six feet by six feet across, and maybe four feet high. The roof was made of what looked like two-by-fours beams over which had been laid corrugated tin. Carr guessed that at least of foot of packed earth covered the tin.

More detonations rocked the earth around them, the explosions seeming nearer and even larger. Carr's rational mind told him that only a direct hit would destroy the bunker and injure him, and the chances of a direct hit were relatively small, but he was scared nonetheless. Only his pride and lofty status as a second lieutenant kept him from showing the fear.

"Sounds like one-oh-fives and one-five-fives," Samples said loudly but conversationally. "Maybe even eight-inchers." The 105-millimeter howitzers were the smaller size artillery that could be pulled by jeeps. There was a battery of them at Fire Support Base Wood. The larger 155-millimeter cannons could be found at Dau Tieng. The giant 8-inch guns were divisional assets, probably based at Cu Chi, and fully capable of reaching any target in the division's Area of Operations. Carr didn't really care which were involved, since any of them could kill him just as easily as the others. Size didn't matter, only accuracy.

While projecting a calm demeanor, Aaron Samples was beginning to feel like an endangered species himself. The deafening roar of the explosions assaulted his ears, and the invisible pressure waves pounded through the entrance and bounced around like deadly beach balls. He had been through rocket and mortar attacks before, but had never experienced an artillery barrage this closely. It wasn't something he would want to repeat. He wasn't really worried about dying—he had long ago accepted that it was inevitable—but he did want to avoid being maimed or disfigured. He would rather be dead than have to depend on others.

Across the small underground room Lieutenant Carr was huddled with his arms around his knees. His face looked pale to Samples, and his jaw was clamped shut, but otherwise he was maintaining. Samples gave him credit for that. This was a bad situation, the worst that Samples had ever been in, so he could understand anyone's terror, especially that of a green lieutenant like Carr. Yet the other man just sat there looking at the floor, perhaps praying.

With his eyes now fully adjusted to the dimness of the bunker, Samples scanned the walls through the eddies of dust and smoke, watching for potential collapses of the earthen bulwarks. For the first time he noticed the rectangular cubby hole in the back wall near the entrance, next to Carr. It was only about a foot wide and half that tall. Squinting his eyes, he thought there might be something in it. If this arty ever stops, he thought, I'll have to check that out.

A huge explosion, nearer than the others, jolted the ground so hard that Sample's butt lifted off the floor a couple inches before crashing back down, and a shower of dirt from the wall flowed down the back of his neck. A quick glance around confirmed that the bunker was still intact.

"Close one," Carr called out. Samples nodded. He wondered how long the bombardment would continue. While the U.S. forces had an almost limitless supply of ammunition and a willingness to use it profusely, the gunners would be getting tired, and their immediate supply of ammo would need to be replenished from the ammo dumps. Samples figured the barrage would end sooner rather than later. Just how much sooner, however, was unknown. It was difficult to tell with all the smoke and dust in the air, but he thought he detected a change in the ambient light as the sun began to set. Darkness was coming, but what that meant for him and Carr was a new question they would have to deal with.

After what seemed like hours, there was a change in the tone of the shelling, and somehow it sounded slightly more treble than bass. The spacing between blasts was lengthening. Samples hoped this indicated that the bigger guns had dropped out of the action, leaving only the smaller guns still firing. Then even the smaller explosions sputtered to a halt. The only sound Samples could hear now was the ringing in his ears. A tremendous wave of relief washed over him. He had survived, at least for now.

"Is that it?" Carr asked too loudly.

"Shit, I hope so," Samples replied, noticing that he, too, had spoken too loudly. It would take a minute for their ears and voices to adjust to the new silent reality. Samples watched the dust settle and listened for the dreaded resumption of the arty strike. It didn't come.

"There might be an air strike," Samples warned, forcing his speech down to a normal level.

"You think?"

"I hope not. If they hit this area with napalm, this bunker won't do us much good." Samples saw Carr look worriedly out the entrance. All they could see were shattered tree branches and a darkening sky.

"Maybe we should go up and take a quick look around," Carr suggested tentatively. Samples figured he was feeling a little claustrophobic. He didn't want to tell Carr, but he, too, wanted to get out of the confining space.

"Let me check it out," Samples told him, duck-walking toward the doorway. The steps up to ground level were littered with broken twigs and shredded leaves. Cautiously Samples crawled up using one hand and his knees, the other hand holding his M-16 by the pistol grip, ready for action. As his eyes topped the lip of the passage he paused and scanned the area behind the bunker. Drifting smoke was the only movement he could detect. With a sudden burst he scrabbled the rest of the way up and squatted beside the upper opening, swinging the barrel of his rifle in a 360-degree arc, his boots scuffling in the dirt and debris. Slowly he stood up, still searching for any movement around him.

"Come on out," he said down into the hole. Carr emerged a little clumsily, slipping on the leaves, until he was standing beside Samples. Together they surveyed the damage to the woods around them. Most of the remaining branches on the trees were bare, blasted clean by the artillery. Some trees were shattered and split, and others tilted or completely knocked down, their dirt-encased roots showing. The bunker had been denuded by the explosions, and its rectangular mound was now far more obvious than before. What was left of the stricken APC was still burning, but not as hotly, and there were smaller pieces burning in several spots yards away from the main hulk. Only the treads and road wheels were recognizable, and on one side they were twisted out of shape. A molten lump smoldered where the engine had been.

"Looks like one-four took a direct hit," Samples commented. Carr nodded sadly. The devastation around them was humbling.

Carr began walking away to the southwest. "Where you going?" Samples demanded.

"To get the radio and Miles' rifle," Carr answered. Both had been left behind when they ran for the cover of the bunker. Samples wanted to stop him, but instead followed him to where they had hidden under the bush, a bush that no longer existed. Recovering the radio and rifle was now totally pointless, but Samples had no other plan at the moment.

They found the radio lying where they had left it, partially buried by dirt and twigs. Carr lifted it by the backpack straps and inspected the case. It still had a bullet hole in it. The coiled cable for the handset was still attached to the top of the radio, but the handset itself was gone, leaving only loose wires hanging down.

"It's junk," Samples said. Carr nodded and dropped the radio to the ground. They found the rifle several feet away, its plastic stock and front handgrips shattered. They stared down at it.

"Think the armorer could fix that?" Carr asked. Samples wasn't sure if he was joking or not.

"Sure," Samples said. "Give him a call on the radio."

"I'll get right on that," Carr replied in almost a monotone. They were trying to be normal, but after what they had just been through, it wasn't easy.

Though his ears were still numb and whining, Samples heard a distant rumbling sound. "Is that a jet?" he said with concern. He was still worried about an airstrike. Carr and he both scanned the sky, twisting their heads to see every quadrant. Then Carr chuckled.

"There it is," he said, pointing to the south. The setting sun glinted off the Boeing 707 that was climbing and turning to the east.

"Freedom Bird," Samples noted. A plane taking soldiers back to the World. He hated the irony.

"Think they'll come looking for us?" Carr asked, changing the subject.

Sample shook his head. "They think we're dead," he said glumly. "You had Chacon report that we were in the track. As far as they know, we were inside it when it went up."

Carr had a guilty look, but Samples wasn't really blaming him, just explaining what happened. "But they'll come for the bodies," Carr said hopefully.

"What fuckin' bodies?" Samples said with a touch of exasperation. "That Cobra saw how it was burning. They know there's nothing gonna be left. Even the dog tags will be melted."

With his shoulders slumping, Carr nodded. "So what do we do?" he asked dejectedly.

"We're going to have to walk home," Samples said, admitting it to himself for the first time. "And it's a long fuckin' walk."

"Guess we better get started, then," Carr replied.

Samples noted how low the sun was in the west and shook his head. "Too late today," he said. "We'll start out first thing in the morning. Don't want to be walking in the woods at night."

"I'm not Little Red Riding Hood, Sergeant," Carr admonished him.

Samples gave him a brief sour look, his grip on his rifle tightening. Then he forced himself to consider the lieutenant's inexperience and kept his voice calm and reassuring. "The gooks come out at night," he said. "The woods will be crawling with them. There's probably going to be arty H&I fire, and maybe even another B-52 strike. And what if we ran into a Wolfhounds ambush patrol in the dark? Not to mention the chance of getting lost." The last was a not-so-subtle dig at Carr about the ambush patrol he had led the night before last.

While Samples spoke, Carr had opened a small pouch on his web belt and felt around inside. His expression was now one of surprise and a little panic. "Shit!" Carr said vehemently. "Lost my compass."

"Well that settles it," Samples told him. "Can't travel at night in the woods without a compass." Carr nodded in defeat.

ELEVEN

Carr's shoulders slumped as the precariousness of their situation sank in. Standing there amid the devastated and desolate woods, the sun already below the tops of the trees, he experienced an almost overwhelming depression settling around him. He was miles from safety, surrounded by dangers, and had only an antagonistic sergeant to depend on. Much as Carr hated to admit it, Samples had been right: trying to hike back to Wood at night was out of the question. But what was the alternative? They couldn't just stand or sit here in the open waiting for dawn. Before he could raise the issue with Samples, the sergeant turned and walked back toward the bunker.

"Where are you going?" Carr asked him.

"There's something in the bunker," Samples said over his shoulder. Carr followed him, puzzled because he had seen nothing in there but dirt.

When they reached the entrance, Samples dropped down inside. Carr remained outside, standing guard. He rotated his body slowly in a circle, eyeing the surrounding forest for any unusual movement. By the time he had made a full circle, Samples climbed back out, holding a small flat package wrapped in black plastic.

"What's that?" Carr asked.

"Don't know," Samples said, cradling his M-16 under his bicep and over his right forearm so he had both hands free. He unwrapped the plastic, which turned out to be a narrow bag, and shook out a thin wallet and a small notebook. After stuffing the plastic bag in his pants pocket, Samples handed Carr the notebook to hold while he inspected the wallet. Carr moved close beside Samples so he could see what was in it. The first thing revealed was a photo of a young woman, a black-and-white picture with water stains.

"Nice-looking girlfriend," Samples commented. He flipped the plastic sleeve containing the photo to reveal another photo, this time of an elderly couple standing in front of a rough farmhouse. "And the folks back home," Samples said. A third sleeve contained what appeared to be an ID card of some sort, with printing over a government symbol of some sort. Samples then opened the bifold to reveal a couple pieces of currency. One had a "1" prominent displayed and the other a "5". Both featured a portrait of Ho Chi Minh.

"We're rich," Carr said flatly.

"What about the notebook?" Samples asked.

Carr repositioned his rifle the way Samples had and thumbed open the little book, bound in genuine imitation red leather. It appeared to be a diary, the first few pages filled with cramped pencil writing in Vietnamese. One page featured an amateurish but recognizable drawing of an M-113 armored personnel carrier. "Target recognition?" Carr mused out loud.

"Could be," Samples agreed.

"Can you read Vietnamese?" Carr asked, paging through the journal.

"Sure," Samples scoffed. "Hell, I can't speak it either, except for a few words that I'm probably saying wrong. Fuckers need to learn English." Carr wasn't sure if that last remark was said in jest or in earnest. Carr closed the book and put it in his shirt pocket.

"We'll give it to Intel when we get back," Carr said, buttoning the pocket. "Maybe they can get something out of it."

"Give 'em this, too," Samples said after a moment, handing Carr the wallet. Carr unbuttoned his shirt pocket again, slipped the wallet inside, and rebuttoned. "Probably won't get much," Samples said. "Looks like they came from a lowly grunt private who doesn't know anything."

"You never know," Carr replied. "Might be Uncle Ho's grandson or something."

"Hmph," Samples grunted dismissively.

Both men re-gripped their rifles in a ready position and looked around them at the darkening forest. The sun was now dipping below the horizon, leaving deep shadows and reducing their range of vision.

"So where do we spend the night?" Carr asked.

"I forgot to make reservations at the Howard Johnson's," Samples said.

"Not much choice, is there?" Carr considered the possibilities, which were few. "Bunker looks to be the best bet."

Samples looked down at the entrance and shrugged. "Not if the gooks come back," he offered.

"How likely is that?"

"Fuck if I know."

"Then what, sleep on the ground?" Carr was again getting annoyed with Samples' attitude.

"Or up in a tree," Samples countered. "Course, then you can't fall asleep without falling out."

"Exactly. And on the ground, we'd still be vulnerable to arty fire or ambush."

"Okay, okay," Samples surrendered. He stared at the bunker for a minute, and then looked around at the areas still visible in the dying light. "Maybe we ought to camouflage it," he said.

Carr thought about that for a minute. Would the camouflage look too artificial, and unnecessarily draw attention to it? Would it make any difference in the dark? If no one came around, it was pointless anyway. He needed to keep Samples on his side, though, so maybe agreeing with him on this would help.

"Sounds like a good idea," Carr told him. "But not too much. It still needs to look like the rest of this area."

Samples nodded and walked over to pick up a fallen branch that still had a few leaves on it. He carried it to the front of the bunker and laid it over the gun port. Then he stepped back and eyed the result judiciously. He leaned down and moved the branch six inches, then nodded approvingly. He looked up and saw Carr watching him. He raised his eyebrows and said, "You gonna help?" Carr sighed and walked away, looking for more fallen tree limbs.

It took a few minutes, in part because they could only use one hand, the other filled with their rifles. Leaves were scattered randomly but artfully over the roof and around the edges to soften the bunker's rectangular outline, and together they dragged a ten-foot tree limb to be draped across the bunker diagonally, as if it had fallen there naturally. While Samples scattered more leaves and twigs to cover their tracks, Carr pulled a small bush up by its roots and dug a small hole in the ground just in front of the bunker's entrance.

"We can plant this after we get inside," Carr told Samples. The sergeant nodded as he wiped his dirty hands on his pants. Then he turned and walked away, headed toward the smoldering remains of the one-four track. "Where are you going?" Carr called after him.

"Take a piss. Do you mind?"

Carr watched him approach within ten feet of the smoking hulk before he stopped and did his business. When he returned he gestured with his head toward the wreck.

"Better drain your lizard now, while you got a chance. Don't want you pissin' in the bunker with me."

Carr walked a few feet away and stopped to fumble with his fly.

"Not there, di—lieutenant," Samples chastised, correcting himself in mid-sentence. "Go all the way over by the one-four."

"Why?"

"Cause the gooks got good noses, and American piss smells different than gook piss. Over there the smoke and, uh, other stuff will mask the odor." Carr guessed that Samples was referring to the smell of burned flesh that was noticeable even at this distance. Recognizing the wisdom of Samples' suggestion, he moved on and got as close to the hulk as he could stand before relieving himself. When he returned Samples was already down in the bunker. Carr followed him down inside, pausing to pull the uprooted bush into position. At the bottom of the steps he leaned his rifle against the wall and set his helmet down on the floor, then crawled back up the steps to jam the bush's roots into the hole and sweep dirt over them.

Carr backed down the steps and sat down against the side wall opposite Samples, who was still wearing his helmet and had his rifle lying in his lap. Even in the deepening gloom of the bunker, Carr could tell the sergeant was watching him closely. Twisting around some, Carr reached back to his right hip, unsnapped the cover, and pulled out his canteen. Unscrewing the cap, he took a slow sip of the tepid chlorinated water, surprised at how good it tasted.

"Better go easy on that," Samples warned. "It'll be a long time till we can get more."

For Steve Carr, that was the final straw. It had been a very long and extremely stressful day, and he was finally fed up with Samples' condescending and antagonistic attitude. With his jaw clenched, he glared at Samples and spat out, "I'm well aware of that, *Sergeant*! And I'm tired of you treating me like an idiot! What the fuck is wrong with you?"

Samples visibly recoiled at this verbal assault. "I'm just trying to help," he answered defensively.

"Bullshit! You go around me whenever you can, you don't keep me informed, and you act like I haven't got the sense God gave a screwdriver. And you never say 'sir'!"

"That's not true," Samples replied with increasing fury, "and now is not the time."

"I am your superior officer, and if I say now is the time, then it is. And goddammit, say 'sir'!"

"Yes, *sir*!" Samples said with hoarse sarcasm. "Shall we invite the neighbors in as well, *sir*?"

Carr was instantly abashed. He realized he had raised his voice to a level easily audible beyond the confines of the bunker. Worse, he had lost his temper with a man that potentially could save his life. Carr consciously slowed his breathing and calmed himself, fully aware of the judgmental gaze from Samples.

"Look, Sergeant," Carr began again in a more conciliatory tone, but stopped to gather his thoughts. Beginning again, he said, "I know we have our differences. I realize you have a ton more experience than I do, and I've only been here a couple weeks. I didn't ask to be here. But the Army, in its infinite wisdom, made me the platoon leader and you the platoon sergeant, and there is a long-standing tradition and many military policies about how that is supposed to work. I'm sorry you don't like me, or like my being here, but it's a fact of life and you'll just have to deal with it."

"There's not a problem, sir," Samples said, but his tone was not apologetic.

"Clearly there is. Is it me, or all officers, that you hate?"

"It's not you, sir," Samples admitted reluctantly. "And it's not all officers. Just lieutenants."

"Lieutenants?" Carr said. "Why lieutenants?"

"I got my reasons," Samples said.

"Well, what are they?"

Samples shook his head. "Don't want to talk about it," he said, taking his helmet off and setting it down beside him so he could rub his short hair.

"I heard that your last platoon leader had some problems. Is that it?" Carr was truly curious, and his tone was as encouraging as he could manage.

"Nope," Samples said. "I mean, yeah, he was an idiot, but no more than most butter-bars."

"Then why?"

"Like I said, sir, I don't want to talk about it."

Carr wanted to pursue the issue, but decided to accept the small victories he had just won. The tension was defused, and Samples was using 'sir' in a natural manner. They had a long night ahead of them, and Carr suddenly realized just how weary he was. He leaned his head back against the wall, oblivious to the particles of dirt that dribbled down the back of his neck, and closed his eyes.

Aaron Samples rubbed his head some more, then brought his hands down to rub his face and eyes. He was disgusted with himself. He had treated Carr poorly, but had been unable to stop himself from doing so. The events of a year ago still dictated his actions and attitude, and not in a positive way. He probably should have seen a shrink or a counselor, but that was a career killer. Army sergeants were supposed to just suck it up and drive on.

Carr wasn't really a bad lieutenant, better than most Samples had known. He had put up with Samples' shit for only so long before dressing him down, which earned him a measure of respect. Now they were stuck in this gook bunker in enemy territory, where anything could happen. Maybe, Samples admitted, it was time to let his past go and move on, while he had the chance.

"I'm married," Samples said out loud, "sort of." Carr's head jerked up. He had apparently fallen asleep. Carr brushed the back of his head and neck before replying.

"Sort of?" Carr asked.

"Got married in '65 at Fort Ord," Samples began. "She was good looking, and I was horny. Then I got shipped out to Nam, MACV. We wrote back and forth, I thought things were fine." He paused as he remembered the good times. "When I got back, I was transferred to Polk, cadre in the AIT. We got post housing. I thought everything was going good with her. Yeah, we had some arguments, but nothing big. She hated Louisiana, but so did everyone else."

"So what happened?" Carr asked.

"We took a cycle to Tigerland for their Nam training, supposed to last a week. One of the kids got meningitis, so they brought everyone back in and quarantined the barracks. I went home two days early, brought some flowers, going to surprise my wife. I was the one that got surprised." Samples stopped again, replaying the events in his head. Emotions welled up in his chest.

"And?" Carr urged.

"The front door was locked, but there was a light on in the bedroom. I unlocked the door real quietly and went inside. I could hear the bed squeaking. I snuck down the hall and looked in, and there was some naked guy humping my wife like there was no tomorrow. I was really pissed. You know that saying, 'if you grab them by the balls, their hearts and minds will follow'?"

"Yeah."

"That's what I did. I grabbed him by the nuts and hustled him out the front door, then locked it."

"So he's standing in the front yard buck naked?" Carr asked with a chuckle.

"Damn straight. Then I called the MPs. Told them there was a naked man prowling in the neighborhood." Carr laughed out loud.

"They caught him a block away, trying to break into his car," Samples said, now laughing as well. "I would have loved to hear that conversation."

"Then what happened?"

"They took him to the brig. I imagine his First Sergeant or commander had to go identify him and pick him up."

"What'd you do?"

"My wife was hiding in the bathroom, so I went through the guy's clothes, found his wallet and keys. He was a butter-bar from the Basic Training brigade. Threw the clothes in the trash, and left his wallet and keys on top of a neighbor's car. Packed my shit and went to the BEQ." The Bachelor Enlisted Quarters had rooms for senior enlisted men who were single or unaccompanied.

"Did you get a divorce?"

"Nah. I was too pissed off. Didn't want to give her the satisfaction. Instead I put in my papers to come back to Nam. She had to go live with her mother in California. Still gets my allotment, but she can't marry that asshole lieutenant."

"So that's why you hate lieutenants, huh?" Carr sympathized. "I can understand that."

"Yeah," Samples said, "but I guess it's not fair to blame you for what happened." He couldn't quite bring himself to actually say he was sorry, however.

"Does she write to you?

"Sometimes," Samples admitted, remembering the last letter he got. "She's always saying she's sorry and wants to make it up to me."

"Have you written her back?"

Samples shook his head. "Can't do it. Besides, what would I say? 'It's okay that you were fuckin' around on me'? Shit, I'll bet that wasn't the first time, either."

"Then you ought to get a divorce. Make a clean break. Move on with your life."

"I know you're right," Samples admitted sheepishly, "but it's hard. I really loved that girl. Hell, if I saw her, I'd probably take her back."

"But you'd always remember what she did," Carr pointed out.

"Yeah." Samples sighed. "Well, I've got four more months to think about it." He didn't want to think about it, however. To change the subject, he said, "You're married, right?"

"Yep," Carr answered, sounding happy about it. "Two years."

"Any kids?" Samples didn't really care; he just wanted to talk about something other than his own problems.

"Not yet," Carr said. "We want to wait until I'm out of the Army."

"That'll be a while, won't it?"

"Not really. When I DEROS they'll probably let me go into the reserves. I'm ROTC"—he pronounced it 'rotsey'—"so I only have a two-year active duty commitment." DEROS—the Date of Estimated Return from Overseas Service—was the most important date in the mind of every soldier in Viet Nam. Everyone knew exactly how many days remained before they would DEROS. Many had short-timer's calendars on which they tracked the days remaining.

"So," Samples said, "basically you're a draftee officer."

"Kinda, yeah."

Samples figured that was why Carr got along well with the troops—he was only in for the short-term, not a lifer like Samples. Samples wasn't sure how he felt about that personally. On the one hand, that meant Carr wasn't part of the oppressive officer establishment, but on the other hand he wasn't a professional leader either. Maybe, Samples realized, he shouldn't try so hard to fit people into stereotypical boxes.

"So how did you get into 'rotsey'?" Samples asked, still steering the conversation away from himself.

"My freshman year it was required," Carr explained. "At state universities all able-bodied males had to take ROTC the first two years, either Army, Navy, or Air Force. They changed the rule after my first year, but I stayed in it to keep from being drafted."

"But you had a student deferment, didn't you?" Samples asked.

"Yeah, but to keep it you had to keep your grades up, and mine weren't so good at first. As long as I was in ROTC, my grades weren't as important."

Samples had joined the Army right out of high school, and hadn't been aware of the requirements for college students. Hearing about Carr's grades made him seem less elite and different.

"But you got your degree?" Samples inquired.

"Oh, yeah. BA in Sociology, for what good that will do me. After I met Sarah, my wife, I got my act together and started studying."

"What kind of job can you get with that degree?" Samples was actually interested, for reasons he couldn't identify.

Carr huffed dismissively. "Nothing good. Social worker, maybe advertising or customer service. Pretty much worthless."

"Then why did you get it."

"Seemed like a good idea at the time. No, actually, I wanted to get into movie production, like scripts or set decoration, but they don't offer that as a major. So I chose Sociology because it looked easy."

"Was it?"

"Not really. But at least now I have a degree. It'll help me get a better job when I get out, working at a business or for the government." Carr sounded wistful and perhaps a little disappointed at how his education had turned out. Samples envied him, though. After this enlistment, he thought, he could get out and go to college on the GI Bill. Or maybe not. He had found a home in the Army, and the security of the service would be hard to give up.

They were both silent. With the setting of the sun the bunker was as black as a coal mine, with only a barely perceptible lightening of the murkiness coming in through the gun port and entrance. It smelled of freshly-dug earth and human sweat, with a hint of cordite and dead fish. Outside Samples could hear insects and an occasional rustle of leaves when a slight breeze gusted through. Samples thought about his wife, remembering the good times they had had, then despising her for the infidelity. Being married was incredibly difficult, not like being a combat soldier. Here he knew who his enemy was, and knew what to do to protect himself.

"Why don't you get some sleep," Carr said. "I'll stand watch."

Samples nodded, and then realized Carr couldn't see his gesture. "Okay. Wake me in an hour."

TWELVE

Steve Carr felt his head sinking toward his knees and jerked it up, aware he had almost fallen asleep. Again. Sitting in the total darkness of the bunker, listening to Samples snoring gently across from him, was so soporific he could hardly resist. He drummed his fingers on the dirt floor and twisted his head back and forth, hoping the activity would help keep him awake. He brought his watch up close to his face, but the hands had already lost most of their luminance, making it impossible to tell the time. He was certain it had been more than an hour since he had told Samples to get some sleep, but he wanted to show the sergeant he was just as hard core as Samples was. He also wanted Samples to actually get some rest, for he knew he would be totally dependent on him tomorrow.

Carr pondered what Samples had told him about his marriage, and for the first time since they had met he had felt some sympathy for the hard-bitten soldier. He now understood where at least some of Samples' combative nature had originated, wondering how he himself would have handled such a situation. Sarah would never cheat on him like that, he was almost positive, but if she did, he didn't know how he would deal with it. Probably not as cleverly as Samples had.

Over the sound of Samples' breathing, the clicks and chirps of insects, and the rattling of leaves in the wind, Carr thought he heard a different vibration in the air. He held his breath and strained his ears. There it was again. It sounded like someone had spoken.

"Pst!" he hissed at Samples. Immediately the snoring stopped and Carr could sense that Samples had become fully alert.

"What?" Samples whispered.

"Voices," Carr whispered back. They both held their breaths and listened intently. The sound came again, this time a little closer. Someone out in the woods spoke, and another voice answered. Carr couldn't make out any words, but the cadence and tone were distinctively Vietnamese.

"Gooks," Samples breathed in confirmation.

There was more chatter, and the speakers were getting closer and closer. Carr could detect the different voices of several men, all talking happily as if they were on a picnic outing. One man's remark garnered a burst of laughter from the others. Carr estimated there were at least eight or ten men out there. "At least a squad," he whispered to Samples.

He heard Samples move around and pick up his rifle. There was a slight click as he took the weapon off safety. Carr did the same, moving into the corner farthest from the entrance. Outside, the group of men, undoubtedly NVA soldiers, was now within a few yards of the bunker. Car could hear the fall of their tennis-shoe-clad feet and the thunks and clanks of the weapons they carried. Hoping they would continue walking and leave the bunker far behind, Carr breathed as shallowly and quietly as he could.

The gooks stopped, and what sounded like an argument ensued. Finally a conciliatory voice made a suggestion, and others grunted their acquiescence. To Carr's horror, the men sounded as if they were spreading out and searching the area, calling to each other to report what they found, or didn't find. Carr was sure they were looking for the bunker, probably so the one soldier could retrieve his wallet and notebook. One of the men walked right by the bunker's entrance, without apparently noticing it, and then tripped on a tree root and cursed loudly. He said something that sounded angry, and a distant voice answered with a command. The voices all gathered again, and another argument arose. There was a sharp command, and Carr thought he heard the word "di," which he knew meant "go."

Carr could hear the group of men departing, but after going only a few yards one of them called back. A voice closer to the bunker answered. Although he couldn't understand a word, Carr believed he understood what was transpiring. One soldier wanted to stay and search some more, and the others wanted to continue their journey or patrol. There was a warning or admonition from the distant group, and a promise from the nearer soldier. The voices of the group moved away, and the lone soldier began stomping around muttering to himself. Carr pointed his rifle at the entrance and tried to shake off the fear. He heard Samples scoot closer to him, and felt the sergeant's hand find his forearm and follow it down to the rifle, firmly pushing the barrel down.

Carr understood. They couldn't afford to shoot. It would bring the group of soldiers back in an instant, leaving them trapped. Outside they heard a scratching sound, and then there was a tiny flare of light. The soldier had lit a match, and through the branches of the bush covering the entrance they could see the pool of sputtering light float around as the soldier used it to search the area. They heard a sharp yelp of pain when it burned his fingers, muttered curses, and then another match was lit. This time the flame itself was briefly visible through the lacework of the bush. Carr heard the man say something that sounded suspiciously like "Aha!"

The shrub was suddenly pulled aside and the match was blown out. Their hiding place had been discovered. Carr tensed his muscles, though he had no idea what he would do. It sounded like the soldier took off his helmet and set it on the top of the bunker, and then laid his rifle on top of the helmet. Feet dimly appeared on the top step and began descending. Quickly the man's body blocked the entrance, sealing off the dim moonlight and starlight from outside. Then there was a fumbling and a scratch, and a match flared right in front of Carr's face. The flame revealed a young NVA soldier, slender, dark-haired, and almond-eyed. His eyes widened in surprise as he saw the two Americans, but he was so shocked he just crouched there holding the match.

"Don't move!" Carr commanded in a whisper, and then added "Chieu Hoi!" in the hope that would encourage the man to surrender quietly. Instead he dropped the match and took a deep breath so he could yell. In the dying glow of the match on the floor, Carr saw Samples jump forward and grab the young man's face, sealing his mouth and nose with his hand. Samples pulled the struggling soldier further into the bunker, grunting with the effort to control the boy who was thrashing wildly. Carr moved over to help, ignoring the kicks that assaulted his legs and abdomen. He swung his M-16 in a butt-stroke aimed at the gook's midsection, but with the poor visibility and the man's antics, he only grazed the man's chest. The gook's flailing hands found the stock of Carr's rifle and pulled on it, his fingers scrabbling for the trigger housing. Without thinking, Carr went with the flow and pushed the butt of the gun at the man's throat, which had been exposed by Samples' grip on his chin. Adrenaline pumping, Carr pushed with all his strength and felt the cartilage give with brief crack.

Now the young man's body began jerking and pulsing, his fingernails scraping against Carr's hands and the rifle, his legs twitching spasmodically. The air was filled with the smell of urine, but Carr didn't know if it was the soldier's or his own. It didn't matter. He just kept pushing against the man's neck, crushing his windpipe and preventing him from making a sound. Then, with one last heave, the gook's body went limp. Wary of a trick, Carr kept the pressure on. The smell of feces joined the odor of urine.

"You can let up now," Samples whispered. "He's dead."

It took a moment for that to sink in. Carr pulled the rifle away and sat down, his back against the wall of the bunker. He checked his crotch and was relieved to find it was dry. His body was electrified by the action, but the effect was beginning to ebb away. He knew he had just killed another human being, but he didn't want to think about it right now. He replayed the action in his head to determine how much noise they had made, but it was all a jumble. He heard Samples push the body to the center of the bunker.

"Think they heard us?" he asked Samples in a hoarse whisper that was louder than he expected.

"Hope not," Samples replied with more control. "If they did, we'll know in a few minutes."

"God, he stinks," Carr blurted.

"Shh," Samples warned him. They both listened intently, worried they might hear the return of the patrol. The forest was quiet, the insects undisturbed by what had occurred below ground. They waited for what Carr thought must have been fifteen minutes. There were no threatening sounds.

"Looks like we lucked out," Samples said quietly.

"Yeah, but now what?" Carr was shivering as he came down from the adrenaline high.

"Don't know," Samples admitted. "Can't stay here."

"Why not?"

"They'll come looking for him eventually. Besides, as you pointed out, he stinks."

"We could take him out and dump him somewhere else in the woods," Carr suggested.

"As soon as they find him, they'll search the whole area."

Carr knew Samples was right. And if they left him here, they could collapse the firing point and entrance enough to bury the body and cover up the odor. But the night was only half over.

When Samples climbed out of the bunker and stood up, he took in a deep breath of fresh air. The stench below had been nauseating, and the bunker had become very claustrophobic. Carr followed him out, accidentally kicking the AK-47 left by the entry and making a slight clatter as the gun slid from the top of the pith helmet. Both men froze and picked up their ears, wary that someone might be close enough to hear. After a moment of silence, they resumed breathing.

"Should we take the AK?" Carr asked quietly, bending down to pick it up. There was just enough moonlight for Samples to make out Carr's shape and actions.

"What? You want a souvenir?" Samples detected the snideness in his own voice and instantly regretted it. In a nicer tone, he added, "No, just toss it inside, sir. The helmet, too." Carr lowered the rifle to the bottom of the steps and let it down gently. The pith helmet was tossed in, making only a soft clunk as it hit the floor.

Samples kicked at the edge of the opening with the heel of his boot, and knocked a few clods of dirt loose. The ground was hard after a long dry season, and filling in the entry wasn't going to be easy. Carr walked away and came back with a tree branch about six feet long. Laying his rifle down on a nearby stump, he began chipping at the opposite side of the hole with the pointed end. It knocked only small chunks of earth loose, but it worked better than Samples' heel. Samples set his own rifle down next to Carr's and went in search of his own make-shift pick. It took some pawing around in the dark, but eventually he found a suitable section of limb and came back to the bunker. Carr had already made considerable progress on his side of the doorway, so Samples attacked the other side with all his strength, determined to catch up.

At Carr's suggestion, they paused every few minutes to toss twigs, leaves and small bushes into the hole to give the fill more bulk. After about half an hour of work, the entry was just a shallow depression. Using the sides of their feet, they pushed more loose dirt onto it and brushed the area with leafy branches, afterward laying those branches across it in what they hoped was a random way. The same was done to the firing port on the other side, but it took only a couple minutes to seal that opening. Samples sniffed the air, and could no longer detect any foul odors emanating from the bunker.

"Let's go," he whispered, walking back around the bunker to retrieve his rifle. He picked up Carr's as well and handed it to him.

"Which way?" Carr asked.

Samples pointed vaguely southwest. "There were some bomb craters back that way. Maybe we can hole up in one until dawn." He figured that in a crater they would be out of sight, and gooks would be unlikely to climb down in one. It would also protect them if they got in a firefight.

"What if that patrol comes back this way before we get there?" Carr didn't sound worried, just curious.

"Then we're fucked." Samples led off, going almost directly west until they had passed what was left of the one-four track, which still glowed in places, and then turned more directly south. Or what he hoped was south. There was too little open sky to steer by the stars, but the nearly half moon was sometimes visible through the trees, and he knew that it was setting in the west. All he had to do was keep the moon to his right, and he was heading in a generally southerly direction. He hoped.

Moving through the woods at night was slow and tedious. The pale moonlight barely penetrated the canopy, and brush and vines clutched at his ankles and midsection. When he pushed a branch out of his way, he had to turn and hold it so it didn't slash back and hit Carr in the face. He tried to follow the path left by one of the APCs during the initial sweep, but the seedlings and bushes crushed by the treads had already sprung back up.

Samples estimated they had gone only a couple hundred meters when he heard something. He stopped suddenly, and Carr bumped into him.

"Sorry," Carr whispered.

"Sh!" Samples said, turning his head different directions as he listened for more sounds. Carr caught on immediately, and did the same. Samples heard it again. A voice—no, several voices—calling out in Vietnamese. They said the same word over and over. The patrol had come back, looking for the soldier they had left behind. Samples prayed that they didn't find him.

Frozen in place, Samples and Carr listened to the distant voices and tried to guess what they were saying. The tone of the words seemed to slowly change from the sound of someone seeking someone else to a tone of annoyance and even anger. There was a brief conversation as a couple voices offered opinions, and then a louder command and subsequent silence. The louder voice now gave another command, and the voices resumed a quiet discourse as they moved away. When they could no longer be heard, Samples heaved a sigh of relief.

"Guess they didn't find him," Carr whispered with evident satisfaction.

"Guess not," Samples agreed. "Let's keep moving."

After another half hour of dodging trees and shoving their way through the underbrush, they burst out of the blackness of the forest onto the edge of a bomb crater, dimly illuminated by the moon. It was the middle one of three huge bomb craters in a neat row across their line of march. Samples was tired, and he knew Carr must be even more so. Samples, at least, had gotten a little sleep in the bunker, but Carr had been awake since the night before, and had been noticeably shaken by the experience with the NVA soldier.

"This looks good," Samples told the lieutenant. After checking the surrounding area as well as he could in the pale moonlight, Samples half stepped and half slid down the loose slope of the inner wall of the crater. Carr came after him, but lost his footing and started to fall. Samples caught him and helped him regain his balance at the shallow bowl of the bottom.

"Anybody coming," Samples explained in a low voice, "will probably go around the other two craters and not look in this one." Carr nodded and then sat down. Even in the dark Samples could tell Carr was trembling a little. He sat down beside him and thought about reaching out pat him on the shoulder, but held back. Carr might take it wrong, somehow. And Samples just wasn't a touchy-feely kind of guy.

"I'll take first watch," he told Carr. "You need to get some sleep."

"Okay," Carr acknowledged weakly. "Wake me up in an hour."

"Roger that," Samples said. He watched Carr lay back against the sloping wall of the crater, his head cradled in his helmet, and his rifle lying across his chest. Carr twitched and squirmed to get comfortable, but in less than a minute he was breathing slowly and deeply.

Samples stood up slowly and did a full circle scan over the rim of the crater, but all he could see were dark trees. He sat back down, realizing he would hear something long before he would see it anyway. He gazed at the slumbering lieutenant and felt a brief wave of paternalism wash over him. Carr had done all right so far, especially for an officer. Samples was going to protect him, not only because it was his duty, but also because he truly wanted to. Samples gave his head a quick shake. His thoughts were getting too deep and personal; he forced himself to listen to the forest and think about what they would do when dawn came.

Suddenly the events in the bunker replayed in his mind, forcing him to come to terms with the death of the enemy soldier. Samples had never killed someone with his bare hands before, and it wasn't pleasant. At the time he had been too scared and angry to even think about it, but now he found himself analyzing his own reactions. He hated that the boy had to die, but knew there had been no choice on their part. He briefly rationalized that it was Carr, and not himself, that had actually ended the young man's life, but recognized that was a cowardly excuse and dismissed it. They were equally guilty, but this was a war, after all, and that's what happened in a war—people died.

Taking off his helmet and setting it down beside him, and then resting his rifle on top of the helmet, Samples crossed his arms over his upright knees and laid his head on his arms. He knew from experience he could sleep in that position for only a few minutes at a time before the pain in his neck and back brought him back awake. Technically he should remain totally awake, but he knew that would be almost impossible, and probably pointless. Even asleep his mind would recognize unusual noises and bring him back to total consciousness in an instant. In base camp he had learned to sleep through an outgoing artillery barrage, but awaken instantly at the sound of incoming mortars or rockets.

Seated uncomfortably in the dirt, drifting in and out of sleep, Samples stood guard over Lieutenant Carr and prayed for the arrival of dawn.

THIRTEEN

It was an incredibly vivid dream. Carr was back at college, although the campus looked subtly different. He was late for an important class, but for some reason he couldn't find the right building. It was night time and no other students were around as he jogged down the tree-lined sidewalks, looking for the Liberal Arts building where he was supposed to take a final that would allow him to graduate. And then he saw the zombies. There was one, then two, then four zombies, all chasing him with their jerky shambling gait. Despite the slowness with which they pursued him, Carr could not outrun them. He felt stiff and weak, his legs stumbling over the curbs of narrow streets. He kept looking for his car, which he had left parked somewhere nearby, but couldn't find it. Then one of the zombies pitched forward and grabbed his ankle.

Waking up slowly, he heard a voice say, "Hey!" A hand that had been shaking his ankle let go. Carr opened his gummy eyes and blinked to clear them. Above him the sky was dark blue, not black, and only a couple stars still twinkled. Suddenly his mind cleared and he remembered where he was—and why. He struggled to a sitting position, rubbing the back of his neck and twisting his head around to remove the kinks. Across from him sat Sergeant Samples, his features almost distinguishable in the waning darkness.

"What time is it?" Carr asked groggily.

"About time to go," Samples answered. Carr looked at his watch, and by squinting he could make out the hands. It was 4:30.

"Why'd you let me sleep?" Carr asked, both angry and relieved.

"You needed it," Samples answered. "Don't worry, I dozed a little, too."

"Well, thanks, I guess." Carr wasn't sure what to make of Samples' gesture. It seemed generous, but also condescending at the same time. It was like Samples thought that Carr, a green lieutenant, needed sleep more than him, an experienced combat veteran. Ruefully, Carr thought, that's probably true. Still, he felt a little ashamed that he hadn't awakened on his own to take his watch. His mouth was dry and gritty, so Carr pulled out his canteen and took a drink, swishing the warm water around in his mouth before swallowing.

"Never thought I'd say it," Carr remarked casually, "but I'd kill for some C's right now." They hadn't eaten since lunch the day before, and now even C-rations sounded good.

"I've got a couple John Wayne bars," Samples told him, reaching into an ammo pouch on his pistol belt. He pulled out two foil wrapped disks slightly larger than silver dollars. They were hard chocolate candy infused with chopped nuts, and came in some of the C-ration cans along with round crackers. They got their name from the fact that they had the consistency of dried plaster, and only a real warrior could bite into them. Right now, they looked wonderful. Samples handed one to Carr, and they both unwrapped the candy and bit into them.

Carr managed to break off a small piece with his teeth and let it soften in his mouth for a moment before he began chewing. He was ravenously hungry, and he quickly devoured the rest of the meager breakfast. Another drink of water to wash it down, and he was as ready to go as he ever would be.

Looking around, Carr could now make out individual leaves on the trees against the steadily lightening sky. Dawn at last was approaching. Having survived the night, Carr was ebullient at the idea they would soon be back with their unit. All they had to do was walk a few miles through the forest. It sounded easy, and far safer than traveling at night would have been.

Carr picked up his helmet and rifle and stood up, placing the helmet on his head with a confident one-handed gesture. "Ready to go?" he asked Samples.

"Might as well," Samples said as he stood up, "can't dance."

Side by side they climbed up the south slope of the crater and entered the woods. With dawn only minutes away now, it was much easier to navigate through the woods. They found the crushed vegetation and tread marks of one the APC's that had come through the day before, and followed the path southward. Carr tried to estimate how far they had to go, and how long it would take them, but couldn't reach any firm conclusion. Yesterday they had been advancing slowly and carefully, and there had been several stops along the way. Today he and Samples were moving as quickly as was prudent, anxious to escape the dangers and discomfort of the forest and rejoin their comrades.

During the night the air had cooled, relatively speaking, to what would be considered a nice spring temperature back in the States. The woods blocked any breeze that might be blowing, however, and the activity of their rapid movement soon worked up a sweat. Carr wanted to get a drink from his canteen, but he was very aware of how little water was left in it, and how long it might be until they could get more. Soon he noticed sunbeams glinting through the tree tops, and sensed the increasing temperature. Just like every other day in Viet Nam—another hot one.

Sometimes Carr led the way, sometimes they walked side by side, and sometimes Samples led. They rarely spoke, saving their breath and energy for the long trek ahead. Their heads swiveled from side to side, searching through the trees for any sign of the enemy. Carr's pistol belt, weighed down with magazines, gas mask, and canteen, banged against his hips, while his helmet pressed against his skull, bouncing painfully when he stepped wrong. Occasionally his mind flashed back to the fight in the bunker, but he would quickly force his thoughts away from that terrible struggle, avoiding any reflection on his part in it. He had not yet experienced the great remorse and emotional upheaval portrayed in books and movies when the good guy has to kill someone, and he didn't want to start now. Once he was safe and had time, he would then contemplate his reaction and explore how the killing had affected him. For the time being, however, all he could think about was escape and survival.

That made him think of the S.E.R.E. training he had gone through in Officer Basic. Survival, Evasion, Resistance, and Escape, the training designed specifically for situations just like this. He had been taught how to find food and water, how to evade capture, how to resist torture if he was caught, and how to escape from a POW camp. During the evasion portion of the training, they had been required to traverse a large stretch of woods at night with only a compass and a map, avoiding capture by drill sergeants patrolling the entire area. Carr and a buddy had violated the rules and boundaries of the exercise and went way around the patrolled area, and then congratulated themselves on their initiative. Here, however, that option wasn't available.

After an hour or so they came to another string of bomb craters, and Carr called for a short halt. Just inside the tree line on the near side of a crater, they knelt down and rested. Carr pulled out his canteen and allowed himself just a sip of the tepid water. Samples did the same, and then took off his helmet to wipe his brow.

"How far do you think we've come?" Samples asked, putting his helmet back on.

"I don't know," Carr said. "Maybe a third of the way?"

"Think so? I'm trying to remember when we passed these craters."

"You remember these craters? They all look alike to me." Carr was still breathing heavily from the exertion of the last hour, and consciously slowed himself down.

"Well, yeah, pretty much," Samples agreed. "But it was around noon when we hit the first craters, and if these are them, then we might be almost halfway."

"I hope you're right," Carr said. He started to add something when he noticed Samples' expression change to one of alert wariness. Samples held a finger to his lips. Carr raised his head and opened his ears to the sounds of the forest. He detected something, but he wasn't sure what it was. The sound was not unlike the rustle of leaves in the wind, but it was a little too regular, and seemed to come from a single location, somewhere to their east. Carr saw Samples slowly and quietly lower himself into a prone position, so Carr did the same.

Carr looked east along the line of bomb craters, squinting against the sun that was now topping the trees. At the far end of the string, skirting around the farthest crater, he detected movement. A lone North Vietnamese soldier, armed with an AK-47, strolled southward, nonchalant and unconcerned about possible enemy ambush. The soldier's confidence was probably rooted in experience, Carr realized. Any American night ambush patrol would have departed by now, and a daytime patrol by straight-leg infantrymen would have been spotted long before it reached this area deep in the woods. And an ARVN patrol was simply not conceivable.

The man disappeared into the woods, and Carr was just wondering why a lone soldier was roaming the woods when another man appeared, this time toting an RPG launcher. Behind him came another soldier, carrying a pack, and then a third and fourth. It was a steady stream of NVA, all bearing weapons, all moving south. Carr counted twelve men in total. One had carried a heavy machine gun, followed by a man carrying the tripod for it, and two others toting cans of ammo. After the last man had moved out of sight, Carr and Samples waited for a good ten minutes, in case there were stragglers.

"Ambush team," Samples said in a whisper. "Maybe going for the convoys."

Carr nodded. Although it was a small detachment, it was too big for Samples and him to tackle. They needed to get back and warn someone. But now the enemy unit was between them and safety. "Can't keep going this way," Carr said.

"Cut southwest?" Samples offered. "Then cut back south. Can't go east, that's for sure."

"Think so," Carr agreed. He gathered his legs beneath him like a sprinter at the start line. "Cover me," he told Samples, then ran across the jagged berm that divided two of the bomb craters. Once he was again in the trees, he turned and signaled Samples to follow. The sergeant jogged across the open area and took cover behind a tree. They both watched the east end of the crater string, but there was no reaction.

Carr took a bearing from the sun, as best he could, and led off into the woods at an angle from their previous direction. He reduced his pace from what it had been before they saw the NVA team; with the enemy definitely active in the Crescent today, they could take no chances. Carefully, with as much speed as he dared, Carr picked his way through the woods, crossing at an angle the beaten-down areas where APCs had passed by. Samples followed a few paces behind him, constantly turning and sometimes even walking backwards to ensure they weren't being followed.

Suddenly there was a rapidly rising roar of helicopter blades, and several Hueys flashed overhead, skimming the treetops as they flew to the east. In less than a minute their sound faded away.

"Eagle flight," Samples said. That was what they called a group of troop helicopters carrying a straight-leg unit for an insertion somewhere. All Carr could think about was the fact that American forces had been just above them, but now they were gone. So near, and yet so far. They had had no opportunity to signal the choppers, and even if they had, the aircraft couldn't land to pick them up. The forest canopy that protected the movement of enemy troops also prevented any rescue of Carr and Samples. Carr cursed underneath his breath and pushed on.

An hour later they stopped to rest in a small glade. Carr sat down and leaned back against a tree trunk while Samples squatted gook-style, leaning his rifle against a bush so he could pull out his canteen. Each took a couple sips of water before putting the canteens back in their holders. Carr looked up at the small patch of blue sky framed by the trees.

"Think we can head back south now?" Carr asked conversationally.

Samples shrugged. "No way to be sure. These woods are crawling with gooks."

"But we should be far enough from those guys we saw," Carr mused out loud. "We need to get to the highway as soon as possible."

"Yeah, it looked like they were headed straight south. If they don't veer over this way, we shouldn't run into them."

"That's what I was thinking." Carr took off his helmet and scratched his head. "Wonder what the battalion's doing today?"

"Regrouping, I hope," Samples said. "We took a pretty good beating yesterday. They'll need fuel and ammo, track maintenance, and general recovery."

"They'll need to get a replacement for one-four," Carr said.

"The word we got last month was that there wasn't going to be any replacement tracks," Samples said, shaking his head. "We figured it meant they were planning to pull us out soon."

"And the Army never changes its mind," Carr said sarcastically. Samples gave the remark the small chuckle it deserved. Carr rubbed his face, fingering the bandage on his cheek. It was peeling up at the edges, but had stayed on well enough.

"How are you wounds?" Carr asked.

Samples felt his abdomen, then undid a couple buttons on his shirt and explored stomach. "Okay, I guess. They itch a little, which is supposed to be good."

"Well, have Doc Allman check 'em out when we get back, put clean dressings on them."

"Yes, sir," Samples said with a smile to show he wasn't being a smart-ass. He buttoned his shirt back up, put on his helmet, and stood up. Carr checked his watch as he, too, replaced his helmet and rose. Without saying anything, they had agreed it was time to continue moving.

"I'll take point for a while," Samples said, glancing around to orient himself. He strode off into the trees, and Carr followed. Carr realized that they were working together as a team much better now than they had before last night. He hoped it would continue.

Samples pushed yet another branch out of his face as he simultaneously stepped over a projecting tree root. They were now moving through a much denser patch of the woods, with limited visibility and slower going. It was approaching noon, and it was increasingly difficult to judge direction, even when the sun glinted through the roof of the forest. At this rate, he thought sourly, they might not make it to the road before dark. Thus, when he broke free from a particularly nasty batch of vines onto some sort of path, he decided to throw caution to the winds. Infantry training emphasized the policy of avoiding trails, as they could be booby-trapped, as well as a likely place to meet the enemy. Today, Samples believed, the reduction in travel time on the path outweighed its potential danger.

The trail wound in a vaguely north-south direction, and looked lightly traveled. It could even have been a game trail, if there was a lot of game in the woods, but Samples didn't think there was. Made by animals or humans, it didn't matter; it was a quicker and easier way to get where they were going. Samples glanced back at Carr, and the lieutenant nodded his agreement; he was obviously glad to get out of the thick brush as well. They strode down the trail at a faster pace than before, but Samples had to hold himself back from going too fast. The twists and turns of the trail meant he could see only a dozen or so yards ahead, and he didn't want to run headlong into a bunch of gooks headed the other way. Then, just as he was congratulating himself on their luck in finding the trail, it happened.

Unlike in the movies, events didn't go into slow motion. Nonetheless, Samples became hyper-aware of his surroundings and the actions that unfolded. He saw each finite movement in extreme detail, and his mind and body reacted with lightning speed to each occurrence.

As he followed the trail in a long gentle curve to the right, he veered around a large tree trunk and looked down the straightened path that arrowed through the brush for about twenty yards. Coming around the next curve in the trail appeared two figures who saw Samples at the same time he saw them. All of them came to a sharp halt.

Both of the people were dressed in the "black pajamas" worn by peasants in South Viet Nam. Baggy silk-like pants and a high-collared tunic, the outfits were also the "uniform" of the Viet Cong. On their feet were rubber flip-flops, which seemed totally inappropriate for walking in the woods. Hanging down their backs by a cord around their necks were the typical farmer's conical straw hats. The one in front, Samples realized with only mild surprise, was a woman. Small breasts pressed against the front of her tunic, and a long pigtail hung down in back. In her hands was an AK-47, its 30-round banana clip inserted, its barrel pointed toward the ground. She was young, but Samples couldn't tell how young. To him all Vietnamese women looked about fourteen years old, or sixty years old, with nothing in between. He had always wondered at what age they suddenly transformed from child-like to geriatric.

Behind the woman—or girl—was a young man who carried a filled burlap bag on top of his head, steadying it with one hand while the other hand was held out ready to push aside branches. He looked even younger than the girl. Each of them was small compared to Americans, maybe five-two and a hundred pounds. Slender, dark brown hair, brown eyes, only their different genders distinguished them from each other. Their eyes were wide with surprise at finding American soldiers out here in the woods. For a moment everyone froze, neither side wanting to initiate a skirmish.

Slowly Samples raised the barrel of his M-16 so that it was parallel to the ground, but pointed just to the side of the two VC, not directly at them. He sensed that Carr took a step to his left to clear his own field of fire. With as little movement as possible, Samples used his thumb to move the selector lever on the side of M-16 off 'SAFE'.

"Lai dei," Samples said, using the phrase he believed meant 'come here.' The girl's eyes darted from left to right, as if she was looking for someone else, or for an escape route. "Chieu Hoi," Samples tried next, offering them the repatriation program for VC who surrendered. Again no response.

"Drop your gun," Carr said from his left rear. Samples hoped the girl understood some English. Most young Vietnamese did.

The girl let go of the pistol grip of the rifle, allowing the barrel to rise and the stock to sink as she held the gun only by the front hand guard. Samples felt a surge of hope that she was going to surrender. Behind her the boy with the sack on his head was beginning to visibly tremble.

The girl looked down and her right hand shot to the side of the bolt housing, grasping the cocking handle and pulling it to the rear.

"Don't!" Carr shouted. She ignored him, but was having trouble with the weapon. She jerked on the cocking lever a couple times, then grasped the pistol grip and tried to bring the weapon to her shoulder. Samples was pretty sure she had not cleared the jam, but couldn't take the chance. He fired from his hip, squeezing off three rounds quickly on semi-automatic. His left ear was battered by the sound of Carr firing his own M-16, which the lieutenant had brought to his shoulder before firing. He felt Carr's spent casings bounce off his helmet and shoulder.

The wooden stock of the girl's AK splintered and she dropped it like a hot potato. Behind her the boy dropped the heavy bag and turned to run. Cursing the necessity, Samples raised his own M-16 to his shoulder and fired two shots at the retreating boy. The girl still stood there, a look of shock on her face. Slowly she turned and stumbled after the boy, then collapsed in a heap.

"Watch her!" Samples told Carr as he sprinted after the boy. He couldn't let the boy escape to tell others about the two Americans. He ran down the trail, spotting the red liquid drops that splattered in the dirt and on fallen leaves. He rounded another bend in the trail and skidded to a stop. The boy lay sprawled in the middle of the trail. He wasn't moving. Samples approached cautiously, prodding the boy's hip with the tip of his boot. There was no reaction. The boy was clearly dead.

Carr came up behind him. "She's dead," Carr told him.

"So much for the stopping power of the M-16," Samples said with disgust. When the Army had chosen the M-16, with its .223-caliber bullets, many soldiers had raised concern about the effectiveness of the small round. The official line had been that the bullet was designed to tumble when it hit flesh, thus providing a greater shock and increasing the destruction of the muscles and internal organs of the target. In actual practice, however, soldiers had not found much "tumbling" or real stopping power, as had just been amply demonstrated.

"A girl?" Carr asked plaintively.

"I heard there's a whole company of female VC around here somewhere," Samples replied. "Never thought I'd see one, though."

"They're just kids," Carr complained to himself.

"Dead kids now," Samples said, knowing how callous he sounded. "Better them than us."

Both of them stood there silently, staring down at the young boy's body.

"It was another bag of American rice," Carr said.

"No shit," Samples replied in a tired voice. "What else is new." The stupidity of the war was almost overwhelming.

"Think anyone heard the shots?" Carr asked, looking around anxiously.

"Fuck if I know," Samples said, adding "sir" without emotion. "We need to get out of here anyway." The question now, he knew, was whether to continue down this trail or not. It provided a faster route to safety, but clearly there was a risk of running into other enemy soldiers. The thickness of the woods undoubtedly muffled the sound of the gunfire, and it probably couldn't be heard more than half a click away, but there could have been NVA or VC within a half a click. There was no way to know for certain. Samples weighed the options and concluded that they needed to get away from this area as quickly as possible, and that meant staying on the trail.

He explained his logic to Carr, who reluctantly agreed. Samples released the partial magazine in his rifle and replaced it with a full magazine from his ammo bag, slipping the partial magazine into one of the cargo pockets of his pants. Carr emulated him. Stepping around the body, they moved out down the narrow trail, this time even more carefully than before.

FOURTEEN

Carr let Samples lead as they continued down the trail. His thoughts were skittering around like a pig on ice, and he didn't trust himself to make good decisions. He had participated in the killing of two more human beings, and he just didn't know what to think about that. Sure, Samples had been shooting, too, and it was possible that all of Carr's shots had missed the mark. But that didn't change the overall circumstances. Whether or not he had fired the fatal shots was irrelevant; he was complicit in the killings, and he had had every intention of killing them. That made three deaths within twenty-four hours. Plus however many he had unknowingly caused during the previous three days of battle. What did that make him?

Of course, he could rationalize that he was simply taking revenge for the deaths of Chacon and Jones, especially since the man they killed in the bunker had presumably been the one who fired the RPG that destroyed the one-four track. Carr was a little ashamed that he hadn't been filled with grief over the two American soldiers' deaths, which made the revenge logic a little lame, but he just wasn't able to deal with all this death on an emotional level yet. And none of that justified, at least morally, the death of the two VC kids.

Yes, it was a war, and supposedly that made it all right, but did it really? Back home college protestors railed against just this sort of logic, and it was hard to dispute their stance. Carr thought about the words to one of his favorite Eric Burdon songs: "A young soldier, so ill, looks at the Sky Pilot, remembers the words, 'Thou shalt not kill'." Yet here Carr was, killing with almost abandon. And what made it worse, he realized with self-contempt, was that he wasn't really sorry about it. He felt confused, he regretted the necessity, he deplored the circumstances, but he was not emotionally distraught over causing the deaths of the three young people. He felt little empathy for them, and even perhaps blamed them for forcing him to kill them. And what kind of person thought that way? Was he a psychopath, a homicidal maniac? He refused to believe that, if only because he felt no desire to kill anyone. It wasn't pleasurable, but it wasn't truly repulsive, either. He didn't want to be required to kill someone, but knew, now, that he could. It was a heavy realization.

These painful ruminations came to a sudden halt when Samples stopped suddenly in front of him. It took Carr a moment to figure out why, but then he saw the dilemma. Ahead the trail forked, and both paths looked equally well-trampled.

"What do you think?" Samples asked, staring alternately down each path, his head turning slightly back and forth.

Carr thought about it. "Wouldn't the left one take us back toward that patrol we saw?"

"To be honest with you," Samples said, "I'm not sure what direction either one is going. I think we're still headed south, but with the sun directly overhead, I've kinda lost my sense of direction."

Carr felt a wave of disappointment. He had lost his bearings as well, but had suppressed the worry in the belief that Samples knew exactly where they were going.

"Shit," Carr said, "me, too."

"There's no moss on the north side of trees here," Samples said morosely, "so that's out."

"Yeah, well, if only I hadn't lost my damn compass."

"No use crying over spilt milk," Samples offered. It was a trite homily, but Carr was glad that Samples wasn't holding him accountable. They stood there silently for a moment, listening to the subtle sounds of the forest. Carr closed his eyes and tried to somehow detect the points of the compass through an imagined sixth sense, but no magic arrow appeared. But he did hear the distant sound of a jet.

"Is that a Freedom Bird?" he asked. Samples tilted his head back and listened.

"I think so," Samples said.

Carr tried turning his body slowly in a circle, trying to judge where the sound of the distant airplane was the loudest. The dense canopy and tree trunks both muffled and echoed the sounds, so Carr made a second circle. He saw that Samples was doing the same. They both came to a stop facing down the right fork of the path. Assuming the airliner was taking off from Tan Son Nhut airport, it was somewhere to the south of them, which meant the right fork was the one to follow. Samples gave Carr a questioning look.

"The right one," Carr said more definitely than he really felt. Samples nodded, turned, and headed down the trail. Carr followed, hoping they had made the right choice. If not, they might find themselves hopelessly lost, walking in circles out in the Crescent until they died of thirst or were killed by gooks or friendly fire.

They followed the trail for several hundred yards, and Carr noticed that it was getting steadily narrower and slightly overgrown. Then they broke out into a small clearing and paused to take stock and rest a minute. Even though he could now see the sky, or at least a small portion of it, Carr was unable to tell which direction was which. The sun was burning directly overhead, and no aircraft were visible. Both men took small sips from their canteens.

"How much do you have left?" Carr asked, as if it were idle curiosity.

"A couple swallows," Samples answered. "You?"

"About the same. I'm getting really thirsty." Carr licked his dry lips and imagined an endless flowing fountain of pure spring water.

"Wish they had issued us two canteens each, like they do the straight-legs," Samples said. "But nooo, mech guys don't need two canteens, 'cause we got the water cans in the tracks. Except when the tracks aren't around."

Carr nodded his concurrence. It was a common complaint among the mechanized infantrymen that they were underequipped. No backpacks, no bayonets, no rifle slings, only one canteen, and two ammo pouches that were the wrong size for M-16 magazines. And for comfort items they had to scrounge, "finding" things they needed like poncho liners and cots to sleep on. A popular saying was that the infantry was called the queen of battle because they were always getting fucked.

"At least we've got our health," Carr said with a wry grin. Samples responded with a grim chuckle.

Carr looked around the rim of the clearing. "Do you see the trail?" he asked. Samples looked around as well. Both men walked the perimeter, seeking a continuation of the path that had led them there. Samples finally stopped and shook his head.

"Looks like this is the end of the trail," he said with a mock cowboy accent.

"Great," Carr moaned. "I guess now we're back to busting jungle."

"Yep. Uh, you want to take point for a while, sir?" Carr detected a touch of pleading in Samples' voice. Perhaps the sergeant felt he had led them down the wrong path, and didn't want the responsibility for taking them further astray. Or maybe he was just tired of being in front and making all the decisions. Carr could sympathize either way.

"Sure," Carr said easily. He looked back at the opening where they had entered the clearing, and estimated where the trail would have reentered the woods, had it continued in the same direction. He stepped over to the wall of bushes and shoved his way through. On the other side the woods closed back in, the deeper shade limiting the growth of the underbrush, and he only had to dodge around the tree trunks. Maintaining a straight line was more difficult than before, when they had a trail, but the chances of running into an enemy patrol were far less. Carr decided to be grateful for small favors.

Carr noticed that he wasn't sweating, which worried him. He was hot, tired, and terribly thirsty, and feared he might come down with heat exhaustion. He had been trained to recognize the symptoms, but the recommended treatment was out of the question. He should be taking salt tablets, drinking lots of water very slowly, and lying down with his shirt off while someone fanned him. That certainly wasn't going to happen anytime soon. Behind him he could hear Samples breathing heavily through his mouth; even the battle-hardened young sergeant was feeling the strain. Carr was glad to know that he wasn't the only one feeling the effects of their deprivation, but he was also concerned that Samples wouldn't be able to help Carr if he faltered. They had to rely on each other in equal measure, so Carr would just have to buck up and keep going.

Pushing aside what seemed to be the millionth branch of leaves that threatened to hit him in the face, Carr noticed the woods to his right seemed less shadowed. Perhaps there was another clearing over there? Or better yet, they had reached the edge of the Crescent somehow, and would soon be out of the woods. Fifty meters further he recognized the truth, and it did not improve his mood. They had reached the edge of the Rome Plow area, which was disappointing for several reasons. First, they had arrived at the long, thin, rectangular clearing at a very acute angle, instead of perpendicular, as they would have if they had been traveling straight south. That meant they had been wandering even more than they had feared, wasting time walking in large curves. Secondly, they now knew approximately where they were, and it wasn't as close to the road as they had hoped. They had crossed the Rome Plow two days ago, but not yesterday. So they had veered quite a distance west from the battalion's sweep route.

"Shit!" Carr cursed, sitting down on a fallen tree trunk that had penetrated the shade of the edge of the woods.

"God-mother-fuckin'-damn!" Samples said wearily, plopping down on the log beside Carr. It was now past noon, and they still had a long way to go. He took off his helmet and dropped it on the ground in front of him, and then leaned his rifle against the log. Using both hands he rubbed his itchy head and his face, rotating his head to get the stiffness out of his neck. "At least we know where we are now," he offered grimly. "Sort of."

"That's what I was just thinking," Carr said.

"Assuming this is the same Rome Plow as two days ago."

"Looks the same," Carr said, twisting his head to look up and down the stretch of jumbled trees.

"They all do," Samples remarked. "Are we east of where we were yesterday, or west?

"West," Carr replied. "Our night ambush went through the west end of it where it connected with the rice paddies north of the base. Our sweep day before yesterday hit the eastern end of it."

Samples tried to remember the activities of the day before yesterday, but everything that had happened since crowded them out. Then he thought about his dust-off, the trip in the helicopter to Dau Tieng. It had begun in the Rome Plow, and he closed his eyes to picture what it had looked like from the air. It was like a giant lawn mower had cut a swath through tall grass, but had somehow started in the middle of the lawn and ended near the edge. The clearing didn't connect with the Ben Cui, and barely with the rice paddies to the west. He had tried to figure out how they had brought the huge bulldozers in, and why they had cleared just that long strip, but gave up the effort as futile. There was frequently no reason why the Army did things the way they did. As soldiers often remarked, there were three ways to do anything—the right way, the wrong way, and the Army way.

"Seems like it wasn't that far from the road," Samples said judiciously. "Maybe a couple clicks." He stood up and looked up and down the length of the Rome Plow, trying to judge where they were in relation to either end. Through the heat haze he could see a line of tree tops off to the east, maybe a click away. To the west the clearing seemed to go on forever, the sides converging in the distance. He started to sit back down, but caught a flicker of movement. Several hundred meters to the west, on the north edge of the Rome Plow, he saw a green pith helmet briefly pop up above the clutter of trees and branches.

"Gooks!" he whispered to Carr while he ducked down. The lieutenant moved over beside him in a crouch.

"Where?"

Samples pointed along the edge of the Rome Plow. Now he couldn't see anything. He duck-walked out farther into the Rome Plow, wending his way between tree trunks until he found some branches sticking up in the air. Slowly he raised his head and gazed through the limbs. Carr followed him out. Samples realized he had left his helmet and rifle behind, but put that concern aside. From this angle he could see better. NVA soldiers appeared like magic in the edge of the Rome Plow and moved into the tree line to disappear again.

"Must be a tunnel," Samples said quietly. One of the soldiers popped up, then reached back and was handed up an RPG launcher. Then he too melted into the woods.

"Looks like the same guys we saw this morning," Carr suggested.

"Could be," Samples agreed. "But the little fuckers all look alike to me."

"Yes, but how many patrols of that size would be running around in this area right now?"

Samples shrugged. It made sense. "Regardless, we're fucked even more than before."

"Why?" Carr asked with a puzzled frown. "They're headed the other way."

"Those guys were coming out of a tunnel that probably goes all the way across the Rome Plow. That's how they can travel without being seen."

"Yeah?"

"They've got routes that go all the way from Cambodia to Saigon that are always covered, either by jungle or underground. Shit!" Samples was suddenly amazed and perturbed that he hadn't thought of it before. "They must have tunnels under the road to Dau Tieng, too."

"Okay," Carr said, "but what's that got to do with our current situation?"

"We know where this end of the tunnel is," Samples explained, "but we don't know where the other end is. Or who might be there." Samples could see from Carr's expression that he was rapidly grasping the potential complications. First, crossing the Rome Plow area would leave them exposed to anyone watching from the tree lines. Secondly, they might reenter the woods and stumble upon the other end of the tunnel, which might be guarded by the enemy. And third, they might inadvertently cross the trail that leads to that entrance and meet up with yet another gook patrol. Sure, that was a lot of 'maybes', but the accumulation was daunting.

Samples scuttled back to the tree line to retrieve his helmet and rifle. Carr joined him, and both knelt on the ground scanning the Rome Plow area and pondering the possible courses of actions.

"Little fuckers are good with tunnels," Samples said with reluctant admiration. "Got thousands of 'em, and they're almost impossible to find. I talked to one of the tunnel rats in Cu Chi."

"Tunnel rats?" Carr asked.

"We've got guys whose only job is to explore the tunnels. They go down in them with nothing but a flashlight and a .45. Man, I couldn't do that. The guy told me they've got whole camps down there, barracks, stores, hospitals. The tunnel rats go down there, kill anyone they find, and then blow the fuckers up."

"Jesus," Carr breathed.

"Not that it does any good. The gooks just build new tunnels." Samples studied the Rome Plow area some more, and finally spotted what looked like a possible route across it. He pointed it out to Carr. "What do you think?" he asked.

"I think anything we do could be wrong, but it's better to do the wrong thing than to do nothing. Let's go." Staying as low as they could, they crept out of the tree line and headed across the clearing, winding their way around, over, and under the fallen trees. The sun beat down on them, and Samples felt a tingle in his back as he worried about some gook spotting them and taking pot shots. Several times he led them into dead ends and cul-de-sacs of horizontal timber, forcing them to backtrack to find a different route that still afforded them some cover.

When they were about halfway across, they heard a helicopter buzzing far overhead. Samples thought about trying to signal it, but knew it was useless. Even if the people in the chopper saw them they would assume they were gooks in stolen American uniforms, and either ignore them or shoot at them. This was a free-fire zone, and no Americans were supposed to be there right now. There was nothing to do but push on.

FIFTEEN

Lieutenant Carr heaved a sigh of relief when he crossed the final log in the bright sunlight and slipped into the shade of the forest, and not just because it was slightly cooler. He had felt frighteningly exposed out in the Rome Plow, and by comparison the woods felt like a fortress. There were no enemy soldiers waiting for them, and no obvious tunnel entrances. Instead they found partially crushed bushes and broken branches that had apparently resulted from the battalion sweep of two days earlier. Tread marks were still visible in the forest floor. All they had to do now was follow those prints back to the road.

The lane trampled down by the APC was wide enough that Carr and Samples could walk side by side most of the time. Within a few minutes they had left the Rome Plow far behind, and Carr felt a tingle of optimism, hope that they would soon be out of the Crescent and back in what passed for civilization. It couldn't come too soon. His thirst was all he could think about now—the dryness of his mouth, the weakening of his muscles, the burning sensation of his skin. There was still around an ounce of water in his canteen, and it called to him like heroin to an addict. Carr convinced himself that they were now close enough to the road and to salvation that he could afford to take that last resurrecting sip.

"Break," Carr uttered, staggering to a stop. Samples didn't argue. Carr unsnapped the canteen cover and withdrew the brown plastic vessel. Unscrewing the top, he told Samples, "This is the last of it. How about you?"

Samples pulled out his own canteen and shook it like a bell to judge its contents. "Maybe one swallow," he said. He, too, unscrewed the lid. Looking at each other, they both raised the canteens in a silent toast and then drained them. Carr would never before have believed that hot chlorinated water would taste so wonderful, and he held the canteen upside down to his lips, tilting his head back, to wait for the last drops to trickle down into his mouth. When it became obvious that the canteen was truly empty, Carr reluctantly lowered it, screwed the lid back on, and put it back in the carrier. Samples had already replaced his own canteen and was snapping the cover back on.

"Hope there's some Coke kids out at the road," Samples said. "I'd kill for a cold soda."

"Me, too," Carr said fervently. Then he chuckled. "I don't know why, but that reminds me of a joke I read in Reader's Digest." Samples gave him a strange look, but Carr decided to push ahead. "A guy in Viet Nam has been writing to his new wife, telling her how horny he is, and she's been writing back saying the same thing. Just before he DEROS's, he writes her that when she meets him at the airport, she better have a mattress strapped to her back. She writes back and says she'll do that, but he better be the first man off the plane."

Samples actually laughed out loud, and Carr was extraordinarily pleased with the reaction. They both needed cheering up. Incongruously grinning, they resumed their march through the woods.

About an hour later the woods quickly thinned and they broke out of the tree line. Fifty yards away, across a strip of waist-high weeds and brush, was the red-brown dirt highway stretching off to left and right. It was mid-afternoon, and the road was deserted. The lack of traffic was disappointing, and perhaps a little unsettling. "Where is everyone?" Carr asked rhetorically, wading forward through the weeds.

"Siesta, maybe," Samples answered with no conviction. "Vietnamese take a two-hour break for lunch."

"Are you shittin' me?" Carr wasn't really surprised, but wanted to keep the dialogue going, to take his mind off his concerns.

"When I was with MACV," Samples said, "we had to plan around the lunch break. Even the VC and NVA stopped the war at noon."

"That's crazy."

"Well, they been fighting this war for over twenty years, so they probably figure they might as well take it easy, because it ain't gonna end tomorrow."

Carr shook his head at Samples' cynicism, while recognizing the wisdom in the observation. Maybe those cultural differences were the root cause of the lack of American progress in the war. Americans were too concerned about short-term success, while the Vietnamese were more patient and ready to take the long view.

They reached the highway, crossing the ditch and climbing up on the raised roadway. They looked both ways, staring through the heat shimmer at the vacant road that stretched off in the distance. Nothing moved.

"Fuck me," Samples said. "I was hoping for rush hour."

"Bound to be someone come along pretty soon," Carr told him encouragingly, although he didn't really feel it himself.

"Ought to be some of those Lambrettas or mopeds," Samples observed. "Something." The local Vietnamese used three-wheeled Lambretta scooters as buses, the tiny benches behind the driver crammed with people, some hanging on to the outside.

Carr checked his watch. "It's after three. Lunch break should be over."

Samples shrugged. "Might have to hoof it," he said. "Think we're closer to Dau Tieng, or to Wood?"

Carr looked east and west, trying to figure out exactly where they were. "Probably Wood," he surmised. "Don't you think?"

"Six of one," Samples said, not bothering to finish the saying. Tilting his rifle up and back to rest on his shoulder, he turned and strode down the middle of the dusty highway toward the west. Still not sure if they were doing the right thing, Carr followed. He quickly caught up and fell into step beside his sergeant. They didn't speak—there was nothing to say.

Slowed by fatigue and thirst, they slogged on, barely lifting their boots from the ground, and occasionally stumbling over small rocks or potholes. Carr figured they were at least two miles from FSB Wood. He wasn't positive he could make it.

Behind him Carr heard a whine, like a mosquito buzzing his ear, and absently he swatted at it. The whine got louder, and deepened in tone. Samples jerked his head a little, apparently hearing it too. Both men stopped and slowly turned to face the east. There was a dot hovering just above the road, leaving a thin trail of dust. Carr realized it was the heated air from the road that made the object appear to float, and as it got closer, he was able to distinguish a small motorcycle. It was one of the ubiquitous Honda 50 bikes, with tiny engines that rang more than roared. Soon he could make out the driver, a young Vietnamese man with a cowboy hat and a plaid long sleeve shirt, with mirrored sunglasses. Behind him sat a girl wearing black silk pants and a light blue tunic. She was holding on to the driver with one hand while using the other to keep her conical straw hat firmly on her head.

Carr waved his arm and stepped over in front of the bike. He looked right at the driver's face, but the young man stared straight ahead, avoiding any eye contact. Samples stepped up beside him and spread his arms. The young man's gaze never wavered, and he swerved to go around them without slowing at all. As the bike zoomed by, Carr caught the eyes of the girl, and she gave him a look that seemed both sorrowful and worried. Then the couple was disappearing to the west, the bike's rattling whine fading into the distance.

"Why didn't he stop?" Carr complained.

"Because we're Americans," Samples replied, as if it was obvious.

"But he's South Vietnamese. We're on his side."

"Yeah, just like the Japanese in World War II, and then the French."

Carr was a little disturbed at Samples' cynical outlook, even though he recognized the truth of it. He sighed with resignation and resumed walking, following the motorcycle.

"Even if he had stopped," Samples pointed out, walking beside Carr, "what good would it have done? That bike wouldn't carry all of us, and we don't speak Vietnamese."

"He probably speaks English," Carr argued listlessly. "He could have taken a message."

"He's a pimp, so yeah, he probably does speak a little. But who would listen to him?"

Carr knew Samples was right, but it annoyed him just the same. He tried to think of a good come-back, but failed. He was too tired and thirsty. He stared down the ruler-straight road, hoping to see some sign of the American presence. At first he didn't believe it, and blinked his eyes rapidly to clear them. Sure enough, there was a black speck approaching them through the haze.

"He's coming back," Carr said hopefully.

"Don't think so," Samples said. "Listen."

Instead of the tinny hum of a Honda, there was a deep rumble of diesels. That meant big vehicles, almost certainly American.

"Yes!" Carr chortled happily. They stopped to await the arrival of the distant vehicles.

"Convoy," Samples said. "Pretty late in the day for them, and why are they going so slow?"

In his exultation at the impending rescue, Carr hadn't noticed the speed of the approaching vehicles until Samples commented on it. Indeed, they were coming at what seemed a snail's pace. Convoys normally roared down the road as fast as they could, to minimize their exposure to ambush.

Out of habit Samples kept glancing around, searching the tree lines on either side of the road for anything suspicious. Everything seemed normal and quiet. The convoy was rumbling up toward them, and he was now able to make out some of the individual vehicles. In the lead was one of the Commando armored cars used by the Military Police for convoy escort. An angular lozenge-shaped vehicle perched high on four huge wheels, it was a curious but interesting piece of lightly armored hardware. As it got closer, he saw the small cupola turret on top that housed a couple small-caliber light machine guns, and on top of the turret was a pedestal mount with a .50-cal machine gun as well. The driver had his hatch open and his head sticking out while he drove, and another MP stood in the cupola holding on to the fifty.

Behind the armored car was a string of trucks, deuce-and-a-half's and five tons, all crawling along at less than ten miles an hour. The first truck in line, a five ton, was belching black diesel smoke like a train in a Western movie. There were about ten trucks in all, and at the tail end Samples could see a jeep with a pedestal-mounted M-60 machine gun. Samples waved his hand at the Commando, signaling for them to stop. The vehicle rolled to a stop beside them, and the line of trucks accordioned as it, too, came to a halt.

The Commando's driver was a black man wearing a boonie hat, and he stared at them with mild curiosity. The man behind the machine gun was freckle-faced with a pug nose, a look Samples always associated with people of Irish descent. He was wearing a shiny helmet liner emblazoned with a stripe and the MP lettering. His lapels held the rank pins for a staff sergeant, the same as Samples'.

"What's up?" the gunner asked, releasing the gun and leaning over the edge of the cupola. "Sir," he added when he saw Carr's collar.

"Can we catch a ride?" Samples asked. "We're tired of walking."

"Sure, if you're going to Dau Tieng. That's where we're headed." He had a southern drawl, Samples noticed, perhaps Texas or Arkansas.

"Thank you, sergeant," Carr said. "Dau Tieng will be fine."

The MP dropped down inside and then reappeared at the side door. The door on the Commando was a two-piece affair, like a Dutch door; the upper part opened sideways and was already latched open. The sergeant released the lower part of the door, which dropped down and formed a step. He climbed down and stepped over to Samples and Carr, brushing dust from his uniform as he did so. His nametag identified him as Sergeant Canady. His uniform, other than the accumulation of road dust, was clean and pressed, and his boots were impeccably polished. He wore a pistol belt that held only a holster containing a .45 pistol. He didn't offer to shake hands, instead hooking his thumbs in his belt.

"So what are y'all doin' out here by your lonesome?" he asked. He was smiling, but there was a hint of officiousness in his tone. Typical for a cop, Samples told himself.

"We got separated from our unit yesterday," Carr explained. "Had to walk home."

"They didn't come lookin' for you?" Canady was clearly surprised, and maybe even a little suspicious.

"Thought we were dead," Samples told him. Canady frowned, and then shrugged. He glanced down the road at the convoy and winced.

"Shit!" the MP cursed. The driver of the first truck, the one that had been smoking, had climbed out and opened the hood. The truck was no longer smoking, evidence that it had stopped running entirely. "That son of a bitch has been draggin' ever since we left Cu Chi," Canady griped. "We'll never get there at this rate. You guys go ahead and climb in, get comfortable. I got to go jack this guy's ass up." Canady turned and strode purposefully off toward the stalled truck.

Samples gestured for Carr to precede him, and watched as the lieutenant climbed into the armored car with some difficulty. Samples followed him, and also had problems negotiating the narrow doorway and tall steps. He realized they were both weak from thirst and hunger. Inside the cramped confines of the Commando, he sat down beside Carr on a short narrow bench seat. The driver had dropped his seat down inside and turned to look at them. He was more tan than black, and had fine features now creased into a welcoming smile.

"Spec 4 Cohen," he said in the way of introduction. "And yes, I know I don't look Jewish."

Samples had to laugh, because that was just what he had been thinking. "Hell, Specialist," Samples told him jokingly, "I had you pegged as Norwegian." All three laughed.

"I'm Lieutenant Carr, and this is my platoon sergeant, Staff Sergeant Samples." Carr looked around the crowded light-green interior of the vehicle. "Have you got anything to drink in here?"

"We ran out of water a couple hours ago," Samples explained. "Been out in the boonies since yesterday."

"I got some sodas," Cohen said, rummaging around in a bin behind his seat. He pulled out a couple cans of Coke, and Samples had never seen anything that looked that good to him before. "They're not cold," Cohen warned as he passed them back. Samples truly didn't care. He handed one to Carr, then lovingly popped the top of his can and glowed as the soda fizzed out and splattered his hand. Closing his eyes, he raised the can to his lips and let the wonderful elixir flow over his tongue and down his throat. It burned, but in a good way. He realized the carbonation was probably a good thing, as it kept him from drinking too quickly. Nonetheless, he had drained the can within a minute.

"God, that's good!" he breathed when he was finished. Beside him Carr shook the can and tilted his head back, trying to get the very last drop out of it.

"Damn straight," Carr agreed. "Got any more?"

Cohen shook his head. "We were supposed to be in Dau Tieng a couple hours ago. We've already drunk up the rest we had. Might be something in one of the trucks."

"We can wait," Carr conceded.

You got anything to eat?" Samples asked. With his thirst partially satiated, he now realized how hungry his was.

Cohen dipped into the bin again, pushing stuff around. He came up with two very short cans, each less than an inch tall. "Got a couple cans of peanut butter," he offered. Both Samples and Carr shook their heads. They were still thirsty, and the peanut butter would be like glue in their mouths. Cohen looked around some more, and came up with a Hershey bar. It was the extra dark candy that came in the SP packs, more like baking chocolate than anything. It was the only kind of chocolate that wouldn't melt in the heat of Viet Nam. It barely melted in your mouth. But Samples was so hungry he reached out and grabbed it. He stripped off the paper and broke the hard bar in half, handing the larger section to Carr. The both broke off pieces with their teeth and crunched the chocolate into smaller pieces until it began to melt so they could swallow it.

Canady appeared and climbed into the vehicle, then bent down and pulled the door up until it latched. "Got the fucker runnin' again," he told Carr and Samples, then turned to Cohen. "Let's go," he ordered, then climbed up into the turret. Cohen turned to the front, raised his seat so his head was above the hatch opening, and put the vehicle in gear. With a slight lurch it moved forward and was again rolling down the highway. The upper doors were open on both sides, and a hatch on the roof at the rear was open. The air rushing through was a welcome relief from the stifling heat that had built up inside while they were stopped.

Samples removed his helmet and set it on the end of barrel of his rifle, which he held vertically between his knees. He took another bite of the chocolate bar. Carr set his helmet on the floor, and Samples saw that the lieutenant's eyes were closed as he slowly chewed on his portion of the Hershey.

"Beats the hell out of walkin'," Samples said. The slow speed of the convoy, along with the relatively even surface of the roadway, let the armored car rock gently like a boat on a lake. He felt relaxed for the first time in a couple days, and had to fight to stay awake.

"Not much faster, though," Carr commented. Samples had to agree. Through the open upper door he could see the tree line flowing by at a glacial pace.

"So how'd you get left behind?" Canady yelled down at them from above. All they could see of him was from the waist down.

"Our track got blown up," Samples shouted back over the engine and tire noise. "They thought we were in it."

"That's the shits," the MP yelled sympathetically. "So you been out in the woods since yesterday?"

"That's right."

"Musta been rough. Well, we'll get you to Dau Tieng pretty soon. That okay?"

"Sure," Samples replied. "Our company headquarters is there."

"Come on!" Canady pleaded, apparently talking at the truck behind them. "Better slow down, Art," Canady said to the driver, "you're getting' ahead of 'em again." Samples felt the deceleration and gritted his teeth in frustration. He wanted to get back to the unit, and this was taking far too long. Carr seemed equally impatient.

"How far?" Carr yelled. At first neither of the MPs responded, and then Cohen held out his hand for them to see with three fingers raised.

"About three clicks," Cohen shouted back.

"We might get there before dark," Samples muttered grumpily, "if we're lucky."

"Mother fuck!" Canady barked. "Stop. Stop." Cohen applied the brakes and brought the Commando to a gentle halt.

Canady dropped down inside and wrestled with left door latch. "Fucker stopped again," he complained as the door swung down. "Jesus H. Christ!" He climbed out of the vehicle and ran toward their rear. Up front Cohen picked up a paperback book and started reading. With no air flow, the inside of the armored car began to heat up again. Samples put on his helmet and moved to the door.

"I gotta get some air," he told Carr, climbing out onto the road.

SIXTEEN

Although Carr hated to admit it even to himself, the security of the armored car around him allowed him to relax for the first time in days. He had no obligations, no responsibilities, and no concerns about being spotted and shot at. He felt a little guilty about his temporary retreat from the real world, but wanted to enjoy it while he could. Then the heat started to get to him, and he began to wonder what the situation was outside. He didn't want to stand out in the open, like Samples, but he felt like a coward for hiding inside the Commando, as well as cut off from whatever was going on around them.

At the back of the vehicle, on the right side of the roof, was a small square hatch that was open. Leaving his rifle and helmet by the bench, he maneuvered around the inner wheel wells, supports, cables, and random equipment to poke his head out. A very light breeze cooled his head just enough to feel better than inside, so he pulled himself up until his entire upper body was clear. Next to him a pedestal had been welded to the top of the vehicle, on top of which was a small ammunition tray and pintle for an M-60 machine gun. Carr has seen an M-60 strapped to one of the inside walls. He thought that it was unusual, but logical, to have a machine gun that covered the rear of a vehicle like that, sort of like the tail gunner on a World War II bomber. It was just hard to imagine the circumstances under which the gun would be useful.

From this elevated position he had a good view of all the surroundings. About thirty yards behind the Commando was the disabled truck, its hood up and Sergeant Canady arguing with the driver. Further back the drivers and co-drivers of the other trucks were milling around on the road, some checking tires and load restraints, others just looking bored. On either side of the road was a strip of land cleared of trees, now overgrown with weeds and small bushes. Beyond this open area was the forest, dark even in this bright afternoon sunlight. To the north of the road the woods were known as the Crescent. To the south they were known as the Boi Loi Woods, although ecologically they were the same forest, divided by the highway and interrupted only by the Ben Cui rubber plantation somewhere up the road. Carr looked to the east and thought he detected the taller tree tops of the Ben Cui less than half a click away. At the Ben Cui this highway made a sharp left turn to go north for a mile or so, and then turned east again to cross the Saigon River and enter Dau Tieng.

Since he wasn't going to go back in the woods any time soon, or so he hoped, Carr decided to get a little more comfortable. He unhooked his pistol belt, pulled it up through the narrow opening, and laid in on the roof. Then he unbuttoned his shirt, shrugged out of it, and rolled up the sleeves. That done, he put the shirt back on and replaced the pistol belt. It was a small change, but it greatly improved his general attitude. Having his arms bare signified that he was out of the woods, literally.

"Sergeant Samples," Carr called out. He couldn't see the sergeant, his line of sight blocked by the bulk of the armored car. Samples stepped into view and looked up him questioningly. "Uniform of the day," Carr said, pointing to his bare arm.

"Roger that, sir," Samples replied with a smile. He leaned his rifle against one of the wheels and rolled up his own sleeves without taking off the shirt. Doing it that way wasn't as neat and tidy as removing your shirt, but it was quicker and more efficient.

The MP sergeant came striding back and stopped where he could address both Carr and Samples. "He thinks he found the problem," Canady said, shaking his head dubiously. "Be another ten minutes or so. He says." Putting one foot on the step formed by the open side door, he leaned into the vehicle and spoke to the driver. "Art, you got any ass-wipes in there?" A moment later he stepped back onto the road, a couple of the small brown packets of toilet paper from the C-ration boxes in his hand.

"I've had the trots lately," Canady said. "Gonna check on the truck again, then go take a dump in the woods. Can you fellas mind the store?"

"Go ahead, Sergeant," Carr told him. He wasn't pleased that Canady was taking the situation so lightly, but he couldn't really refuse the sergeant's request. As the MP walked away, Carr and Samples exchanged looks of disdain. Nobody in the Army really liked MPs, and this guy was a good example of why.

With his helmet still inside, Carr's lack of headgear meant the sun was blinding. He put one hand to his forehead to shade his eyes and peered at the surroundings, rotating slowly to take in the entire area. He stopped to look at the area to the front right, idly wondering if he could detect any significant difference in the foliage of the Boi Loi Woods from that of the Crescent. Trees and bushes all look alike, he decided. Even back home he couldn't tell an oak from an elm; the best he could do was differentiate between deciduous trees and evergreens. As he turned his head to scan the north side of the road, he caught a flicker of movement where he had just been looking. He shifted his gaze back, and at first didn't see anything out of the ordinary. Then another disturbance in the stillness of the tree line. A couple hundred meters to their front Carr's eyes registered just a microsecond glimpse of a man darting from the tree line in a crouch and disappearing into the low brush of the cleared strip. He closed his eyes for a couple seconds to replay in his mind what he had just seen. It was a man carrying a long thin object that suspiciously resembled an RPG launcher.

"Aaron!" Carr called quietly but urgently. Samples, who had been sitting on the door's step, moved away so he could see Carr.

"Yeah?"

"Gooks." At this warning, Samples crouched down and swiveled his head rapidly back and forth, searching out any signs of enemy activity. "At our one o'clock," Carr told him, keeping his voice down. "Go up in the turret."

Samples nodded and climbed inside, his helmet popping up in the machine gun cupola a moment later. He kept his head low, peering around the base of the machine gun mount. "Where?" Samples asked.

"About two hundred meters. See that one tree that leans out at an angle?"

After a moment, Samples said, "Yeah."

"Just past that. I saw a gook with an RPG launcher come out of the woods and head toward the road."

"See any others?"

"No," Carr said. "I barely saw the one."

"There's bound to be more," Samples said grimly. "Setting up an ambush."

The highway was swept every morning for mines, with troops guarding the engineers and simultaneously searching the areas on either side of the road for ambushes. But that had undoubtedly been done earlier this morning, and with this convoy running so late, the gooks had had plenty of time to move in after the American troops were gone. Carr knew there was probably a platoon outposting somewhere along the road, but it might not be close enough, even if they could contact them.

Carr dropped down inside the armored car and moved forward enough to retrieve his helmet and rifle. "Cohen," he called to the driver, who was still reading his novel. The soldier looked up. "There's an ambush up ahead. Call for help."

"Ambush?" Cohen said disbelievingly. "No shit?"

"About two hundred meters in front of us. Get on the horn."

"Yes, sir," Cohen replied anxiously, dropping the book and reaching for a headset and mike. "Where's Sergeant Canady?"

Samples heard the question and called down from the turret, "Taking a shit. Call it in."

Cohen starting calling, and while he waited for a response, Carr asked him where the ammo was for the M-60. Speaking urgently into the mike, Cohen pointed to a cabinet next to Carr. Carr opened it and found two boxes of 7.62. Leaving his rifle on the bench, Carr grabbed one of the boxes and set it nearer to the rear hatch. Fumbling with the buckles, he unstrapped the M-60 from the wall and pushed it barrel-first up toward the hatch.

Behind him Samples squatted down and looked at the two machine guns mounted in the base of the cupola. "How the fuck do these work?" he asked with frustration.

Cohen finished what he was saying into the mike, and then told Samples, "They don't. We just use the fifty." Samples straightened up, and Carr heard him open the ammo box and check the mechanism on the heavy machine gun. Meanwhile Carr maneuvered the M-60 out the hatch and fumbled with the mounting pin until the gun was locked onto the pintle. Ducking back inside he grabbed the ammo box and pulled it up to slam into the tray. Surprising himself, he got it in the right way the first time, and quickly popped the release and flipped back the lid.

With a twist of a lever he released the top cover of the machine gun and held it up with one hand as he reached into the ammo can and found the first round on the belt. He laid the end of the belt into the bolt mechanism and carefully closed the cover down to hold it in place. He pulled the charging handle to the rear sharply and pushed it back forward to load the first round into the breech. Cocked and locked, he was now ready to fire.

Samples made sure the fifty was ready to fire, and glanced back to see Lieutenant Carr preparing the M-60. He was gratified that Carr seemed to know what he was doing. He looked down into the driver's compartment ahead of him, and saw Cohen putting on a CVC helmet. "They comin'?" Samples asked.

Cohen looked up, a touch of panic in his eyes. "They said they'd be here in fifteen minutes."

"Who? Who are they sending?"

"I don't know," Cohen admitted.

"Sergeant Canady!" At the back Carr was calling for the MP, but there was no response. Samples saw Carr waving at the truck drivers to get back in their trucks, but they just looked confused.

"Here they come!" Cohen yelled. Thinking Cohen meant the gooks were attacking, Samples grabbed the machine gun handles and searched for a target. Then he small the distance shapes on the road raising a cloud of dust. He realized that Cohen was talking about the reinforcements he had requested, and felt a surge of hope. Until he realized that the approaching column was in fact just another supply convoy, led by a jeep.

"Fuck!" Samples cursed. He turned to Carr and said, "We can't wait. We've got to bust the ambush." He realized Carr couldn't see the oncoming convoy, his view blocked by the turret. "Another convoy is coming this way," he added in explanation.

"Rock out," Carr told him simply.

Samples dropped back down inside and stretched out to pull the lower door closed. "Cohen," he barked, "get this fucker moving. Drive right down the tree line." Cohen gave him a blank look. "Now!" he screamed. Cohen nodded and turned to his controls. Samples stood up to grasp the handles of the fifty as the armored car suddenly lurched forward. The vehicle bounced off the raised roadway and through the ditch at an angle, tossing Samples from side to side, and then Cohen gunned it toward the tree line. Bushes and tall weeds scraped along the angled underside of the Commando, the huge wheels and knobby tires rolling right over the brush in a headlong rush.

When he reached the wood line, Cohen turned to run parallel to it, and simultaneously lowered his seat so he head was no longer exposed. Now he would have to drive using only the limited vision ports to guide by. Samples didn't care, he was too busy seeking out the enemy. He couldn't see them, but he knew they were there, so he opened up.

Pressing the butterfly trigger, he fired a short burst at the ground directly ahead of them. Then another burst, and another, shifting his aim first to the cleared strip, and then the tree line, spraying the area at random. The jerky motion of the armored car made aiming difficult at best, but he kept firing. If he didn't hit anything, at least he might keep them from returning fire. From the corner of his eye he saw someone rise up from the bushes to his left, an RPG on the man's shoulder. Samples pushed the machine gun's handles to the right, turning the barrel to the far left, but it wouldn't swing far enough to bear on the gook. At that moment he decided he was well and truly fucked.

Lieutenant Carr also saw the RPG gunner pop up out of the weeds, and he was in a better position to do something about it. Throwing his body back against the right side rim of the hatch, he swiveled the M-60 by the pistol grip and brought it to bear on enemy soldier just as he took a stance and aimed at the speeding Commando. Carr pulled the trigger and held it down as he sent a stream of bullets at the gook, walking the rounds toward him by observing the flight of the tracers. Unnerved by the onslaught, the man jerked as he pulled the trigger on his launcher, and with a boom and a whoosh the rocket spewed from the launcher and zoomed just over the top of the armored car. A millisecond after the launch Carr's bullets found their target, and the gook crumpled in a heap. Carr heard the explosion of the RPG in the woods, but didn't bother to look at it. He was too busy seeking new targets in the tall grass and brush.

No more enemy could be seen, but Carr knew they had to be there, hidden in spider holes or hastily dug bunkers. He kept firing in short bursts at any clumps of bushes or logs that looked like they might hide someone, watching the ground recede as the armored car jolted along the tree line. The heavy thumping of the 50-cal stopped, and Carr heard Samples shout at the driver to hold up. Carr stopped firing, too. It appeared they had passed through the ambush area completely. Carr watched the area closely, his finger on the trigger, ready to blast any movement. With his left hand he felt inside the ammo can, and decided it was still almost half full. Behind him he heard the clanking and snicking of Samples loading a fresh can of ammo for the fifty.

"Another pass?" he said over his shoulder.

"Roger that," Samples answered. "And, hey, thanks for getting that RPG."

"No sweat," Carr told him, smiling to himself. "I figured it was the least I could do." Carr glanced around close to the Commando, in case someone was sneaking up on them, and noticed the shiny oval divots in the dark green paint on the sides of the armored car. It took a second to sink in. Those were bullet marks, which meant someone had been shooting back at him. He hadn't heard them at all. Reflexively he ran his hand over his upper body and face, checking to see if he was bleeding, but when he looked at his palm, it remained dirty but dry. "Wow!" he said to himself.

"Cohen," Samples commanded the driver, "make a U-ey and head back down the tree line, as close to it as you can get."

If Cohen responded, Carr couldn't hear it, but the vehicle began moving again, making a tight circle out toward the road and then back to the wood line. When they were making the turn, Carr saw that the other convoy had stopped, undoubtedly alerted by all the shooting. As instructed, Cohen guided the Commando right up to the trees, so close they were in the shade and branches were swiping the sides and occasionally the top of the armored car.

"Watch for the limbs!" Samples yelled at Cohen, ducking to avoid a branch that caught on the machine gun mount and slid past it like a whip aimed at Samples' face.

"You get the woods," Carr shouted at Samples, "and I'll get the open area." Samples nodded his understanding, and began firing short bursts between the trees as they passed by. Carr awkwardly maneuvered the M-60 around and opened up on the semi-cleared area between them and the road. He saw the barely perceptible flicker of a muzzle flash from under a small shrub, and swung the machine gun to spray that area as they sped by.

The Commando swung out toward the road a few yards to avoid a low tree limb, and suddenly there seemed to be an echo of Samples' fifty-cal in the woods. Carr heard the snap of rounds breaking the sound barrier and felt the shudder as large bullets slammed into the sides of the vehicle. The gooks had a heavy machine gun in the woods, probably a .51 caliber, and it was aimed right at them. Samples swung the fifty around and sprayed the woods, while Cohen stepped on the throttle to get them out of range. Carr dropped down inside to take cover, and noticed with alarm an irregular line of holes in the left side wall through which sunlight glinted. Like the M-113 armored personnel carriers he was familiar with, the Commando apparently also used the aluminum alloy armor that was only effective against smaller caliber rounds. Like a jack-in-the-box, Carr popped back up in the hatch and grabbed the M-60, ready to fire.

They were almost back to where they had started, and the armored car slowed and came to a stop.

"Cohen!" Samples barked. "Cohen! Turn it around."

Carr ducked down again and looked to the front of the vehicle. He could see Cohen's back up in the driver's seat, but his head was hanging to one side. Blood was running down his neck.

"He's hit!" Carr shouted at Samples as he scrambled through the crowded interior to the front.

"How bad?" Samples asked, crouching down on the turret stand.

Carr reached the young man and touched his neck to feel his pulse. It seemed to be steady, but Cohen was unconscious. There was a huge gouge in his scalp from which blood was flowing steadily. "He's alive," he reported to Samples. "But just barely."

Without prompting, Samples pulled out his only field dressing and handed it forward to Carr. Carr knew there was probably a first aid kit somewhere in the vehicle, but they didn't have time to search for it. Quickly he tore open the plastic cover, unwound the gauze strips, and pressed the pad onto Cohen's head wound. He wound the strips around the boy's jaw and neck and tied them off on top of the pad. It was a sloppy job, but it did the trick.

"We gotta get that gook machine gun," Samples said.

"Yeah," Carr replied. "Let's get Cohen to the back and lay him on the floor. I'll drive." He pulled on Cohen's shoulder and tilted him off the seat, while Samples reached forward and grabbed the bloody shirt. It was frustratingly challenging to maneuver the limp body through the cramped confines, and both Carr and Samples were grunting and wheezing at the effort. Sharp corners jabbed Carr in the arms and sides, and various cables kept getting tangled around Cohen's arms and legs, but eventually they were able to stretch him out on the rear floor, using a seat cushion as a pillow. During the attempt Carr's helmet had come off and rolled away somewhere. He didn't bother looking for it.

"You know how to drive one of these things?" Samples asked.

"Not really. Do you?"

"Never been in one before," Samples admitted.

"Then I'll figure it out," Carr assured him. "You're better on the fifty."

Carr made his way back forward to the driver's compartment, trying, and failing, to avoid getting any of Cohen's blood on his hands. Climbing into the driver's seat, he wiped his bloody hands on his pants and studied the controls. There was a steering wheel, a couple pedals on the floor, and round instruments on the dash. It appeared to be just like a car or truck. Carr took hold of the steering wheel and pressed lightly on the gas pedal. The engine note rose and the vehicle began creeping forward. Okay, he thought, that works. There were four vision ports with thick bulletproof glass, two that looked straight forward, and one on either side at a 45-degree angle. Carr could see, but not very well, and only within a limited field of view.

It took him a minute, but he finally figured out how to raise the seat until his head was above the rim of the driver's hatch. He had no helmet, no hat, and no protection, but at least he could see where he was going. He looked up behind him where Samples was poised behind the fifty. "Where you headed?" he asked like a taxi driver.

"To Hell, probably," Samples replied with a grin. "Meanwhile, we've got to get into the woods and hit them from the flank."

"Roger that," Carr said. "Hold on."

Samples had both hands on the grips of the fifty-cal, his eyes scanning both the wood line and the open areas for any signs of the enemy. With a couple jerks and stops Carr got the Commando moving and swung it around in a circle until it was facing the trees.

"See that gap just to the left?" Samples called down. Carr nodded. "Let's go in there." As the vehicle jolted over the cleared area, aiming for an opening in the trees that appeared to offer an entrance to the forest, Samples fired off a couple bursts into the gap. Off to his left a figure rose from the underbrush and ran for the woods. Samples swiveled the machine gun over and fired a burst just as the man reached the trees. The soldier's AK-47 flew up in the air and the man slammed into a tree trunk and collapsed. The armored car passed into the shade of the trees, and Samples' eyes took a moment to adjust to the relative darkness.

The woods here were not as heavy as some they had seen in the last few days, but still visibility was limited by the trunks and bushes. The vehicle slowed a little as Carr maneuvered it between the trees. He had to swerve and steer around the thick trunks, penetrating deep into the forest. Samples fired a couple burst at any open lanes that appeared. After they had gone about fifty yards into the trees, Samples said, "Take the next left."

"Hope I can," Carr answered. Unlike the tracked APCs, which could literally spin in place, the Commando had a large turning circle which made piloting it in the woods difficult. Samples held fire and mentally coaxed the vehicle around as Carr swung wide and turned between two trees, crushing a sapling and bushes with the oversized tires. Now they were headed east, straight toward the part of the woods where the enemy machine gun emplacement was located. Samples sprayed the area ahead of them, knowing that most of the rounds would end up embedded in the tree trunks, but hoping to suppress any return fire.

Here, deeper in the forest, there were fewer low branches to dodge, for which Samples was very grateful. Once Carr hit a tree with the front right corner of the Commando, jolting Samples and stopping their forward movement. Carr quickly reversed a few feet, then put it back in drive and steered around the tree, scraping against another tree in the process. Then a lane opened up to the right, angling deeper into the woods. With no gaps wide enough for the armored car directly ahead, Carr steered down the lane, and then found another opening leading back toward the road. When they rounded a small cluster of young trees, Samples suddenly was able to see all the way to the road, and directly ahead of them was the machine gun nest. A shallow hole had been dug in the forest floor, and two men were hunched behind the tripod-mounted gun. They had moved the gun around to face the west, where they had expected the armored car to come at them, but were taken by surprise when it appeared where it did.

They were already lifting the tripod to move it around to the south when Samples pressed the butterfly trigger of the fifty. A stream of rounds erupted from the barrel and poured toward the machine gun nest. Every fifth round was a tracer, and the red streaks, readily visible in the dimness of the forest, helped Samples direct the fire to the target. Both men fell backwards as they were hit, sprawling on their backs in the dirt, and the machine gun toppled over as it was hit by multiple rounds. The Commando juddered to a halt. Samples let off the trigger, and silence reigned in the forest.

His ears were ringing from the gunfire, and his hands were beginning to tremble. Samples took a couple deep breaths, but maintained a wary watch on the woods around him. A snapping twig brought his head around to the left where he caught a fleeting glimpse of two gooks running south through the forest. Before he could swing the fifty around, they were gone.

"What do you think?" Carr asked, his own head swiveling back and forth.

"Looks like the gooks have booked it."

"About damn time," Carr remarked. "So now what?"

"Home, James," Samples said with what he hoped was an aristocratic tone. Below him Carr put the armored car into motion, heading for the road. He respectfully steered around the bodies at the machine gun nest, Samples noted with satisfaction. The gooks might be the enemy, but they were still human.

As they broke out into the open, they saw four Huey helicopters zoom overhead and drop down in the cleared area on the far side of the convoy their armored car had been leading. Infantrymen jumped out of the choppers, which lifted off immediately after.

"Here comes the cavalry," Carr said, steering the Commando to the left down the cleared area.

"Well, better late than never," Samples replied, feeling magnanimous. "I hope they've got something to drink. Man, am I thirsty."

"Know what you mean," Carr said. When he reached the head of the convoy column, he pulled it around, up onto the road, and parked it where it had stopped earlier. Samples saw Sergeant Canady stomping toward them, glaring.

"Cohen's wounded," Samples called to him, hoping to defuse the arrogant MP. It didn't work. Canady came up beside the Commando with his fists on his hips.

"What the fuck were you doing with my armored car?" he demanded.

"Your job?" Carr said lightly, standing up in the driver's hatch.

Canady fumed a moment, unwilling to chew out an officer, even a second lieutenant, then demanded, "How bad's Art?"

Samples squatted down so he could see inside and looked back at Cohen; he was surprised to see him sitting up. Canady reached in to unlatch the lower side door and looked in.

"Hey, Sarge," Cohen said groggily.

SEVENTEEN

Lieutenant Carr folded the letter he had just read and stuck it in the cargo pocket of his pants. He was sitting shirtless on a cot nestled against the side of the one-three track, taking advantage of the shade it provided from the late afternoon sun. It was the first letter he had received from his wife since she got the letter he had written after his ordeal in the Crescent. The Army had informed her that he was missing in action the day after the one-four track was destroyed, and she had been in a panic until she received his letter. Carr was glad the Army had been circumspect and not told her he was killed, although clearly that was their belief. Regardless, she was obviously overjoyed at his return to the dubious safety of the American lines. Sergeant Samples came over and sat down on the other end of the cot, maintaining a manly separation.

"Good news?" Samples asked.

"My wife just got the letter I wrote about our little adventure. The Army told her I was MIA. She's really glad I was found."

"Me, too," Samples said, grinning. "Since I was missing with you."

"You heard from your folks yet?" Carr asked.

"I sent them a letter, but they're not much for writing. I'll probably hear from one of my sisters in a day or two. They're used to hearing about me from the Army."

"What do you mean?" Carr was puzzled by the apparent lack of concern expressed by Samples' family.

"Every time I get wounded, they get a telegram. After the third or fourth, they stopped getting upset about it."

Carr shook his head. He came from a close family, and he had a hard time comprehending his sergeant's situation. They sat in silence, staring at the ground, for a minute.

"Ran into an MP over at the mess tent," Samples said. "Told me Cohen said to say thanks."

"He's okay?"

"Apparently. He's out runnin' the roads again."

"Good to hear," Carr acknowledged. "Nice guy."

Carr and Samples had been on the same medevac chopper that came for Cohen that day on the highway. That had been two weeks ago. All three had been flown to the MASH unit in Dau Tieng, where Cohen had been rushed into surgery. The medics had examined Carr and Samples, changed their old bandages, and released them to the mess tent. After stuffing down a huge meal and drinking what seemed like gallons of Kool-Aid, the two men had walked to the company headquarters building and reported in to the First Sergeant. A few minutes later the Executive Officer, a first lieutenant due to DEROS in a couple weeks, returned from the PX with a new watch and got very excited about their return. While the First Sergeant radioed the commander out in the field, the XO insisted they tell him the entire story in detail while he took copious notes. Carr wasn't sure if the notes would be used to draft a report to battalion, or for a book the XO hoped to write.

They were finally shown to one of the barracks tents, empty except for Eberhart and a couple other guys who were recovering from light wounds. Carr plopped down on a cot and immediately fell asleep, even though the sun had just set. During the night he came half-awake during a rocket attack that struck another area of the base camp, but fell back asleep when he realized the explosions weren't close enough to worry about. In the morning they climbed in the back of a deuce-and-a-half along with four new replacements for the ride out to FSB Wood. The new guys stared wide-eyed at the dirty clothes and weary expressions of the lieutenant and sergeant, and one tried to ask them questions. Carr gave the young men with their new uniforms and shiny faces a look that dissuaded them from further interrogation.

When they arrived at the fire support base, the company was out in the field, providing security for engineers who were sweeping the roads for mines. They reported to battalion, and sat around while a clerk typed up a ton of paperwork that officially brought them back to life. Major Moore walked by and saw them, demanding to know why he hadn't been informed earlier about their return from the dead. The clerk smoothly gave a bullshit answer and continued to type. Moore called them into the curtained area of the headquarters tent that served as his office and had them stand in front of his desk while he reclined behind it, listened to their recounting of the events of the last two days. He scowled, insincerely welcomed them back, and told them they would have to meet with the colonel when he returned from Cu Chi.

Lieutenant Colonel Duran was much more pleasant when hearing their story, and congratulated them on their actions and their safe return. Pudgy and starting to lose his hair, Duran was not a striking figure, but Carr figured he must have done something right to make it this far. Some of Duran's remarks led Carr to believe the colonel hoped to bask in the glory of his subordinates. Finally they were released from battalion headquarters and walked over to the company area, arriving just as the company pulled into the compound. There was much whooping and hollering from the men of First Platoon, all of whom demanded to hear their story again and again. The person who appeared the most pleased at their return was Second Lieutenant Stiltz, the battalion assistant S-2 officer who had been filling in as platoon leader. Captain Raymond had rushed over as soon as he heard, and kept slapping them both on the back and beaming proudly. He had heard about them from the XO, so already knew the full story. The captain thanked Stiltz for his help and told him Carr could take it from there. Stiltz couldn't wait to grab his gear and head back to battalion.

Carr now led a much smaller platoon, with only three APCs and fewer men. He tried not to think about Chacon, Jones, and the other guys who had died in the Crescent. Miles had been sent back to the world for a medical discharge. The other wounded would be returning to duty sooner or later. Sergeant Washington had been reassigned to Bravo Company, to replace one of their casualties. All Carr's personal gear had been on the one-four when it exploded and burned, but Samples had scrounged replacements for most of it. Carr and Allman now rode on the one-three, and when Eberhart returned to the field the day after Carr and Samples, he volunteered to be the RTO.

The days following had been spent doing normal tasks in the battalion's AO, sweeping the main road with the engineers, outposting to provide convoy security, and occasional RIFs through the rubber and sweeps through the Boi Loi Woods. There no incidents, no contact with the enemy, and minimal intrusion by Battalion or Brigade. They had formed company night laagers in the rice paddies a couple times, but mostly spent the night at Wood. They had gone into Dau Tieng for one night, allowing the troops to go to the PX and visit the EM club. There had been more and more rain showers, and the paddies were starting to fill up.

"I think Aiello's in love," Carr said, breaking the comfortable silence.

"That Coke girl today?" Samples asked.

"Yeah. She's been showing up for the last week, and Aiello just can't stay away."

"She's a cute girl," Samples admitted. She was a little older than the other Coke kids, with a bicycle painted pink.

"Aiello says she speaks English and French. And he insists she isn't a boom-boom girl."

"Well, as long as he stays out of trouble."

Carr chuckled. "Listen to us. We sound like parents worried about their teenager." Sample laughed, too. Although they were only three or four years older than Aiello, they were definitely more mature. Carr realized he had aged, emotionally at least, a lot in the last few weeks.

Eberhart stepped out of the track onto the ramp and leaned around the side. "Sir, the CO would like to see you at his track."

"On my way," Carr replied, slowly getting up from the cot. He started to put on his shirt, but then left it lying on the cot. Inside the perimeter he no longer felt the need for such formalities.

"AP tonight?" Samples suggested.

"God, I hope not." Carr strolled away, scuffling his boots down the perimeter road that was both muddy and dusty. When he reached the commander's track, Zychowski, the driver, had the engine cover up and was probing around the engine. He didn't look up as Carr went by to the rear of the APC. Ducking his head, Carr stepped up the ramp and plopped down on one of the benches inside, across from Raymond. The captain was scribbling something in a notebook, and looked up just long enough to acknowledge Carr's arrival. Carr waited until the CO finished what he was doing. Raymond then closed the notebook and set it down on the ammo boxes at the front, before looking directly at Carr with an expression Carr found difficult to read.

"I put you and Aaron in for medals," Raymond said bluntly.

"Uh, thank you, sir." Carr wasn't sure what the proper response to that statement should be.

"Don't thank me yet. I put you both in for Silver Stars, which I think is entirely appropriate for what you two did. I gave the recommendations to Major Moore." Raymond raised one eyebrow and waited for Carr to absorb the significance of the last remark. Moore had the reputation as a hard-ass, and Carr's response to the Major's missing tool investigation had done him no favors.

"Here's the deal," Raymond continued, a note of disgust in his voice. "Moore will approve yours, but he insists I downgrade Aaron's to a Bronze."

"What?" Carr yelped. "That's bullshit! He did just as much as me, if not more."

"I know," Raymond soothed, patting the air with his hand. "The S-3 thinks officers should always get higher awards than enlisted. Some nonsense about leadership and career progression. I argued with him about it."

"But. . ." Carr sputtered, the anger rising. "What about the colonel?"

"The colonel says the S-3 is in charge of awards, and won't intervene."

"Well, shit! Look, sir, I won't accept a higher award than Aaron gets. I'll just fucking refuse it. It's just wrong."

Raymond looked at him with amusement. "Are you serious? You'll refuse the medal?"

"Damn straight," Carr said heatedly. "I'll throw it in his damn face."

"We don't want that to happen," Raymond said mildly. "Let me talk to him some more. We'll work something out."

"Thank you, sir." Carr looked at Raymond expectantly, wondering if there was anything else. Raymond picked up his notebook and opened it. Without looking up, he said, "LP tonight for your platoon."

"Roger that," Carr replied. He waited a few seconds, but Raymond starting writing in his notebook again, so Carr got up and left.

The following day the platoon did a road clearing operation down near Trang Bang, sweeping on either side of the road while the engineers walked down the middle of the road with their mine detectors. Once they had finished their assigned sector of the highway, the three tracks were parked in a triangle in the middle of a rice paddy just off the road. This "outposting" was a welcome duty, since it required nothing but to stay ready to respond to the infrequent ambush. The troops took off their helmets, gear, and shirts, and then relaxed. Samples warned them to stay alert for jeeps or helicopters carrying senior officers, and posted a guard fifty meters away toward the distant tree line. Then he, too, found a shady spot and opened a paperback mystery. He noticed that Lieutenant Carr kept his shirt on, but replaced his helmet with his boonie hat and played catch with a couple of the local boys who were out minding the water buffalo.

It was a slow day, with nothing to do but watch Aiello chat up the Coke girl. The convoys roared past around noon, and a sandwich mama-san came by and sold them gook sandwiches—French bread with spam, American cheese, cucumbers, onions, and tomatoes. The more adventurous had her add *nuoc mam*, a fermented fish oil like soy sauce that smelled horrible but tasted okay. Finally, around three, they got the word to return to FSB Wood. After they parked in their spots on the perimeter, Samples put everyone to work cleaning their weapons, checking the tracks, and straightening up their areas. Just another day in the land of the little people, another day shorter until DEROS.

Samples was assembling his just-cleaned M-16 when Carr came up to him.

"CO says for you and me to put on clean uniforms and report to Battalion."

"What the fuck for?" Samples asked, pushing the last takedown pin into place.

"I don't know," Carr said with a shrug. "I was afraid to ask."

"Polish our boots, too?" Samples asked, but not seriously. Polished boots were a liability for infantrymen in the field, who needed to blend in with the environment.

"Just do it," Carr said, slapping Samples on the shoulder. "I hope you've got a clean set."

Samples went into the one-one track, found his waterproof bag, and pulled out his last clean uniform. It was time to send a load off to the laundry and hope it came back. He quickly changed pants, then took a minute to carefully roll up the sleeves of the clean shirt and transfer his rank pins to the lapels. The pins were brass painted flat black, although the paint had worn off along the edges. Three chevrons, and one rocker, the mark of an E-6. When he was satisfied with their placement, he pulled on the shirt and stepped back outside. He found his boonie hat where he had left it on his cot, and slapped it against the cot's crossbar to knock most of the dust off before setting it on his head. Five of the guys were playing cards around a makeshift table between the tracks, and a couple of them let out wolf whistles at his appearance. He ignored them and walked down to the one-three. Carr came out just as Samples arrived, carrying his boonie hat in one hand and his helmet in the other. He looked at Samples, then tossed the helmet back in the track and donned the boonie hat. Side by side they walked toward the center of the fire support base, where the battalion headquarters was located.

"Maybe they're going to send us back to the World to sell bonds," Samples suggested facetiously.

"Yeah, right," Carr grumbled. "That'll happen."

It had taken a minute, but Samples finally registered that Carr had a Combat Infantryman's Badge sewn on his uniform above the left pocket of his shirt. The CIB, a narrow horizontal rectangle framed by a wreath, with a musket image inside the rectangle, was the award most prized by all soldiers. It showed the wearer had survived the worst the Army had to offer, and greatly improved one's chances of promotion. Samples knew it was mostly a sop the Army had devised to placate the complaints of the infantry, but he was proud to wear his anyway. It was only awarded to soldiers with an infantry MOS (military occupational specialty), or officers in the Infantry Branch, who had served at least 30 days in an infantry unit engaged in combat operations.

"When'd you get the CIB?" Samples asked.

"I became eligible today, actually," Carr said. "I had one sewn on this shirt when we were in Dau Tieng the other day, just to be ready."

"The six P's," Samples commented. When Carr gave him a puzzled look, he expounded: "Prior planning prevents piss-poor performance." The Army loved mnemonic devices. Carr chuckled.

They went down into the command bunker, where an admin sergeant sent them back outside and over to the briefing tent. When they got there, the tent was unoccupied. The sides were rolled up halfway for ventilation, and there were two rows of folding chair facing an empty easel.

"Guess we're early," Carr remarked. Samples just grunted.

Lieutenant Stiltz stuck his head in through the flap and said, "Good, you're here. I'll tell the others." He disappeared; Samples and Carr stood around feeling at loose ends. Hurry up and wait. Samples was used to it.

Fifteen minutes later Lieutenant Colonel Duran, the battalion commander, walked in, followed by Major Moore, Captain Raymond, Lieutenant Stiltz, and a buck sergeant Samples recognized as heading the clerical staff. Stiltz was carrying a very nice Nikon 35-mm camera on a strap around his neck, and the sergeant had a stack of thick shotgun envelopes. All of them were bare-headed, so Samples quickly pulled his boonie hat off and stuffed in in one of his pants cargo pockets, and a moment later Carr did the same.

"Gentlemen," Colonel Duran said, coming to a halt in front of them. "How are you doing?"

"Fine, sir," Carr answered for both of them.

"Good, good. Well, we're going to have a little ceremony here. The Brigade Commander wanted to be here for this, but he's tied up at Division, so I get to do the honors." He looked over at the buck sergeant, who opened one of the big manila envelopes and pulled out a medal and a document. He handed the medal to the colonel, and the document to Major Moore. There was a quick reshuffling as Captain Raymond and Lieutenant Stiltz moved to one side.

"Attention to orders," Moore announced officiously. Everyone came to attention. "For conspicuous gallantry in the face of the enemy, Staff Sergeant Aaron Samples is hereby awarded the Bronze Star with "V" device for Valor." Colonel Duran stepped forward and pinned the medal to Samples' pocket flap while Moore continued to read the citation, an elegant but vague description of the events that had taken place in the Crescent two weeks prior. Stiltz raised his camera and took several pictures of the pinning. When Moore was finished, the colonel took a step back and saluted, and Samples returned the salute. Stiltz took more pictures.

They dropped their salutes and the colonel said, "Congratulations, Sergeant," while shaking his hand. Then the colonel side stepped over in front of Lieutenant Carr. The clerk opened another envelope and handed a medal to the colonel. He took the first citation from Moore and exchanged it for another. Samples sensed that Carr had gotten very tense, like a wildcat ready to spring. He also saw Moore's eyes narrow and a grim smile appear on his face. Samples wondered what was going on.

"Attention to orders," Moore said again, unnecessarily. "For conspicuous gallantry in the face of the enemy, Second Lieutenant Stephen C. Carr is hereby awarded," there was a brief pause, "the Bronze Star with "V" device for Valor." The tension left Carr as fast as it had appeared. Stiltz clicked away with his camera as the colonel pinned on Carr's medal, while Moore read essentially the same citation as the one for Samples. When Carr and the colonel saluted and shook hands, Samples watched Moore pass the citation back to the clerk with a mysterious look of satisfaction.

The colonel stepped back and said, "At ease." Everyone relaxed, but remained in place. "I just want to say, gentlemen," the colonel intoned, "that I am extremely proud to have you in this unit. You are outstanding examples of the fighting qualities of the United States Army, and a credit to this battalion." Stiltz started to applaud, but quickly stopped when Moore glared at him.

"And now we have another presentation," Colonel Duran announced. The sergeant shuffled the envelopes, looking closely at what was written on each. He found the right one and pulled something small out, along with a mimeographed form. He handed the small objects to the colonel and then stepped back.

"Staff Sergeant Samples," the colonel said with a smile, "I believe you are out of uniform." Samples was momentarily confused, and looked down at himself to see what might be wrong. "Those pins on your collar are incorrect," Duran said. "You are no longer an E-6." He opened his hand and showed Samples the two new pins he held, with three chevrons and *two* rockers. "You are now Sergeant First Class Samples. Congratulations." He looked around and said, "Lieutenant Carr, Captain Raymond, would you like to do the honors?"

"Certainly, sir," Raymond replied, coming around the colonel to stand on Samples right. The colonel handed one pin to Raymond, and one to Carr. The two officers removed Samples' worn Staff Sergeant stripes and replaced them with the new Sergeant First Class pins. Then each shook his hand and congratulated him, followed by the colonel. Stiltz had been taking pictures, but he, too, stepped forward to shake Samples' hand, as did Major Moore.

Samples was grinning and couldn't stop. The medal was nice, but the promotion was better. Higher rank brought more money, and more prestige. It also brought additional privileges, like the right to buy hard liquor and go to the senior NCO clubs. He couldn't wait to go back to the platoon and impress them. He hadn't expected this; he wasn't due for promotion for at least a year. He wondered if the colonel had manipulated the system somehow. However it happened, he was extremely glad.

Everyone was now milling around aimlessly. Carr slapped Samples on the shoulder and told him it was about time. Then the colonel spoke again.

"That's not all, folks. We've got one more presentation." The clerk opened the last envelope, dug around inside, and passed the colonel another small black object. "Second Lieutenant Carr, you are also out of uniform. Your orders came through yesterday. You are now a First Lieutenant." The colonel showed Carr the single black bar of his new rank pin. Carr's face showed the surprise he felt. Duran stepped forward and reached for Carr's collar, but the lieutenant stopped him.

"Sir," Carr said hesitantly, "I know it's not protocol, and no disrespect to you, but would you allow Sergeant Samples to pin that on?"

Samples was thunderstruck. He couldn't imagine what Carr was thinking. Asking the colonel to let an enlisted man pin on an officer's new rank totally violated Army protocol. It just wasn't done. The colonel was obviously caught completely off guard by this request himself. He paused with his hands in the air, confusion on his face followed quickly by disappointment and then acceptance. Without a word he turned and handed the pin to Samples and took two steps back.

His head swimming, Samples moved over to face Carr, and their eyes met. Carr nodded encouragingly. Samples reached up behind the lapel and squeezed the clips to remove them from the pins that penetrated the fabric. Holding the clips in his left palm with two fingers, and the new pin in his right palm, he pulled the dull gold bar free, wondering what he should do with it. Carr held out his open hand, and Samples gratefully dropped the old pin into it. Using the tiny holes left in the lapel by the previous insignia, Samples inserted the sharp pins on the back of the new one and pushed on the clips to secure it.

For Samples, the other men in the room faded into the background, their presence of no consequence; it was just him and Carr. Samples took one step back and came to attention. He brought his right hand up in the smartest and sharpest salute he had ever mustered.

"Congratulations, sir," he said. Again their eyes met, and Samples thought he saw a glimmer of moisture. Carr returned the salute and held it.

"Thank you, Aaron," Carr said quietly and warmly. They continued to hold their salutes, staring into each other's eyes. After a few seconds, as if at an invisible signal, they both dropped their salutes and shook hands. Samples felt his own eyes burning. It was a very emotional moment, even though he couldn't really say why. What he did know was that he and Lieutenant Carr now shared a kinship that was stronger than anything he had ever known. It was more than familial, stronger than that of brothers, and even stronger than that of a married couple, but in a different way. It was the unique bond between two men who had walked through the valley of death together, fearing the evil, but guiding each other through to safety on the other side. It was a mutual pride and respect that transcended common friendship. They both knew, without saying so, that they would always be connected, would always trust each other absolutely, and could always depend on each other. It was a relationship that would last as long as they lived.

Made in the USA
Lexington, KY
17 November 2018